I0719833

DUST UP

AN ANTHOLOGY

Publisher's Cataloging-in-Publication data

Title: Dust up : an anthology by New Mexico writers / curated and with an intro by Jennifer G. Edelson ; [written by] Andee Baker, Cristina Browne, Sue Bryan, Jennifer Edelson, P.J. Christman, Melinda Cross, [and nine others].
Description: Santa Fe, NM : Bad Apple Books, 2024.
Identifiers: ISBN 978-1-7335140-4-0 (paperback) | ISBN 978-1-7335140-5-7 (ebook)
Subjects: LCSH: Short stories. | Essays. | Creative nonfiction. | Paranormal fiction. | Romance fiction. | Fantasy fiction. | New Mexico--Fiction. | BISAC: LITERARY COLLECTIONS / Subjects & Themes / General. | LITERARY COLLECTIONS / Essays. | FICTION / Anthologies (multiple authors) | GSAFD: Short stories. | Occult fiction. | Fantasy fiction. | Love stories.
Classification: LCC PS595.C38 D87 2024 (print) | LCC PS595.C38 (ebook) | DDC 811/.6--dc23.

To our families. Our friends. Our people. Our readers.

THE
CONTENT

THE INTRO

Welcome to *Dust Up,* aka the magic that happens when a bunch of Santa Fe writing nerds conspire to let their imaginations run wild in the Northern New Mexico desert. Every writer who contributed to this anthology and I are excited to share it with you.

Before you dive in, I hope you'll take a beat and allow me to wax poetic for a moment about how this anthology came to be. Way back when, before *Dust Up* was even a seed, I dreamt of launching a social space for writers where creativity flowed as freely as the Rio Grande—which, because of drought, sometimes doesn't flow at all (trust me when I say it's an apt analogy). As a writer who too often grapples with existential dread over the process, I imagined pulling together a sort of writers' 'safe space' devoid of pretense and ego, a sanctuary for oddballs who hear sonnets in the silence and find prose in the mundane, or at least who want to. So I started a writers' social, called it the Kooks Writing Group—because it's Santa Fe, and why not—and crossed my fingers that other people who fancied themselves writers would join me.

To my delight, people turned up. And they continued to join. And our group blossomed. Soon enough, we gathered regularly to contemplate every unique voice, bizarre plot twist, and word we dared write (or struggled to). In a world often marked by competition and discord, our little collective became a haven of support and mutual respect. A group of regulars and drop-in writers, we traded ecstatic, subversive, peculiar, and exuberant stories against the backdrop of the oft-pink-hued Sange De Christo Mountain Range and a city drenched in history—the magic of it all imbued in our laughter-peppered conversations, empathetic feedback, and every encouraging nudge (or push off the cliff). And eventually, *Dust Up* was born.

Inspired by a state where Coronado's ghost strays the land searching for his famed Cibola and the spirits of Ancient Puebloans roam free, *Dust Up* is both a testament to the power of unity *and* a wild ride through life's kaleidoscope of weird and wonderful experiences. Think of it as a literary potluck with a dash of rebellion and a pinch of southwestern spirit; every dish as surprising and eclectic as the next—like stumbling into a New Mexico speakeasy where Georgia O'Keeffe slams shots with Montezuma and Billy the Kid. Dying for a story about axe-wielding directors, exiles with mysterious sun allergies, or dead ewes? We got you. Jonesing for tales of off-world mining expeditions and alternate-universe fashion choices? We're here for it. How about shadowy glowing ladybugs and fugitive computer codes? Or mini-mart robbers and serial killers? And what would an anthology be without angsty romance, a touch of humor, and existential essays about life's minutia? Whew!

We thank you for choosing to embark on our continued literary journey. For honoring our esteemed collective by reading the works inside, many of which are award-winners. We thank you for choosing to purchase a book in a world that increasingly values digital dopamine dispensed in convenient fifteen-second media chunks over long, lazy reads. Albert Camus once said, "The purpose of a writer is to keep civilization from destroying itself." It's a mighty task, but even just entertaining or distracting you for a few hours is a big win.

Split infinity

JENNIFER EDELSON

Under the hot sun, the shanty bus stop does little to stave off the heat baking the arid, dusty ground. The grimy bus is just up ahead; it won't take long before it groans to a halt, belching its sooty breath into the cloudless sky, polluting my senses with the smell of burning rubber and the screech of squealing gears. Slowly, it inches toward the sparse portal, coming to a standstill just after the dilapidated metal structure. As it stops, I look down the road ahead, at a long, golden stretch traveling through Nothing, Kansas, lost until a *tsking* sound brings me back to reality.

From his high seat, the driver winks down the stairwell, waving me on.

The first step is the hardest. That's the way those old Greyhound buses were made. It takes a large stride to reach level ground. Today, that first step is special, my hundredth Greyhound stair since I set out to see America. Five steps a bus equals twenty towns so far.

Sighing, I grab my backpack and sling it over my shoulder along with my newly acquired duffel bag—the one I pinched from the Kum and Go in Friendly, Tennessee. I close my eyes and lift a foot, pausing midair, waiting to slip as I step up onto the worn green runner, splitting the bus between the left and right sides of town. But I don't fall. I land solidly, two feet on a carpet that leads to an empty seat near the restrooms at the back of the bus. A seat next to no one, the way I like it.

Out the window, empty fields cup Oakley, Kansas, like a worn baseball glove, closing in on the failing town. Oakley is a blip, but outside, beyond its dusty main street, the land is starkly beautiful and stirringly desolate. Once upon a time, America felt like this sweetened parcel of promise waiting for me to cultivate for my own. But most of what I've seen is vacant, and tribal, and vast enough to distance its citizens from its ideologies. The country's enormity makes me shake. Like space, it swallows me up, a molecule in an atomic ocean.

"This seat taken?"

A massive body looms over the aisle, pointing to the seat beside me. The seat is piled high with my bags, a sure tell that it is not, in fact, available.

"What's wrong with one of the ones up there?" I point toward the front of the Greyhound, toward the seat the boy occupied before the bus pulled away from the station.

"Nothing." He shrugs.

I want to say, *'Yes, it's taken. Can't you see all my stuff, you idiot?'* But I'm curious. The boy followed me through five overnight stops already, trailing behind at each like a shadow, only to disappear until the next bus to nowhere pulled into town. He hasn't said a word to me until now.

"Fine," I answer, looking out the window at waning fields of dried cornhusks.

Grunting as if my one bag and backpack combined weigh more than the bus itself, the boy pulls my items off the seat, throwing them in the frail overhead bin before sitting down with a thump.

He taps his ratty blue Converse repetitively against the seat back, driving me crazy.

"How old are you?" I ask.

"Twenty," he says to the seat in front of him.

Twenty. Not a boy, not a man.

As the bus makes its way into the setting sun, the sky spreads out in fuchsia ribbons that glow against golden cornhusks and dried farmland. I envy him. We're almost the same age, and yet, he seems . . . unspoiled.

The boy stares straight ahead, peeking sideways when he thinks I'm absorbed by whatever it is we're passing outside—panoramas stretched like taffy by motion. I hate meeting people's eyes. Peripheral vision is a gift from God. I can't count the times it's saved me.

In the distance, Oakley is a blur of grain silos. We ride silently beside each other, and I wonder what he's up to, pretending with his frayed knapsack and beat-up guitar case that he's got nothing better to do than sit with some stranger. That guitar, like a prop from a movie—I wonder if he plays it or just carries it around.

My seat is hard and springy, but I've come to expect that. In front of me, blue fabric stretches across the seat's backrest, a visual racket speckled with colorful polka dots that burst across the frame. It's a pattern that's neither comfortable nor attractive, but I've pretty much stopped caring about things like aesthetics after seeing so many ramshackle towns.

"Where are you going?" The boy asks earnestly.

"Santa Fe for a couple weeks." I lie because I don't now, and never have had a plan. "Next though, Plains, Oklahoma. Then Clayton, New Mexico."

"I mean in the end."

He's attractive, and that bothers me. But he's also awkward. Too tall and too big, as though still a child trying to inhabit a man. His fair eyes are innocent despite rugged features, and his soft, slow voice, tinged with southern inflection, makes me want to strangle him.

Where am I going?

"Nowhere," I shrug. "Just like you." I grin at him disingenuously, then close my eyes against the glare outside. Small talk is worse than truck-stop coffee.

"Mind if I go with you?"

"To nowhere?" I raise my eyebrows.

"Yeah. Why not?"

The boy's gray eyes are unguarded but not simple. They're sweet. Unaware. They smile openly above his delicate nose, the only other fragile thing about him. He reminds me of a puppy patiently waiting for a bone.

"Where were you headed?" I ask.

"Santa Cruz. At least, I was."

"You've been following me?"

I already know he has been. I first noticed him back in West Virginia, in line for a Minneapolis-bound bus. Then suddenly, there he was again, sitting four aisles ahead of me, headed down Interstate 64 for Kentucky. He got off with me in Lexington, then got on with me heading for St. Louis.

"Kind of."

"That's creepy."

He shakes his head. "Not really."

"Yes, it is. It's called stalking."

"I'm not stalking you. You just . . . you seemed alone."

"We're all alone."

He smiles sheepishly. "Sure. But we don't have to be lonely."

Shielding my forehead, I meet his stare. The bastard looks sincere; he smiles a small, genuine smile, totally unaware I'm packing a .45 and will probably rob someone, maybe him when we stop for the night in the next town. "You have pretty eyes," he says, holding his pointer finger near enough to my face to actually poke me. "Like amber."

"What's your name?" I ask, pinching the bridge of my nose as though my head hurts, hoping to shut him down.

"Octavian."

"Seriously? Like Caesar and all that?"

"Seriously. Like Caesar and all that. Octavian Orion Xavier August Navarro. What's yours?"

"Do me a favor." My name is transient. It has no meaning beyond what other people assign it. Like me, it's a ghost. Grimacing, I change the subject because I can't even care enough to take back the awful things I've done, which means I probably shouldn't get to know him better. "Grab my backpack."

Octavian stands up and pulls my pack from the overhead carriage, snagging it on a jagged piece of plastic jutting from the bin before sitting down again. He fidgets beside me, flicking at a flap on his denim jacket as he stares up at the tiny television screen suspended from the ceiling above us. He's obviously waiting for me to say something else. But I don't, and he doesn't either.

There's a small travel alarm in my duffel, and I set it to ring in an hour. The last part of the day's trip takes us through the Prairie National Grasslands before stopping in Oklahoma, and I don't want to be sleeping then. Land is my one indulgence. I'm not ashamed to admit it's my only love.

I revere roads especially. Even before I knew what escape meant, highways and all their tributaries haunted me—all that infrastructure leading somewhere I wasn't. All that violence. A day on a dusty stretch of empty highway tamps the humdrum noise inside my head. Movement keeps me sound, and that's stellar because reason feels like it's become a dirty concept.

The bus's tires hum against the tarmac. It's a soothing sound, and I drop my forehead against the hot glass, letting the sun-warmed pane sear my skin. Drifting, I keep my eyes mostly closed and furtively squint out the window. My reflection in the grimy pane makes me anxious. I know my face well, but the rest of me is so unpredictable.

Minutes later, we pass over a pothole, and I realize Octavian is sleeping beside me like the dead. As we head southwest into Oklahoma, rows of cornfields give way to prairie grass, and I wonder about him. I wonder whether to change seats or take him back to my motel room when we stop for the night. I decide to change seats. But then take it back. I'm too intrigued by his credulous nature.

In Plains, Oklahoma, storm tentacles like dark streamers wind through the late prairie light, stalling over dry corn stalks in the near distance. Lingering above a small dearth of land, the storm washes the golden fields in white hot flashes of electricity. The highway splits the grimy town down its middle. On one side, tall silos loom over railroad tracks and an open field of grass dotted with park benches. On the other, abandoned warehouses stand like sentries on the edge of town.

The air is static, and the area eerily immobile. We stand under a tin roof, sandwiched between the early evening sounds of crickets, and buzzing electrical lines, and hushed obscurity. Up the street, perpendicular to the highway, a neon motel sign blinks Good-Sleep-Inn at us against a mostly dusky backdrop. Together, we make our way toward it, past a ramshackle Stop and Go I think about robbing later and a shanty aptly named Bar Nowhere. I wonder if once Octavian figures me out, he'll turn me in. It's not too late to send him packing, but he's such an anomaly. Tomorrow, we'll reach Clayton, full of empty spaces and beaten-down people; a good place to bury mistakes and secrets, or ideas that follow you cross-country. I could change my mind. But I'd rather gamble.

DEAD HERMAN

PATRICK X.L. LEE

Herman wakes with a start.

He is in a vast, limitless white space. No up or down, no horizon, no features of any kind.

Herman is immediately disoriented and shuts his eyes to avoid a sensation of vertigo.

"Sorry, man, force of habit. My bad."

The voice is not Herman's. It's male, soothing, casual.

Herman opens his eyes again. He is sitting on a rock in a forest glade. Water gurgles in a nearby brook. Oddly colored butterflies flit overhead, backed by fluffy white clouds. Sunlight dapples through the leaves, a cool breeze ruffles Herman's hair. The air smells of lilacs or roses or violets. Herman doesn't know flowers.

"Better?"

Herman looks around for the source of the voice. No one.

"H … Hello?" he stammers.

"Oh, crap, sorry, not used to this. Over here."

Herman turns around. Behind him stands a dark figure. Dark, as in jet black. As in a hole in the fabric of space-time itself.

"Hi, I'm Death." The dark figure extends a hand.

Herman recoils. "Wha … What?"

The figure sits down, crosses his legs. He's hovering about two feet off the ground, like a sinister Buddha.

"This is all very confusing to you, I know," he says, waving his hand dismissively. "Sorry, I just feel like it's been ages since I did a check-in with the clientele. Guess I'm a little rusty. As I was saying, I'm Death. You know, the Grim Reaper, the Sandman, the Destroyer of Worlds, Azrael, Hella, Santa Muerte—I quite like that one—the Big Sleep. You know, Death!" He sticks out his hand again.

"You expect me to shake hands with Death?" Herman says, rising to his feet and scanning the forest for a place to run.

Death slaps what would be his forehead if he had a face. "Yeah, duh, sorry again. Like I said, it's been a while."

He flashes a Vulcan "live long and prosper" salute instead. He attempts a smile, but it looks more like the gaping maw of a corpse.

Herman blanches.

"Anyhoo, thanks for taking the meeting." He gestures for Herman to sit down.

Herman slowly sits back down on his rock, keeping his eyes on the black figure.

"So, as I was saying, it's been a while since I checked in with the clients. You know, see how they're doing, ask if they have any questions or concerns, rating their user experience, you might say." He pauses, looking for any sign of response.

"Where the hell am I?" Herman says, the panic rising in his throat.

Death chuckles at this. A disturbing sound, like the rattle of a giant snake.

"Yeah, hell, that's a good one. No, you're not in hell. Such a curious concept anyway. No, you're in, well, let's just call it the afterlife for short."

"You mean I'm dead?"

Death utters a "ding ding ding" noise, like the peal of an iron bell.

"But I can't be dead! I've got a job interview tomorrow!"

"You know, everyone says the same thing," Death replies. "Well, not exactly, but, you know, it's always, like, 'I can't be dead! The King is going to knight me!' 'I can't be dead, I'm to be wed on the morrow!' 'I can't be dead; I was just elected Pope!'" Death laughs heartily at this last one.

Herman is getting a bad feeling about all of this. "If I'm dead already, then why are you here?"

Death sighs deeply. This one's not too bright. "So, on occasion, I like to talk to the recently departed," he says evenly as if talking to a four-year-old. "That's you, my friend. Things change a lot, and sometimes it's hard even for me to keep track of where y'all are at. Think of it as a debriefing after the mission."

"Wait, so how did I die?"

Death rolls his eyes. Not that he has any eyes.

He snaps his fingers.

Herman finds himself back at Arby's on Colorado Boulevard. Now that he thinks about it, it's the last thing he remembers. He's about to take another bite of his Smokehouse Brisket sandwich with extra crispy onions.

Suddenly, it comes flooding back to him. The big bite, the sudden panic as the greasy gob of meat goes down the wrong pipe, his fingers scrabbling at his throat as he feels the blood rushing to his face, people turning to gape. He tries to cough, tries to inhale, but nothing.

An Arby's employee runs over, tries to reach around Herman's torso to administer the Heimlich maneuver as Herman frantically gestures at his throat.

"I can't reach around," she yells to the manager. "HE'S TOO FAT!"

Then everything goes black.

Then, that vast, white space.

Herman clenches his eyes, forcing tears out of the corners. Just as suddenly, he hears the gurgling brook, smells the lilacs. He opens his eyes.

Death is sitting in front of him, as serene as before. He looks at what would be his nails then looks up.

"So?"

Herman breaks down, sobbing. Death leans over and gives him a "there, there" on the shoulder while looking at the nails of his other claw.

After a while, Herman stops sobbing. He just sits there, whimpering now and again.

"All better?" Death sighs.

"So that's it? That was my life?" Herman's lower lip trembles.

"It wasn't so bad, was it? Your mom loved you. You had that date one time. You got a high score in Grand Theft Auto! What, you were expecting a Nobel Prize?" Death is starting to get a little impatient.

"But I was such a LOSER!" Herman starts to cry again.

Death tries to maintain his calm.

"Let's not assign judgment," he says reasonably. "I mean, what's the point? So, here's the thing," Death adds, brightening. "It's not entirely over for you! There's still things you can do!"

Herman stops weeping. He looks at Death like a shelter puppy looks at a little girl.

"I can?"

"Sure!" Death says. "*And* you have all the time in the world."

"To do what?" Herman says hopefully.

Death pulls a sheath of papers from underneath his flowing black cloak.

"For starters, you can help me with this survey!" Death clicks a ballpoint pen. He hands the papers and the pen to Herman.

Herman receives the papers, frowning. The top sheet says, "After-Death User Survey." It's filled with questions followed by boxes labeled 1 through 5. There are about a hundred pages.

Herman begins to cry again.

• • •

Page 28, Line 33: "On a scale of 1 to 5, 5 being the most, how closely did the death experience match your preconceived notions?"

Herman puts the pen down and rubs his eyes with his thumb and forefinger.

"What's really the point of all this?" he asks.

Death, who has been filing his claws this entire time, looks up. "Sorry?"

Herman is about to repeat the question when Death speaks up. "Oh, well, I'm trying to put together a manual for anyone who wants to do this job. It helps to have the user feedback."

"Anyone who wants to do the job?"

"You, know, someone else."

Herman frowns and says nothing.

"I've been doing this a long time," Death says by way of explanation. "I might want to take some time off. You know, book a cruise, lie on a beach." He resumes filing.

Herman doesn't know how to process this information.

"You mean you want to train a temp?"

Death keeps filing.

Herman stands up. He's starting to feel panicky, like that time in school when Jim, his roommate, rushed in with a purloined copy of the final exam answers, stuffed it in Herman's backpack, and told him not to tell anyone.

Herman begins to pace. He walks to the gurgling brook, turns around, comes back to the rock, stands there, turns, walks to the brook, turns, comes back to the rock. Beads of sweat form on his upper lip.

"Are you talking about me?"

Death stops filing, looks up. Somehow, the figure is smiling again. The effect is chilling. "You're not as thick as I feared," Death says. "Yes, ya got me. Busted! Sorry about that. The user survey was just a diversion. I was waiting to see if you'd go along with it or what you'd do. Also, I've been monitoring your answers."

"You've been filing your, um, nails the whole time!" Herman says irritably. He sits down on the rock.

"I can multitask! But I have been following your answers. It's curious. You don't seem to like what happened to you, even though, logically, death should have been a blessed relief to someone like you. Someone so, um, well …" Death trails off.

"Someone so pathetic as me?" Herman says indignantly.

"… someone so sad as you," Death says.

Herman looks hurt. "I wasn't sad."

Death says nothing.

"I mean, okay, my life wasn't *that* great. But I had friends! I did stuff!" Herman says.

Death cocks his head in sympathy.

"I even had a girlfriend. Well, she was a friend who was a girl. Penny. She lived next door to me after I graduated from college. Well, dropped out of college. She'd come by most evenings to ask me to take a walk with her through the neighborhood as the sun was setting.

"She'd tell me about her day at the insurance company, and I'd tell her about the ants in my kitchen. She'd say something rude about her boss, Paul, and she'd laugh. I'd say something rude about Paul, and I'd laugh. And then we'd be laughing together."

Herman grows silent, thinking about Penny.

Death shifts but says nothing.

"Then she moved to Israel," Herman says.

A beat.

"Yes, you're right, you're not sad," Death says, waving that dismissive hand. "My mistake. So how about it? Would you like to learn the trade?"

Herman returns to the present.

"Why me?" he says.

"It's like I said: You seem sorry to have passed on, however your life was going," Death says. "And, no offense, I mean, it's not like you were George Clooney. But I get it. Life is precious to you. Or was, whatever. Maybe you'll have a lighter touch than me. I've been doing this so long it's like flipping burgers, you know? Oooh, sorry, too soon?" Death grimaces with embarrassment as Herman flinches.

"See, that's what I mean. Maybe I'm losing my touch here, ushering you guys into the next phase. I'm not a bad guy. I feel for you. For all of you. It's not my idea that you have such short lives. I want to do what I can to make the transition easier, but, you know, maybe I need a break."

Herman gives this some thought.

"So you think I'd be a … nicer Death?"

Death smiles again in that faceless, non-smiling way.

Herman considers this. He looks up.

"Why *do* we have such short lives?" he asks Death.

Death rolls his non-eyes. "Oh, that. Yeah. That's above my pay grade."

Herman nods.

Another beat.

"Okay."

"Okay?" Death says.

"Okay. I'll try it."

Death stands up and claps his claws with glee. "I *knew* it. I had a good feeling about you, Henry. You won't regret it."

Death vanishes in a puff of smoke.

Herman sits alone in the forest glade.

For the first time in a long while he feels at peace. The oddly colored butterfly flits overhead. The brook gurgles.

"Herman," he says quietly.

• • •

Herman adjusts the black cloak draped over his sloping shoulders. It contrasts with his blue Captain America T-shirt and tan cargo shorts.

"Is this really necessary?" Herman asks Death.

Death stands back, cups what would be his chin with his right hand, taps his cheek with his index claw.

"It works. You gotta represent, you know what I mean? You're not just Henry anymore. You're Death now! The Pale Horseman! Lord Shiva! Thanatos! The Babadook!"

"You just made that last one up, didn't you?"

"My point is, there's a gravitas to this job, and the black duds sell it. It's part of the service. Think of yourself as a concierge into the afterlife, and this is your uniform."

A full-length mirror appears in the forest glade. Herman regards himself, turns this way, that. He feels silly.

"You don't think this is a little on the nose?"

Death waves his hand. "You're killing it."

Herman shrugs the cloak off. "I think people will feel a little more at ease if the first thing they see on this side is someone like me. Not someone like you. No offense."

Death raises what would be his eyebrows. Maybe the kid has a point.

Herman sits on his rock. "So what's next?"

Death waves his arms theatrically.

Herman and Death are suddenly in the enormous master bedroom of a suburban mini-mansion. There's a guy lying in a California-king-size bed surrounded by chip bags. A whiskey bottle and glass sit on the nightstand. The guy is cycling rapidly through TV channels, clicking his remote at a gigantic flat-screen on the opposite wall. The screen's blue glow offers the only light in the room.

"Jim," Herman says, recognizing his old classmate.

"He can't see us or hear us," Death says.

Herman walks over to his old roommate. It's been ten years since college, but it may as well be thirty. Jim's hair, never that robust, has thinned to a few wisps on top and a shaggy mullet in the back. His gut swells up like a breaching whale. His breath is labored, the influence of the bottle of amber liquid on the nightstand, Herman surmises.

Herman looks at Death. "Jim, too?"

Death smiles that smile. "I thought it might be nice if you're the first one he sees."

"Why now?"

"Look at him," Death says. "He's been preparing for this moment for ten years. It takes a lot of work to get in the shape he's in."

They stand there for a bit. The TV drones. Jim has settled on some soft-porny costume drama set in 18th-century Scotland. A lot of heaving bosoms.

Jim's breathing slows. His eyelids droop. Spittle dribbles out of his mouth. His head slips to the side, and his breathing grows irregular. He begins to snore.

Another few minutes. Jim remains unconscious, but his breathing suddenly picks up: short, rapid gasps, then a couple of deep inhalations, followed by a couple of shuddering exhalations. Then nothing.

He lies still.

Death scratches his butt.

"What're you guys looking at?" Jim says.

Herman whips his head around. It's Jim, standing behind them, looking at his body lying in the bed. Jim's wearing the same clothes as his corpse. (Why are we wearing clothes? Herman thinks to himself. Huh.)

Jim realizes to whom he's talking. "Herman? Buddy? What the hell are you doing here?"

Death chuckles to himself. "Hell, ha."

Herman gives Jim a big bear hug. Jim recoils at first, then settles into the hug. It goes on for a minute.

When they separate, Herman smiles at Jim. "It's kind of hard to explain," Herman says.

• • •

The brook gurgles. Herman is gesturing as he fills Jim in on current events. They're sitting on matching rocks, facing each other. The butterflies flit overhead.

Off to the side, Death floats cross-legged, picking at something under his hood with his right claw. If he had a watch, he'd be looking at it.

"So, are we good, guys?" Death says.

Herman looks over and gives two thumbs up. Jim gives Death a wary look, then a wan smile that's more like a grimace.

"Jim's okay. Truth is, he wasn't really happy in his life and feels a lot of relief that he's ended up here. Right, man?" Herman looks at his old classmate with a grin.

Jim gives him a tentative thumbs up.

"Okay, grand," Death says. "Well then, I think we can send good old Jim to the next processing level. You ready, big guy?" Death looks at Jim.

Jim looks at Herman. Herman gives him a wink. Jim turns back to Death, gives him a little nod.

Death unfolds himself, walks over to Jim, and puts his bony arm around Jim's shoulders. "You'll be fine, don't worry. Say good-bye to your pal Henry, and let's hit it."

Jim gives Herman the 'sup nod they used to share in school. Herman returns the gesture.

Death turns Jim to face him, puts a claw on each shoulder, and leans in. His blank face is inches from Jim's. "This won't hurt a bit," he whispers menacingly. Jim begins to sweat.

There's a thunderclap, a gust of wind, and the two disappear in a flash of light.

Herman is alone again.

"That's new," he says.

• • •

"I thought you were going on a holiday," Herman says.

It's been a few months. Months? Years? Who can tell.

In that time, Herman has seen a lot of people cross over here. Young people, old people, sick people. A few children. They were sweet, Herman thinks to himself.

Death is lying on the grass with his claws behind his head, his ankles crossed. He's gazing at the puffy clouds overhead. He'd be chewing on a grass stalk if he had a mouth.

"That is the plan," Death says. "But I had to make sure I was leaving … all this," he gestures grandly, "in good hands."

Herman looks around. "You had me thinking this was going to be hard," Herman says. "But it's actually the easiest thing I've ever done. I mean, it's like being the host at the best party ever. Everyone is so happy to see you. Me. I didn't think it would be … so nice."

Death leans up on an elbow and regards Herman. He says nothing, but Herman can feel that mouthless grin.

"What?" Herman says.

"It's that thing I said," Death says. "It's you."

Herman is confused.

"I once said that I thought you were sad," Death says. But I was wrong. You weren't sad. You were melancholy. Lonely." He sits up, crosses his legs.

"In life, that loneliness was a burden. It was a millstone. But you're not alive anymore. You're dead. And in death, that loneliness is a gift."

Herman is having a hard time following.

"Everyone dies alone," Death says. "It's the core experience of your passing. It's the one thing you all know about death, maybe the only thing.

"Now that you're me—now that you're Death—your loneliness is the gift you share with those who find their way here. Those who have passed. And that is the best gift the recently departed can receive in this place. The knowledge that Death itself knows their pain and shares it."

Herman thinks he understands. For some reason, this makes him think of Penny. He smiles, but he also feels like he might cry.

Then he grows alarmed.

"Wait a minute. I thought I was a temp," Herman says.

Death smiles that non-smile. "Right. You're right, kid. When you're right, you're right. That was the deal." He stretches. "Well, I guess I'll be going then. Knock 'em dead, Henry."

Herman stands, suddenly anxious. "Wait, when will you … "

Death snaps his fingers. A puff of smoke, and he's gone.

Herman sits down on his rock. He rubs his forehead anxiously.

"It's Herman," he says with irritation.

• • •

Years later, Herman has ushered countless more people to their greater reward.

At some point, Herman realizes he's been doing things as if he's always done them. It's not as if anyone gave him that manual Death was supposedly writing. He just suddenly knew when to do his thing, and where, and with whom.

He smiles at the thought. He thinks of the people he's met and the time he's spent with them. First, the fear, then the relief, then the awe, then the serenity.

And so it is that Herman knows one day, while he sits on his rock in that forest glade, that his next appointment is in Tel Aviv.

In Israel.

He finds himself aware of a small urban apartment. It is cluttered but tidy. Full of books and plants. A big dog sleeps on a braided rug. And an old woman, alone, sits at a kitchen table with a big mug of tea, looking out the window at the bustling city. She's thinking of something that makes her smile wistfully.

Her mug says "Penny" on it.

Herman feels warmth fill his being.

No rush, he thinks to himself. We'll have all the time in the world.

THE LADY IN THE GRAY SPACE

SUE BRYAN

There is an empty space at the edge of awareness, a silent gray space where we collect impressions that don't make sense, perceptions of flitting spirits around us, or sure knowledge of extraordinary magic. In the tragedy of maturation, we replace our curiosity about what may or may not be real with a patterned narrative that we call truth. A swearable affidavit we repeat ceaselessly to create the impression that we know how the world works.

I couldn't even read yet when I trudged along with my sister and her friend, Gayle, into the undeveloped area beyond our neighbor's expansive backyard, where we played pick-up baseball games and held neighborhood clam bakes in the summer months.

Today, autumn leaves fluttered around our ankles as we entered the cold shadows of the woods. The older girls were giggly as if we were doing something we shouldn't. Maybe we were. We walked slowly through the thick litter of leaves and the tangly ferns, some of which were almost as tall as me. I gripped tightly to my sister's hand. Just last Saturday, I had lost my grip on her in the corn maze and had to sit down and cry before she came back to find me.

In front of us, Gayle stopped suddenly. "What's that?" she whispered.

We looked and crept forward, stopping just short of a clearing in the trees. I jumped at my sister's side, anxious to see what Gayle was pointing to.

My sister's voice was hushed and shaky. "I didn't know there was a house here."

"There isn't!" Gayle shook her head as if to clear it. "At least there hasn't been for, like, a hundred years."

"I want to see." I broke away from my sister's protective hand and ran into the small clearing. It was a house all right. Even a pesky little sister like me could see that. A big house, too. White. Clearly old. The porch roof was sagging to one side. The wide steps were rotten through in some places. I wanted to climb up those steps, but the girls held me back.

"It's the widow's house," Gayle whispered, shrinking back.

"That's not a thing," My sister's voice rang out and echoed back. She stamped her foot.

"Look!" Gayle pointed to the wide picture window in the porch recesses next to what must be the front door. "Did you see that? The curtain moved!"

Gayle's hushed and trembling voice was beginning to scare me. I stared at the window. It was framed by white, wispy curtains. Even from here, I could see that the curtains were tattered and hung lopsidedly across the window. In the center of the glass, we could see a huge white pitcher, like an old-timey wash basin jug. It looked too big to be real. It looked like it was big enough to hide in. I started forward. The girls screamed and caught up with me at the foot of the porch steps.

"You can't just go in there!" my sister scolded.

"Why?" I hadn't been alive long, but I knew that in my neighborhood, I could go into anyone's house if I needed to pee or get a drink of water—a privilege of suburbia, I suppose.

"It's haunted, is why." Gayle sounded out of breath.

While the older girls argued about the house, I watched as the curtain inside the picture window fluttered. I waved.

"Let's go!" My sister tugged at my arm. But at that moment, there was a movement at the front door of the decrepit manor house. I stared and tugged back.

The door didn't seem to open, but suddenly there was someone there. On the porch. A woman in a long white dress. Try as I could, I couldn't see her face clearly. She clutched at the decaying porch railing, heedless of the peeling paint and splintery wood.

The older girls seemed frozen.

The white-dress lady raised a hand to her brow and peered outward toward the woodsy area we had come through. She didn't seem to see us at all, right here at the foot of her steps.

I shook my hand loose from my sister's and took a step forward. "Hi."

But the women acted like I wasn't even there. This was not a new experience for me, so I did what I always did when I was invisible. I *felt* into the situation to learn what I could about the world around me. I could hear the traffic on the distant highway. And I sensed the dank earthiness of the woods behind us. I felt a wave of sadness, tinged with what seemed like a drop of hope radiating from the woman on the porch.

Poor lady. The husband who was supposed to paint the porch and repair the steps and the curtains wasn't there. Everything was falling apart. I felt her resolve to wait, to be faithful.

I tried to send the pretty lady a prayer of love. Tried to tell her not to wait anymore. *It's been a hundred years (if Gayle is right). He's probably not coming. Probably not going to fix the stairs. Probably not going to paint the porch.*

For just a second, I swear she stopped gazing into the trees and looked down at me. Right into my eyes!

But then Gayle and my sister unfroze and grabbed at me, screaming. They yanked me back through the woods, through ruthless scratchy branches, back into the safety of the manicured lawn. They collapsed on the grass, breathing heavily, and I sat down next to them, a crossed-legged yogini, serene amid their chaotic fear.

"What was that?" Gayle pounded the ground with her fist.

"She was lonely," I said.

"Don't be ridiculous." My sister's voice was severe.

"She is waiting," I tried again.

"Shut up!" She sat up and grabbed my shoulders, looking intensely into my eyes. "That was nothing. Nothing happened. You're making stuff up, and you need to stop it right now." My sister nodded affirmatively in Gayle's direction. I watched Gayle nod dumbly.

Young as I was, I already knew the rules of the game. There are some things you never talk about. Like when grown-ups are lying. When Jesus visits you at night. The fairies that live near the creek. The hatred and sadness that people feel even when their faces are smiling. And now, the sad lady in the woods. These things live in the gray area where things might or might not be real.

"Let's go home," I said and grabbed my big sister's hand.

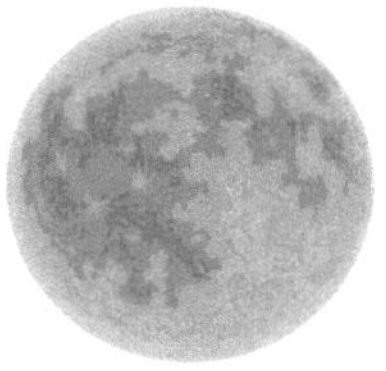

THE POWER OF LIGHT

GREGORY L. WAGNER

Alejandro pedals away from the sparse city lights and into the darkness of night. Up the winding road and into the lower hills he rides, the vestiges of sun-warmed sand fading as the night envelops the piñon and juniper. He stops among the conifers and spreads a blanket on the sand below a small opening to the sky. Stars twinkle against the black curtain of the cosmos. Alejandro lies on his back and stares into the depths of the Milky Way. He can feel the sparkle of starlight on the skin of his face, beckoning him to the infinite. Infinite space. Infinite darkness. Infinite freedom. He can sense the suspended tick of time, the clockwork of the sun and moon, resting and hidden. But not for long. Moonrise is in half an hour. He'll need to be safely home by then. But for a few precious minutes, he slides off his shirt, closes his eyes, and relishes the warmth of the starlight on his bare skin. And freedom.

• • •

Light from the darkroom bulb paints the white bathroom a dim, flat red. Alejandro slides the button through the eyelet of his cuff with swift, fluid ease. The vertical blue stripes on the white dress shirt emphasize the breadth of his shoulders and the narrowness of his waist. He turns sideways and inspects his profile in the mirror. The early-morning hours of weights and cardio have paid dividends over the last year. He faces the mirror head-on, back straight and shoulders square. His eyes track down to the crumpled tube of prescription sunblock neatly stacked at the back of the vanity. SPF 110. His shoulders sag.

He grasps the tube and squeezes thick white paste into the palm of his left hand. With years of practice, he begins to apply the ointment to his face with smooth, even strokes. Creating a uniform white mask is a hard-won skill. He caps the tube, dons his wide-brimmed fedora, pulls on thin tan gloves, slips his wraparound sunglasses on, and shuts off the red light. He opens the door to the brightness of morning.

• • •

Alejandro slides into his seat at the back of the classroom, farthest from the windows. Miss Grisham gets up from her desk and strides to the center of the room, black-heeled boots striking the floor tile and a long, pleated linen skirt swirling around her legs. She smiles at the students as she scans the room, meeting each individual's eyes. Many years ago, Miss Grisham was counseled to promote stronger teacher/student interaction in her classroom. She took the advice to heart.

"Good morning, class!" Straight white teeth gleam as she continues her ritual greeting. Her eyes come to rest on Alejandro's opaque sunglasses beneath his Indiana Jones hat. She doesn't stare at his white-painted face or his gloved hands. Her smile nearly falters. She moves on.

THE POWER OF LIGHT

• • •

The Mitchells' dog barks at Alejandro as he turns the corner, the rhythmic strain of his bike's unoiled chain marking time and his passage in the dark. The brakes squeal lightly as he stops beside the oak tree in the middle of the block. It's late for his ride into the hills. That's been happening more lately. He adjusts his sunglasses and looks up at her light, beaming between the gnarled and crooked branches. Each time he sees her, the impact of her beauty strikes his chest. The potential of her danger strikes his stomach.

Darkness is the only place his circumstance doesn't make him an outcast, a pariah, a spectacle to be stared at and whispered about. For years, he has dealt with the danger the sun poses, the consequence of his rare condition, the blisters, burns, and pain from the slightest touch of its harmful rays. Sunlight can kill him. But he doesn't know about the moon's light. He has never tested her consequence. For years, he and the moon have danced around each other, eyed each other with curiosity. And there was a draw, a longing, that was inescapable. But at what cost? What would happen if the moon's light touched his nakedness? Would his skin boil? Would he acquire more scars to pock his appearance further? Sunlight killed. Starlight tingled and tickled. What about the moon? What price for the knowledge?

He continues to the sanctuary of the hills and spreads his blanket. The infinite of the cosmos calls to him.

• • •

The school bell chimes. Quiet halls fill with the white noise of massed teenagers on the move, hustling to their next class. Students jostle, shove, and squeeze through the bidirectional throng, the younger classmen progressing like Plinko chips cascading down a peg board. No one bumps into Alejandro. No one squeezes him aside, blocks his path, presses on him from behind. Sunglasses, wide-brimmed hat, painted white face, long-sleeve shirt, and gloves, he walks through the halls, Moses to the Red Sea.

All here know of his deadly allergy to sunlight, have seen the results when it shines on his unprotected skin. His disease is not communicable. Everyone knows this as well. Most knew him before the onset of his unique condition. The doctors had lots of theories for his malady. The students had more. Best to be careful.

• • •

Alejandro sits perfectly still on his bicycle seat, gazing at the moon's light through the trees. The moon gazes back. He slowly rides up the hill to the quiet clearing of his sanctuary. The moon follows. He spreads his blanket and lies down on the sand. Stars twinkle in the void of space. Fear compresses Alejandro's chest. What path is life? The moon stands over him, her light filling the darkness. Tears leak unheeded from the corners of his eyes. He unbuttons his shirt.

Cottonwood stars

AMBER TRAIN

1.

I snap clean a slim cottonwood branch —
exposed, is a tiny star.

2.

Native Americans told this:

cottonwood stars
populated the heavens,
born aloft on wind from earth to sky.

Cottonwood boughs gave shade beneath
the cornflower-blue
ceilings of ballroom skies
Their pointed leaves were soothing medicine

Their hollowed trunks, sturdy dugout canoes
Their frost-gray bark fed trail-worn horses
Their logs fueled hypnotic campfires.

3.

Watch our star, the sun, illumine their
toothed leaves, jade crowns, gnarled bark.
Catkins swelling with seeds
primed to burst and parachute
earthward on cottoned strands,
bestrewn across sandbars of the rivers:

Chama
Santa Fe
Cimmaron
Grande
Gallinas
Pecos
Purgatoire
and so on.

4.

The cottonwood
knows nothing of the
Convention between the
United States and Mexico for the
Equitable Distribution of the
Waters of the Rio Grande for
Irrigation Purposes or the
Bureau of Reclamation or the

Pecos River Compact or the
Water Masters.

5.

A haunted yarn told over wagon-circled,
bark-sparked cooking fires:

When a cottonwood is river-swept,
you can hear its spirit weep
while its roots cling
to the sanded banks.

6.

Sing Sacred Muse:

as flood plains retreat,
as downed powerlines and rogue campfires
lick up millions of acres,
as salt cedars and Russian olives
invade and overtake
the cottonwoods' thirsting domain,

Will spirits weep?
Will stars fall?

Will I still raise my face and ecstatically
collect cottonwood puffs on my eyelashes?

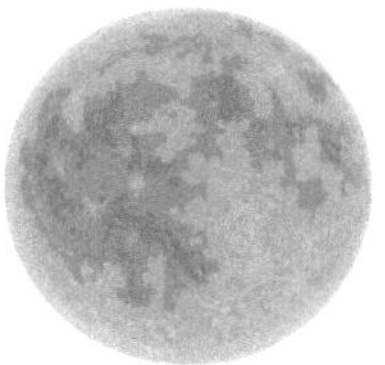

Whۥat these bodies are for

Sue Bryan

We are all one slip away from catastrophe
   one greasy hand on the handle of the frying pan
   one moment—in the forgetfulness of sleep—away from heartbreak.

Are we also one slip away from the Infinite?
One mindless remark away from our fulfillment?

What if you *do* say those words hovering in the shadows of
your lips?

Our "what ifs" confine us, but they could also free us
if we didn't care so damn much.

This body balances on its pointy fulcrum.
what we think we are seeing, what we think we know
tips us one way or the other
out of peace into dismay or delight.

In this game of life, we have decided that it's risky,

that the world thumbs the seesaw and tumbles us.
Some lucky. Some burdened. All suffering.

Our desperate circumstances
are forcing us to look again, to take responsibility.
First for the devastation. Later for the creation—
the capacity we were born with to do things differently
see things differently.

There has never been a more important moment
a more consequential choice.
Yes, you can recycle your water bottle.

But what are you *seeing*?
It is no simple matter to search for the Light
that peers from every corner.
It cannot be an afterthought.
Or this is what we get again and again.
War. Suffering. Disease. Decline.
By our seeing, we make these things real.

The Light glowing behind the headlines
though steadfast and eternal,
is outside the range of our feeble photoreceptors.
We have to train other organs,
those which see through the clouds,
to the stars beyond,
to transmit their data to our awareness—
this centuries-old process of neuro-evolution
that all these bodies are for.

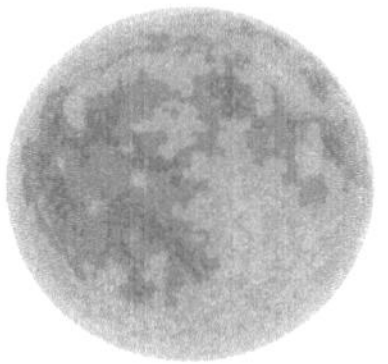

GETTING DISCOVERED

STEF WILLEN

I stared into the director's face and said my lines. I watched for my future in his eyes. He took his time deciding my fate. His gaze crawled around my face, across my shoulders, down my body, even to my feet. He leaned in, close enough to examine my pores. I held my breath.

You are *her*, the director said.

I had been waiting to be her for five years since I moved to Los Angeles. Or maybe I'd been waiting my whole life to be this girl that someone else was so certain I was. I didn't want the director to change his mind. I didn't want him to smell the white wine I'd chugged before the audition. I had an urgent need to scoot away from him, just one inch. Instead, I gripped the couch and said I was honored to be this girl who was supposedly me.

I was being given the starring role in an independent film for an award-winning director. He had been offered a star, but he wanted an unknown. And I was the unknown he wanted.

The director stuffed some papers into the pocket of his track pants and escorted me out of a casting office. He took me for a

Vietnamese lunch special in a nearby strip mall to celebrate. *I need you to lose ten pounds. Can you do that?* I was still deciding what to order. I chose the spring rolls. Yes, I could easily lose ten pounds. His eyes carefully searched my body, even while he ate. He complimented me on my features as though I had selected them. *Where do you get your eyes? Are they Swedish?* What he liked most were my broad shoulders. His eyes swept back and forth between them. *Those are good, those are good*, he appraised.

In the parking lot of the strip mall, the director directed me to walk. I did my best to follow orders. *Relax your shoulders. Step lighter. Take up less space. Even out your pelvis.* Back and forth I went, across the uneven asphalt and its flattened trash, the dirty pigeons darting and bobbing out of my way. Never before had I been so certain I was going somewhere.

The director said, *You've really got something* and drove off in a Cutlass Ciera.

•　•　•

Two weeks later, I arrived at my destination—a modest beige home in the suburbs of Pocatello, Idaho. It looked like every other house on the block, except the roof was caved in, and the siding was licked black from flames. My instructions were: *Do your best to work around debris.* This was my day job. I was an "inventory specialist" of disaster. I traveled all over the Western United States to homes ravaged by fire, dug through charred debris, flipped mattresses to note labels, and reached into the deepest parts of what remained of people's closets and cupboards. My inventory of every last recognizable item in a burned-down home helped owners receive fair settlements from their insurance companies. It was a work environment where the air smelled of acrid rot, and it was possible to fall through a floor or stab yourself with a rusty nail. I'd stepped on loaded guns and dead rats, cats, and dogs. I showered with a scouring pad. Even my snot turned black.

There were other options for "undiscovered talent," but I didn't have bartending or waitressing experience. I didn't want to substitute teach and walk dogs or make lattes and walk dogs. I hadn't wanted to inventory disasters, either, but it paid above minimum wage, there was no experience required, and most importantly, it was a job with a flexible schedule. More than enough homes burned down each month for me to pick my losses and make my auditions.

There were very few auditions and lots of losses. But the director was about to change all of that. In a month, we would begin filming, and I would be the star of a movie. This isn't the same as being a movie star. Still, I sensed the *boom* that was coming. The rumblings of being about to launch to a higher and better place. I was lighter. I had run off four pounds. I was practicing my new walk. I was doing something else, too, something I supposed was preparing me for my entrance into the public eye: I was starring in the movie of my own life, certain moments becoming cinematic, each of my actions and reactions meaningful and set before a vast and silent audience. No view of myself had to be just my own anymore. No moment private.

The camera followed me from my rental car across the yellowed lawn to the beige house. I pushed the water-swollen door open with my shoulder and was hit in the face with a dangling strip of ceiling insulation, but this was not an accident. It was a close-up of me pushing insulation off my face because I was the main character in a compelling drama, one that was leaving audiences wondering, *What's a girl like her doing in a place like this?* I jiggled my measuring tape to make sure it was adequately clipped to my work pants and felt the world's eyes believing I was some kind of expert. Surely, I'd have the attention of even my critics when I lifted my Dictaphone to my lips and said, *Beginning loss. For starters, I'm standing on a doormat that matches the one outside.*

I continued taking in the mess before me as though I were not alone. Me and a sea of strangers were disgusted by the burnt insulation and chunks of drywall that looked like they'd been violently puked from the ceiling onto the floor. We were collectively horrified by the heavy-looking three-piece furniture set strewn across the room, each piece needing to be hefted and pivoted, flipped to a different side, groped for tags, and measured. It was hard for some of us to hear such a talented young lady saying, *One faux-leather office chair with arms, castered, adjustable, exactly like the one I just recorded.*

I moved over to a large collection of books, and the drama I was starring in had an identity crisis. Was this another horror story about a woman who gets slashed in the woods after crossing paths with a paramilitary whack job? It seemed as though a woman with such a fate might be staring at titles like *Ragnar's Big Book of Homemade Weapons*, *The Mammoth Book of Cover-Ups, Shelters, Shacks and Shanties*, *Guerilla Gunsmithing*, *Pit Bulls for Dummies*. I was perhaps doing what critics call "owning the screen" since I was not acting but *re*acting. With every unknown sound, my heart pounded, and I spun around, searching the shadows until I decided I was safe. Eventually, the frame tightened around my false sense of security, narrowed its focus, as I did, on the tediousness of my fingers wiping the soot off each spine, my voice announcing each title and *hardcover* or *softcover*. I was now what's referred to as "lost in the role." I didn't see the man slip into the room behind me. I thought I was alone, and then I heard a crunch. I whirled around to see a man holding an ax. A noise I'd never made came out of my mouth, a new alarm.

The man holding the ax was just standing there, but he seemed to be growing taller and coming toward me. I was just standing there, too, but on legs made of jelly. He slapped the ax handle into his palm. *I'm Phil*, this man said. *Scared ya*, he seemed overly amused to add. Phil dropped his ax and swiped a book off the bookshelf.

Got a lot of mileage out of this sucker, he said, slamming it down on the desk. *His* desk. This was when I realized this man was my client. He'd hired the public adjusting firm who'd hired me. Fear began to release its grasp when it clung to the idea that a dangerous man could act on his compulsions despite the fact that it was not in his best interests. Actually, didn't dangerous men do this all the time? Wasn't this why they were dangerous?

I always wondered what I'd do when faced with possible imminent danger, and now I knew. I stood right next to it, making sure it felt cared for and understood. *You had a lot of great books*, I assured the man who might slowly torture then kill me with an ax. Phil shoved his hands in the front pockets of his coveralls, which stopped just short of his ankles and turned toward his bookcase, his pelvis thrust cartoonishly forward. He began swaying from side to side as if urinating on his collection, marking his territory—a six-shelf, "36 by 18" by 86" inch wood bookcase housing works such as, *How to Build a Good Business with Little or None of Your Own Money; You Can Negotiate Anything; Running Through Walls; Spite, Malice and Revenge; Hide Your Assets and Disappear; The Encyclopedia of Sauces.*

I'm a collector, Phil finally said. He grabbed more books, flipped through them, and slammed them onto his desk. Several fell to the rubble below. I stared at one titled *Surviving a Robot Revolution*. Was he intentionally making my job harder, or was it possible he didn't know what the purpose of me was?

For a moment, I let myself really see his face. I'd expected it to be a hardened patchwork of grimaces formed by years of desperate attempts to express his significance, but it was astonishingly childlike—the face of a boy playing grownup. His large brown mustache and oversized glasses seemed like props clumsily placed over cherubic features. His bowl cut was something shiny and imperfect, just cut by a mother who needed the next larger-size bowl but had to go with the one she had. I'd met parts of this man before, but never the whole him.

Be on this man's side, I thought. *Make him believe you agree with all of his choices.* I cleared my throat and explained how thoroughly I would inventory his books, his bookcase, his desk, his everything that wasn't screwed, wired, or built into the wall. That was structure, I clarified. I was content. Phil slapped the books in his hands on his desk and turned to face me, to stare me down. When he'd done enough of that, he lunged toward his ax, picked it up, and swung it by the handle in big circles. *Swoosh, swoosh, swoosh.* Silence and violence, these seemed to be the conversational wedges Phil stuck between himself and the world. *Thunk*—the ax crashed at the side of his boots.

Laaydeees first! he shouted.

Thanks, I said and picked up *Surviving a Robot Revolution,* and flipped its pages, and nodded my head as though it really had been a good book. *One paperback instructional book*, I recorded and continued my inventory.

Clients often showed up at their losses despite being told by the adjuster to stay away from the inventorying. Some disappeared in silent search of something they hoped to salvage—birth certificates, passports, a signed baseball, a jar of baby teeth. Others followed me from room to room, offering corrections or a kind of eulogy, which I incorporated into my inventory. *Ronald says the sword was a gift from his grandfather, who was born in Hungary and had a furniture-carving business.* Then there were the angry clients. *You have no respect for my stamp collection!* I didn't have it in me to ask someone to leave the remains of their own home, especially an angry person. Especially a person who seemed violent and unpredictable.

Didya meet my neighbors? Phil asked. I was trying to follow his jerky movements in my periphery while recording the title of a book that proclaimed pens could be fashioned into deadly weapons. *They're Mor-Mans. Get it? The MORE mans?*

Ha—I managed and reached for the next book. Several loud whacks issued from somewhere behind me. I turned to see Phil hacking away at a small cardboard box on the rugged terrain of his floor.

Well, this wuz a box of Sudafed. He stood proud and leaned on his ax.

'One box of Sudafed,' I recorded. *Do you know how many capsules?* Phil jumped to his hands and knees and fit together pieces of the box he'd just chewed apart with his weapon.

Twenty-four! He announced this like an auctioneer trying to encourage a higher number. He stumbled to his feet with pieces of the box and brought them to me in open palms. Phil's palms were remarkably clean and pink. Soft, even.

Where had the possible killer gone? Could I trust this ding-a-ling was the real Phil? A certain tenderness came over me, the kind felt toward a scary-looking dog you begin to think just wants to play. The kind of dog you slowly reach your hand through the fence to pet, only to have that fine line between willful ignorance and stupidity gnashed apart.

It was in the next room, the master bedroom, that Phil grew silent and still. I was bent over before him and tugging at his dresser drawers, swollen shut from the water that came after the fire. I'd spent some serious time tugging at people's wood drawers, but I had never turned around to find them standing over me holding an ax.

Phil's face was no longer boyish. It was a face that was sure of what it wanted. I stepped a little to the side so that he was not directly behind me and turned back to his dresser. I hated that he might be seeing the thin waistband of my underwear and the private patch of skin on my lower back. I shifted into my masculine mode like I did when walking past men on dark streets who I hoped glanced my way and thought, *Not worth the hassle.* The first thing I do is hide my hair. Usually, I'm wearing a hoodie, so this is easy. Next, I take my sense of self out of my chest and push it down between my legs. Then I silence my hips and sway my shoulders. I become wider. I land my feet like this is my street. I steer out of the way of nobody. In the present circumstances, I could only make some of the adjustments. I widened. I encroached upon the dresser. I jiggled its nobs with swagger.

Phil remained eerily silent somewhere behind me, seemingly unaware of my change in gender. Should I stop and tell him I can't open this drawer? Was he just standing behind me, trying to think of a great joke? How did I know so little about everything? And why couldn't I stop?

I was so tired I sighed unintentionally. This must have meant something to Phil because his fingers tapped my shoulder, and, for a moment, everything was normal.

I was just a woman stepping aside for a man who thought he could help, but then this man staggered forward with an ax raised high above his head and crashed it onto the top of his dresser. He was both a caricature of a bumbling outdoorsman and someone to run from. He muddled my instincts. This was the scariest thing about him.

Phil climbed on top of his dresser and squatted and grunted until he wrenched the ax free and went tumbling back with it, nearly missing the corner of his hope chest. He shook his head, spit on his floor, strode back to his dresser, and feverishly whacked at it with no apparent plan. I waited, the ground beneath me shuddering, the charred rafters above me shaking. When his blade had mutilated the dresser's three drawers enough for their contents to be viewed, I said, *Thanks, Phil—that's enough.* For good measure, I added, *It's perfect.*

I stepped up to the wreckage, peered through the splintered wood, and made a shocking discovery: a paperback copy of *The Modern Girl's Guide to Life* nesting in a snarl of bras and panties.

My wife's, Phil declared.

A woman loves this man. It was a comforting thought until I remembered women love bad men all the time.

Phil followed me to his office, then his hall closet. He seemed unable to endure the long periods of pacifism that came with detailing the intricacies of junk drawers or sheet sets and tromped off to chop a sliver into his deck railing or demolish the last good leg of an antique sewing machine table. Twice, he was eager to know what it sounded like to drive an ax into the side of a metal filing cabinet. This was a man whose brain lit up with disaster, a man stimulated by destruction. Even his grunts seemed to be echoes of an inner pleasure. I always found a way to feel sorry for a client, but I couldn't feel sorry for Phil.

• • •

I checked into my hotel like I usually did, smudged with soot and smelling like a burnt tire. As always, the desk person asked what brought me to town in a way that suggested they'd really like to know. *Work* is all I ever said. I was not proud of being an inventory specialist of disaster because it was nothing I'd wanted to become. It was a job I kept trying to consider beneath me despite the fact that I was not actually very good at it. The names of common household objects often eluded me, so I described them in great detail. Sometimes, clients overheard and interrupted. *You call that a rotating plate-sized platter with ball bearings on the bottom? I just called it a Lazy Susan.* Or, *That's actually not a pot with a candle type-thing underneath to keep stuff warm, it's a chafing dish.* I saw in their faces that they were wondering whether they had the inventory expert they were promised. If I had wanted to, I could've studied up by browsing online department stores, but I didn't want to. I wanted to believe each loss was my last, and this time I did.

I had six more pounds to lose. I ran from my hotel to downtown Pocatello, along a bike path, around a duck pond, and back. I did twenty pushups and fifty sit-ups. In the shower, I was careful scrubbing soot off my body. My skin mattered now. Not because it was my skin holding me together but because it was my character's skin.

At dinner, the director called to remind me how he wanted me. I was sitting at the bar of my hotel, drinking a gin martini and plucking at a salad. Cameras were on me again. Invisible eyes watched me swallow the last of my martini and nod to the bartender for another.

You're not changing your hair, right?

Right.

And you're losing the weight?

Yes. This was a very important conversation. People were listening.

And you're staying out of the sun? I assured the director everything was the same about me except for the things he wanted to be different. *Good, because you've really got something,* he said and hung up.

It was a distinct specialness, the feeling of being about to become known. I looked around the bar, and people looked back. I was atomized; the whole room felt me. A man in a Hawaiian shirt raised his glass to me. Soon, I was surrounded by four men wearing Hawaiian shirts. Shots were ordered. They were graying and grizzled and celebrating some kind of reunion or new life stage. I said I was an actress. I wrote my name on a cocktail napkin. More shots were ordered. Hairy arms brushed mine. Heavy hands fell on my shoulders. The night blurred and bobbed. The carpet came at me in waves. When everyone seemed to be walking away, I realized the bar was closing and that a guy in a Hawaiian shirt was calling my name from the doorway. I did my best to walk with purpose toward him, then past him.

It was easier to wake up feeling poisoned now that I was starring in a movie. I was not alone, dry-heaving over a Best Western toilet. I was at my mark. My pain was part of the story. What had felt like being lost was only waiting to be found. Even Phil would find me. I drove the long series of county roads to his loss, envisioning the day he would see my face on TV and hit pause and then rewind and realize who I was. He would brag to people that I had once touched absolutely everything he owned, and practically no one would believe him. I pulled into his driveway and was tossed wildly back to the present by what came into view: Phil, waiting for me in his lawn chair, wearing a long-sleeve polo shirt and boxers, his hairy arms and legs spread like a starfish.

I stayed in my rental car, pretending something very complicated was going on in my lap. When I'd done that long enough for a reasonable person to have put on clothes, I peered through the windshield to see there was still a man in his underwear between me and a job I didn't even want to be doing. I got out of the car, punching buttons on my Dictaphone as though something was very wrong with it and not what lay before me, sunbathing pantless in front of his ruined home.

Morning! Phil yelled. He made a slow show of removing his coveralls from a nearby plastic sack and putting them on. Again, my instincts were muddled. Was this sexually aggressive and offensive, or a severe lack of social skills? Was I afraid or compassionate? I felt a welling of what could be the beginning of either emotion. This man was unknown to me.

So, I said casually, *where's your ax?* Phil ignored me and continued buttoning up his dusty coveralls. When he got to lacing his boots, he wanted to know if I'd heard the one about the Mormon and the Jew. I said no. I also said no to *Do you know how many Mormons you should take with you fishing?* When Phil stood up, he looked a lot like the main suspect in a serial killing spree. He winked and said he wanted to show me something in his Tuff Shed, so I followed him into his backyard.

DUST UP

The Tuff Shed only sustained light smoke damage, but Phil insisted this was the place *with the goods* and wanted everything recorded in case it wasn't cleaned to his satisfaction. He unlocked the doors, and I waited for a stockpile of weapons. When he walked out with a tall column of shoeboxes, I thought maybe a ten-thousand-page manifesto. Then he flipped a lid, ruffled some tissue paper, and proudly declared he'd been collecting Avon perfume bottles for three decades.

I had to learn something new about the world now that I knew a guy like Phil collected perfume bottles. But I certainly wouldn't do it by talking to him. I kneeled down in his yard, clicked on my Dictaphone, and opened the first shoebox. I'd inventoried many collections, and the owners usually lurked over my shoulder, eager to point out the errors in my assessment. This was not Phil, who stood over me whistling at squirrels before wandering off and returning with a bottle of water and a beach chair, which he set up directly in front of me. I described the intricacies of his perfume collection, and Phil watched from his front-row seat, gulping his water with gusto and letting out long loose sighs. He appeared indifferent to my clumsy descriptions. So long as I snapped photos of each bottle's certificate of authenticity, his silence on the matter suggested that he, too, agreed that what he'd bought and carefully stored was *an Avon perfume bottle shaped like a woman…no, wait, more like a cat wearing a skirt—but a cat with boobs.*

After Phil's perfume bottle collection was inventoried, he left to *go hunt some lunch,* and I flung myself back into the smokey innards of his home. I had three rooms left and wanted to be done and gone by the time he returned. I moved with speed around his blistered kitchen, jimmying burnt drawers open with a butter knife and rattling off their contents, estimating instead of counting, eyeballing instead of measuring.

Next, I was in the garage, inventorying Phil's wine rack. *Sutter Home Chardonnay…Sutter Home Chardonnay…Sutter Home Char-*

donnay…and again, and again, and again. This was the "wine cellar" Phil had bragged about owning, and though it was not impressively stocked or even a cellar, it was impressively tall. Halfway down the rack, I pushed pause and walked into a shadow with a smoke-glazed bottle. I hunted around, picking through blackened tools, and found a screwdriver. I jabbed the hard cork until most of its dried chunks were floating in the neck of the bottle and took a long, corky swallow. *This is bad,* I thought and hid the bottle, but a more powerful thought kept bringing me back: *I just need a little more.* It was the usual war, but soon half the bottle was gone, and I was again one person wanting one thing.

I strolled around the garage, rattling off descriptions of tools I couldn't name, estimating lengths of cords, wires, and hoses, hitting pause to swig the chunky, soured goodness. My job was almost easy, nearly fun.

I finished the wine in the laundry room, set the bottle among some half-melted bottles of detergent, and began with the washer. I lowered my entire upper body deep into the machine and reached for a moldy tangle of Phil's clothes so my head was in the dark when he came up behind me. I heard his feet stop. I heard a shrill whistle. I heard, *Wuhl! Where'd THIS big bad boy come from?* My heart did a flip. I froze. Other "big bad boys" had been an antler-handled obsidian knife, a vacuum cleaner from the '70s, a four-burner camping stove, and a framed poster of John Wayne.

There was the teeniest, tiniest possibility that Phil was staring at something besides his empty wine bottle. I began banging my knuckles around to insinuate I couldn't hear, that I was busy working. My mind cast frantically about for reasonable ways to keep my upper body in Phil's washer for a really long time. Being bent over before him felt very different this time, like hiding underwater, a fleeting moment of partial existence with a requisite emergence into the harsh, unmuffled world. Once I came up, I would have to be someone else. I told myself I hadn't drunk that wine, that I was someone who only paired wine with meals. I pictured myself loving tea: opening a cupboard and feeling a lightness in my being at the sight of a cardboard box, gently lowering a sack of herbs into a steaming mug, only ever needing one squeeze of honey.

None of this could ever happen. It could barely be imagined. I had to come out of this washer as me. I brought Phil's wad of moldy, tangled clothes along because I needed a layer between the truth and myself, even if part of it was Phil's underwear. I couldn't look at him, but somehow, I saw his eyes moving between my face and the empty Sutter Home bottle, saw him understanding how there were cork chunks at the bottom and clinging to the sides, how the bottle got to be among his detergents, how the bottle got empty. This was not the future I'd intended, but it had happened exactly as I predicted: He would hit pause and then rewind and realize who I was.

I did not tell him where that big bad boy came from. The only words out of my mouth described the clothes in my arms, then the washer and dryer and most everything you'd expect to find in a laundry room, plus two hunting bows. I could feel that I'd had power, that even being uncertain if I should be afraid of someone was the power to exist slightly outside myself, and that I'd lost it all. I made each of my movements as small and impersonal as possible. I was one of those robots Phil had been waiting to battle, except Phil wasn't combative or even really Phil. He seemed to be pulled entirely out of himself by intrigue, thoroughly enjoying seeing something in me he hadn't seen before.

He was silent until I recorded the last item in his laundry room. *Pair of women's cotton underwear, Hanes* I said. *End of loss.*

Nope! Phil sounded excited. *Wait till you see what I got at the temporary house.* My panic stirred under its thick blanket of wine. This wasn't an unusual request. Homeowner's insurance policies typically place people in temporary housing when their homes require more than a month of repair. Most people brought a few items they didn't want stolen or ruined by the elements to these homes. But Phil was not most people. His bottle of wine was empty. He had me where he wanted me—glassy-eyed, guilty, and afraid.

To my great relief, Phil didn't question whether I should drive. I followed his small SUV with huge bull horns mounted on the front, telling myself I could make a U-turn at any moment, even after I was out of the car. It was a weedier neighborhood, a smaller home. Phil tromped across the concrete slab of his temporary porch and held open a squeaky screen door. I entered with careful steps, peering around, assessing the danger. The local news on the TV. A framed print of a fairy feeding bunnies. A pile of clothes on a thrift store couch. A woman bouncing a baby on one hip and folding laundry on the other. I wasn't terrified. *My wife*, Phil said. Her face was cold and young—fifteen years younger than Phil's, my age. She looked at me with suspicion. The baby stared with brand-new blue eyes. I sucked in my alcoholic breath.

I'm the inventory specialist, I said.

Oh! The ice melted from her face. *The wine?* My cheeks got hot. I watched her hand holding a pair of baby socks. *It's our good wine from the garage.* She was blushing like she thought she was talking to an expert. *We didn't want it stolen.* She dropped the baby socks on the couch and looked at her husband, Phil. *Should I show her?*

Phil was somewhere behind me. I heard the floor creak with his shifting weight. I was his no matter what now. My secret had become ours. Either he'd let me live with it, or he'd take his shot. I froze for awfulness.

Phil yawned. *Sure,* he said. His boots clunked away, the screen door opened and closed. Light sprang back into my vision. The brightness of the future.

It's this way, Phil's wife said. I followed her to the other side of the house, the baby's unknowing eyes staring at me over her shoulder. She stopped outside the mudroom and pointed me inside. Pushed up against the back door was a heavy-duty plastic storage bin brimming with sooty bottles of wine.

I dropped to my knees and picked up the first bottle. This wasn't Sutter Home. It was wine people saved for special occasions, wine they might never open at all. *1976 Chateau Montelena chardonnay,* I recorded, *and 1993 Robert Mondavi Reserve cabernet sauvignon…and Dom Perignon vintage 1996…and 2000…and 1995…and 1980…* My voice grew raspy. My knees ached. Fifty bottles later, I croaked, *Now THAT'S the end of the loss* and clicked stop.

I went to the front room, said goodbye to Phil's wife, and made a funny face at the baby. All that was left to do was get past Phil. He was on the porch, stretched out in another lawn chair. His shirt was off, his chest and pot belly covered with a rug of dark hair. I tried to walk past him like a woman on her way to becoming important, but his stare was sifting through the layers of me. It was hard to be important. It was hard to be anything. I stopped just outside the bounds of normal conversational distance. I looked at him looking at me. Was he seeing what the director saw? Or was he seeing the empty Sutter Home bottle? His eyes were the brand-new blue of the baby's eyes, and they told me the truth. They darted to his hand. His hand reached inside a torn thirty-pack of Natural Ice. I saw the trap. I was already inside it. Phil lifted two cans of beer, then his bushy eyebrows. I almost took the bait. Instead, I said my line, my voice clinging to my raw throat like actual grief. *I'm sorry about your loss.* Summoning the broadness of my shoulders and that "something" I had, I walked to my rental car.

UPSET THE APPLE CART

JENNIFER EDELSON

Kelsey stood just off stage, excitedly waiting in her town's Personality Assignment Hall for the Identity Committee to call her name. The Committee had finally reached 'R,' and sometime soon, Kelsey would walk out into the limelight like all ten-year-old Rosedale citizens do on Identity Day every year and assume her position in society. She'd stand under the spotlight, holding her breath as the Committee micro-chipped her with the map that would determine her standing in life before announcing her identity-specific cliché and fashion blueprint to the public.

For months, Kelsey had been hoping for *You Can't Please Everyone* and *Punk Rocker* like her friend Simone's mom, who unapologetically thumbed her nose at society and rocked the world's most kick-ass mohawk. Even a fate like her best friend Sanset, who just minutes ago got *There's No Time Like the Present* and *Eighties English Invasion*, or Sanset's fraternal twin Mac, who'd been assigned *Don't Get Your Knickers in a Twist* and *Skater* would be awesome.

Kelsey's mother and grandmother had both been *Apple Doesn't Fall Far from the Tree* and *Schoolmarm*, and Kelsey knew her mom hoped the Committee appointed Kelsey with the same blueprint. Monotony, it seemed, was a badge of honor in Kelsey's family. But a girl could daydream.

Lost in a fantasy where she scored something like, *And They All Lived Happily Ever After* and *Trendsetter*, Kelsey heard her name called and bounded across the stage to the podium. Nervously, she stood next to Mr. Newman, an *Old as the Hills, Professor* type if there ever was one. She held her breath, fidgeting like a wayward spring, fixated on the thick envelope in Mr. Newman's hands as he slowly tore it open.

Mr. Newman pulled a punch gun from the envelope before fishing out a manual. "Well, this is a new one," he whispered as he crouched and wiped an antiseptic-doused cotton ball over Kelsey's upper arm, raising goosebumps that blanketed her skin like the cache of trendy sweaters or leather jackets she hoped she was about to be appointed. She wrung her hands together. Maybe she'd get *Without a Care in the World* and *Vintage* or maybe *Read Between the Lines* and *Artsy*. She'd always dreamt of a mysterious, carefree life.

Biting back a grin, Kelsey steeled herself against the punch needle, holding her breath for the second it took Mr. Newman to seal her fate. For the rest of her life, the chip in her arm would be her guardian, keeping her from running off the rails as it had every Rosedale citizen since the town's inception. She eagerly accepted the manual Mr. Newman handed her, clutching the sacred text she'd refer to whenever she had questions about what kind of clothing, and classes, and overall role in society, not to mention attitudes she should undertake.

Chip in place, Mr. Newman rose slowly, staring down at Kelsey for a beat before speaking. "Let it be written," he said into the microphone, "that Miss Kelsey Riley will forever be known as *Calm Before the Storm* and *Crinoline*."

Tentatively, people in the audience stood, holding their hands before their mouths, masking their shocked expressions with polite clapping. *Calm Before the Storm* and *Crinoline* might be a new addition to the Committee's manual, but Kelsey read the truth on the townsfolk's faces. As far as they were concerned, she'd just been assigned *Harbinger of Doom*. And *Crinoline*? What the heck was that even?

• • •

Kelsey stood at the end of the school lunch line, waiting like always for everyone else to order and pay before taking her turn. She looked down at her ballooning skirt, bolstered by stiffened horsehair and shellacked linen ribs; she was bigger than a bloody fifth wheel and felt like the boy in a bubble, separated by four feet in all directions from everyone. Kelsey missed eating with her best friend Sanset, who'd stopped lunching with her back in eighth grade because, in Sanset's words, lunch was the one time of the day Kelsey went from *Calm Before the Storm* to *Raging Hurricane*—in direct opposition to the Committee's mandate.

Looking around the lunchroom, where she stood in a corner every day just to eat without knocking into someone or taking up too much space, Kelsey roiled with anger. Some of Rosedale High's other students, like Tylan, a *Love is Blind, Soft Girl*, or Apatha, who brandished *Ignorance is Bliss* and *Bohemian* like an overblown peacock, pissed her off. And being pissed off made things worse. Because for five years now, Kelsey hadn't been able to take a deep enough breath to calm down. Literally, no one in Rosedale knew what being strapped into an iron lung 24/7 felt like. Not that they'd care if they did; ever since Kelsey's Identity Ceremony, she'd been more pariah than citizen.

• • •

DUST UP

On her twentieth birthday, Kelsey waited anxiously in front of Sanset's dorm, secretly suspended by the struts holding her skirt out around her legs. Two years ago, she'd figured out how to rig her crinolines into a secret hammock that supported her weight when she leaned back, allowing her to sit comfortably and still look like she was standing. People in Rosedale called Kelsey a rock; 'solid as they come' and 'legs like a horse' were some of the nicer things they'd said about her. Given the rest of her shitty life, at least it was something. Besides, what was the cliché? 'Fake it till you make it.' Too bad Sanset's asshole boyfriend Tod already landed that label. Tod was a bigger fraud than the statue of the Committee on the college quad, and he still got away with everything.

Gazing longingly at the fancy, red-bricked building, Kelsey wished she could room with her classmates. Dealing with Tod's ego would be worth it. Especially if it meant saving the extra twenty minutes a day it took her to squeeze in and out through the college's abandoned, decrepit dance studio doors, i.e., the only empty building on campus that fit her gigantic wardrobe. All the maneuvering wore her out, but even when things worked, she still felt like burning the college down. Instead, she simmered, glaring at students who gave her a wider birth than necessary with a pointed enough stare—she hoped—to cut them. Kelsey *had* mastered calm, but she related to 'storm' more than anything.

• • •

By Kelsey's twenty-fifth birthday, she and her crinolines had come to an understanding. In fact, Kelsey had made a pretty entrepreneurial penny concocting life hacks and gadgets for herself that other people had no idea they needed until Kelsey invented them. And the money was a godsend because the price of a house able to fit both

Kelsey's lifestyle *and* her wardrobe was astronomical. Kelsey's best friend Sanset and still-an-asshole Tod lived next door. Sometimes Kelsey felt odd about it. Unlike Kelsey, Sanset *had* a mate, but Sanset also never saw Tod for what he was. She never planned ahead or looked back far enough to see the big picture. Despite Tod's obvious duplicities, Sanset never grew a backbone. Being a *There's No Time Like the Present* meant Sanset's life had been full of opportunity but very little chance to reflect or grow from it. Which made Kelsey sad. Jealous as she'd been of Sanset over the years, Kelsey's lot had its advantages.

. . .

Kelsey despised Tod, but on her thirtieth birthday, her consolation prize for putting up with him for years came wrapped in the body of Tod's new best friend, Albert. Most people still crossed the street to avoid Kelsey or teased that she needed her own private zip code, but Albert, a *Rule Breaker* who, in a fitting twist of fate, also scored *Biker*, got in Kelsey's space. In Albert's own words, he preferred to stir up Kelsey's 'after' to sitting with her Zen.

Kelsey fell for Albert on their first date. When her crinoline kept her from riding on Albert's motorcycle, Albert tricked out the bike's seat and sides, assuring it sat them both safely despite her added weight. And Albert wasn't far behind. When a drunk Mr. Newman ran a red light and T-boned Albert's motorcycle, Kelsey's crinoline, fitted with steel girders specifically for traveling, saved both the bike and their lives. Just days later, Albert asked Kelsey to marry him.

. . .

Twenty-five years to the day Kelsey received her identity chip, Kelsey begged Albert to gouge it out of her arm. But after a dose of Lidocaine big enough to down a horse and nothing to show for it, he gave up. In turn, Kelsey searched for Albert's chip, carefully poking around all his tattoos—one absurd cliché for each year of his life since his own Identity Ceremony. But, like Albert, she came up empty. Intrigued by what wasn't there, Kelsey convinced Sanset and Tod to come over and let her play archeologist on their arms, too. But once again, she bombed out.

Sitting in Kelsey's living room, the friends heatedly debated their missing chips, until Kelsey unhooked her crinoline, hoisted it over her head, and dumped it on the couch. She waited for something—punishment, or an alarm, or some horrible cataclysmic event—to end her. Instead, Albert's cat Litmus climbed on top of her crinoline and meowed lazily.

Kelsey stared darts at the couch. "Tonight's the Identity Ceremony."
Albert nodded at her. "I'll start the van."
"Not the van," Kelsey exhaled excitedly. "The bike."

• • •

Hours before the town's yearly Identity Ceremony, Kelsey donned a pair of Sanset's high-waisted, acid-washed jeans, then settled behind Albert on the only motorcycle he'd ever left unmodified, squeezing her legs around its shiny chrome sides. She'd pretended to ride it in the privacy of her garage when Albert wasn't home, but oddly, the seat felt smaller now. Kelsey felt small, and it pissed her off. *Calm before the storm*—well, now she *was* the storm, and she planned on unleashing the truth with a fury.

Locking her arms around Albert's waist, Kelsey fantasized as he pulled down the driveway. Maybe now she could be *Without a Care in the World* and *Japanese Invasion* or maybe *All's Well That*

Ends Well and *Hair Band*. No matter what she chose, she *would* be the tempest that blew the Hall down. But as Albert turned onto the street, cutting through a low-lying fog bank she hoped wasn't a portend of things to come, Kelsey grabbed his arm. Suddenly, she felt naked. Rubbing her shoulder where the chip should be, she waited for Albert to stop. Kelsey hopped off the bike. Shivering, she ran back inside the house and put her crinoline on.

Black snow

P.J. CHRISTMAN

There was plenty she could have done to ameliorate her situation, but spending money was never one of Marlene Sørensson's attributes. When it came to the simplest of expenditures, parsimoniousness imbued every one of her cells, and there weren't as many such composite particles remaining that her significant wealth could easily have increased through the intake of more protein. She barely cast a shadow. Where many individuals of such substantial resources might have become alcoholic or effete, Marlene Sørensson merely exalted in elevating self-pity to a weird form of rapture. She drew great sustenance in remaining hermetic, appearing enigmatic, and having steadfastly withdrawn beyond the reach of the comforts of healthful pursuits and away from those with a capacity for human kindness.

Her small flat had the musty odor of one from which its occupant rarely strays. De Mille, the cat, had been the last animated being to listen with only an intermittent 'meow' to her occasional utterings and mutterings. But with his departure from this world upon being splayed under the tires of a garbage disposal truck,

Marlene had become more resolved that there was no one with whom she wished further to attempt dialogue.

Opportunities would not have been far away. Just outside Marlene's apartment building near the center of Boulder, the fresh air and high-altitude light, even in winter, often illuminated the faces of many moderately happy residents, seemingly in harmony with quasi-urban existence. But Marlene avoided looking out her windows, the blazing Colorado sun kept non-existent by moribund, faded, off-white curtains.

Marlene Sørensson's winter days were spent with the drone of the television providing occasional strident sounds that she would never admit were better than no voices at all. With the TV still on, periodically, she would peruse old photographs of her halcyon Hollywood epoch, the one in which she reached an apotheosis and, at the same time, a growing nadir of despair. For her zenith had been based upon physical beauty, a fleeting characteristic incapable of preservation by elixirs, surgeries, or even the most ardent of prayers.

She was a creature of habit, though diurnal periods were filled more with the avoidance of activities than with those few mundane pursuits she could count on to push the clock onward and get her through another day. The telephone was an annoyance, the sonorous noises from which she no longer had to contend. A permanently unanswered answering machine and an unplugged phone had seen to that. Yet this second-millennium technological advance had pre-empted another avenue to communication with the outside world, facilitating an even greater plateau of solitude and increasing, unrecognized depression. As is the case for many souls lacking any vestige of self-esteem, Marlene's continually deteriorating mindset was converting neurosis into a more serious disease. Whether such pensive alterations of reality were actually disturbing her chemistry became irrelevant because increasing enervation insidiously continued its invasion of her slender frame. Marlene remained one of those millions of urban victims so near, yet so distant, from soothing human interaction.

She might have heated her place. But again, even with enough money to buy the nearby Boulderado Hotel ten times over, Marlene chose rather in the English fashion to wear baggy woolens indoors. After all, she felt ambient heat from the adjoining apartments kept the temperature above fifty degrees most winter days, anyway. During the colder evening hours, she would climb fully clothed in pajamas and socks into bed, propping the pillows up behind her and pulling a weighty Dutch Mother comforter up to a pointed chin devoid of any dewlap. Here, with Dickensian mittens missing the fingertips, in this sepulchral setting, she would often read, while late at night and in the mornings, illumined vapors appeared with each exhalation.

Endless reading filled a life missing human contact with contrived characters, each of whose foibles she accepted as if they were those of long-lost or deceased relatives. Depressing stories were her steady diet. If the protagonists of a book-in-progress fell on hard times, so much the better. There was *schadenfreude*, empathy, or even solace in their misfortunes. Bronte's *Wuthering Heights* and Styron's *Lie Down in Darkness* each had been read countless times. Their characters' plights masked her own deep-seated sadness with a simulacrum of vicarious family life, no matter how distorted or chronically unsettling each proved to be.

Inasmuch as it was Christmas Eve, she had thought of slipping unobtrusively into a neighborhood bar such as the Hungry Toad, but the thought of actually having to appear in public at her age and the probability of having to engage in conversation with some unknown stranger, proved overwhelming. People her age just didn't go unaccompanied to bars. Someone would recognize her or, even worse, stare at her, thinking they knew her from somewhere. Marlene suffered from lofty and misguided self-importance, unattractive in the rich and beautiful but even more so in anyone with the haughty arrogance of those whose charred souls are easily evident upon faces hardened by a loss of any concern whatsoever for others.

So, Marlene was spending Christmas Eve alone. The clock somberly intoned the hour of eleven. In front of the television, she was scarcely aware of the mindless cacophony of four minutes of advertising emanating from it. Earlier, Marlene had lapsed into a protective rhapsody of daydreaming in response to programming laden with seasonal allegorical messages of love and caring. Her pajamas and slippers were propped up on an ottoman. A teacup sat drained in a hand resting upon the arm of a chair whose fabric long ago had faded from the rays of the sun she had once admitted to her chambers with hopeful alacrity. She began to doze while reminiscing about ascending from a limousine to a shower of flashbulbs in front of Grauman's Chinese Theatre. She hadn't bothered to get a Christmas tree. There were no presents to be seen. The three Christmas cards she had received lay unopened on a dusty antimacassar atop the vestibule table.

Just down the hall was an apartment door patched and painted no fewer times than Marlene Sørensson's. Inside this drab barrier, in a more festively decorated apartment, however, Ashleigh Wharton was excitedly wrapping one last gift for her mother, Caroline. Ashleigh was alone, but like all those who have an insatiable curiosity instilled in them at an early age, she was content within her own world of imagination. She was extremely petite for a ten-year-old, but this was more than compensated for by an abundant precociousness, as well as a pleasant disposition and an ability to find excitement or humor in almost any situation. She was a happy, well-adjusted child, even though her unpublished novelist father currently was drinking himself to death in Santa Fe. Most of her resilience was due to the character of her mother. Caroline Wharton was a rare breed of individual raised to look after herself and yet to avoid ever commenting on the acceptance of this same responsibility. She was deeply disappointed that her husband had been unable to discontinue his destructive drinking and gravely shattered when his spirit was seldom, if ever, again to be enjoyed. But to compensate for the loss of his companionship and meager income, Caroline, with little difficulty during the holiday season, had obtained work serving catered food at Boulder's many corporate or private parties.

And so it was alone that Ashleigh quietly snipped the gold cord thread she had fashioned into a crude but thoughtful bow surrounding the navy-blue box and enclosed gift of a tiny horn-rimmed mirror. She smiled as she placed it among the broad array of boxes looming expectantly under the tree. After all, she thought, she could now retire to her reading with great expectations of her mother's broad smile upon discovering that her broken hand mirror had finally been replaced. There was no thought given to the possibility that she would awaken to a Christmas Day apartment, missing this most important person in her life.

As Ashleigh Wharton climbed into her purple metal bunk bed, often the site of late-night discussions with girlfriends sleeping over, she switched on the cream-shaded sconce light just above her pillow. She loved a good read before bed. And the list of books she had recently digested, albeit some without knowing the meanings of a variety of words, would have proved consequential for most adults in a nation addicted to visual imagery and, for the most part, bereft of even semi-literacy. Just then, Ashleigh was slowly devouring *Love in the Time of Cholera* by Gabriel García Márquez. Although empathy with its characters in their declining years proved perplexing, she absorbed their emotions and the tropical descriptions with wonderment.

Just as she had made herself comfortable and her tiny hands positioned the hardback book she had bought in the Boulder Bookstore, she remembered the gift she had prepared for Miss Sørensson.

Ashleigh had failed in her many attempts to talk to the septuagenarian spinster, but not for lack of trying. Her mother had convinced her that Miss Sørensson was miserly and snappish only because of being so terribly alone. Ashleigh knew how that could feel. There was a period when her dad was no longer around at his computer, and her mom was away at work in the afternoons and evenings, that she found herself crying for no reason. Christmas programs on TV had caused some of those same feelings of helplessness to recur. But those diversions were no excuse for Ashleigh to ignore others. Accordingly, earlier that Christmas Eve day, she had gone out and purchased a big card she then had personalized with a drawing, and bits of holly, and a fir branch. Upon the card, she had also composed a poem and had added a hopeful postscript that Miss Sørensson might join her mother and her for some Christmas dinner.

Ashleigh peeked out the door. No one seemed to be stirring, although Frank Sinatra's voice could be heard crooning a Christmas song almost imperceptibly from far down the hall. Nimbly prancing down to Miss Sørensson's door, Ashleigh reached up as high as she could on the badly scarred door and, with a push-pin, attached the card and envelope she had so diligently decorated. She shivered as a cold draft came up from under the ill-fitting door. But with exhilaration, she skipped back to her apartment just as midnight approached. After all, she didn't want her mother to find her awake at such a late hour, especially since her mother might see the mantel stockings she had stuffed with nuts, bananas, and five-and-dime oddments as if Santa Claus had recognized her mother's continuing selflessness.

When Marlene Sørensson awoke on Christmas Day, just for a moment, she lay perfectly still. It occurred to her that the usual intermittent noises from passing cars were not evident outside her apartment. Then she remembered it was Christmas Day. *I wonder if it has snowed*, she thought, *as I don't hear a sound*. Slowly, she turned back the counterpane, swung her wool stocking-clad feet onto the cold floor, and shuffled to the curtained window. Drawing back the material just enough to peep out and unaware of the dust falling from the fabric onto her mottled hand, Marlene noticed that perhaps eight inches of snow covered all but a few car tracks in her street. Large, fluffy flakes still gently wafted down from gray skies. She let the curtain fall back into place. For the past week, Marlene had been fending off an inner battle concerning the resignation that she was alone at Christmas. *Just another day*, she told herself as, with difficulty, she began walking out to the kitchen.

Quite by accident, as circumstances would have it, the answering machine began to click in response to an incoming call as Marlene passed by. She was surprised at how monotonous her own recorded voice sounded given what once had never failed to be projected majestically from the screen. Her message finished, and Marlene felt a frisson of anticipation. She could not stem an increasing curiosity as to who might be calling.

"Ms. Sørensson, this is Mary Paddock at the Boulder Memorial Hospital. I am sorry to trouble you on Christmas Day, but if you get this recording, I wonder if you could call us back as soon as possible regarding an emergency situation of your neighbor, Caroline Wharton—"

Marlene Sørensson's initial reaction was one of being importuned in her sanctum. Quickly, however, she realized that were she not to call back, it would reflect very badly upon her, particularly on Christmas Day.

"—Mrs. Wharton has had an automobile accident, and—"

Marlene plugged the cord into her telephone and took a deep breath. "This is Marlene Sørensson. I'm sorry, but it took me a while to get to the phone."

"I'm sorry to trouble you, Mrs. Sørensson, but your neighbor, Caroline Wharton, has had an automobile accident, and she has asked us to call you. She, and the hospital as well, wondered—until we can release her—if you might be able to look in on her daughter—"

"It's nothing serious, I hope," Marlene asked with an undisguised inquisitiveness.

"We don't think so. Mrs. Wharton was briefly knocked unconscious, but she has regained consciousness. It appears that she may have sustained a skull fracture, and Doctor Rothman has ordered a CT scan just to be on the safe side. He feels there is little probability of any brain trauma, but Mrs. Wharton may possibly have to be held overnight. Just as soon as more is known, we will immediately notify you."

Marlene began in an automatic response to being unwittingly pulled into a situation that could lead to future bother: "Caroline's ex-husband—"

"We have been unable to reach her ex-husband," the hospital nurse interrupted with the realization that she may be losing a necessary contact rather than a patient, "and Mrs. Wharton tells us that most of her other neighbors are away from Boulder for the holidays. Of course, if it would prove to be inconvenient for you to look in on her daughter, perhaps—"

Marlene knew when any further avoidance of this unanticipated responsibility was out of the question. She inhaled in resignation. "I'll certainly look in on her, but on Christmas Day, it might be difficult—"

"We suggest that if you would be kind enough to help us out, you merely tell her daughter that her mother had to go out to a catering job and that she will be home soon. Inasmuch as Mrs. Wharton is a bit groggy and has been slurring her words, we don't feel it appropriate that she call the girl herself just now. It might needlessly frighten the girl. If you would be kind enough to check on Ashleigh—her daughter—the hospital, and I'm sure Mrs. Wharton, would be very appreciative. Would that be possible?"

"I'll just get dressed and look in on her," Marlene answered, at the same time wondering just what she would say to the poor girl without making it apparent something was wrong.

"We'll telephone you as soon as we can determine that Mrs. Wharton is able to come home."

"Very well."

"And thank you for taking time during Christmas to help us out. Goodbye."

It is at such moments, of course, that the deeply lonely find great unexplained relief in the mandate of having to think of someone other than themselves. It felt odd to Marlene Sørensson to experience pathos, but at the same time, she was somehow invigorated with the thought of making sure Ashleigh Wharton's assuredly brief transition could be made a happy one on Christmas Day. Marlene vaguely remembered a Christmas from a long time ago when she had been called upon to visit some sick children in hospital and how she had left the medicinal-smelling premises with a strange peace of mind.

Preoccupation was a normal state of mind for Marlene, so while these and other thoughts pervaded her psyche, it was unconsciously that she dressed in her finest black sheath dress, black stockings, black pumps, and a scrimshaw brooch.

Just as Marlene was leaving her apartment, she saw the card affixed to her door. I'll read it later, she thought to herself, dropping the card back with the three others on the foyer table. Rather than simply feelings of sympathy for the young child, she also considered the difficulty of having to deal with the problem at hand, one that invited distasteful further interactions with other adults in her building. Marlene wished to continue her skillful avoidance of having to say hello to the many unidentified fellow occupants in adjacent apartments.

"Oh, hello, Miss Sørensson," Ashleigh beamed upon opening her apartment door.

"Hello, my dear," Marlene Sørensson answered with the self-importance of one who is used to being recognized.

"Merry Christmas, Miss Sørensson. Please come in," Ashleigh added, pulling the door, dwarfing her in size, wide open and gesturing warmly. "I think my mom's still sleeping because her door's closed. She'll wake up soon, I'm sure. Would you like to sit over here by the tree?"

"Everything looks quite lovely, my dear," Marlene Sørensson commented before continuing on as if matter of fact. "Your mother stopped by early this morning, before you were up, and asked me to look in on you. She was asked by a friend to help serve some Christmas meals at a retirement center, so she asked me to tell you she'll be home just as soon as she can."

"Mm," Ashleigh responded, bravely trying to hide any outward appearance of disappointment. "I hope she gets home soon because I can't wait until she opens my presents for her. Especially the mirror. After my dad went to Santa Fe, she used to spend lots of time combing her hair and looking into it. I think it was one of her favorite things."

This struck an odd chord in Marlene Sørensson for several reasons. It reminded her of how vanity can become a refuge when atop a pinnacle and how such an innocuous habit as combing one's hair can become mesmerizing when despondency has become your best companion. She looked down at Ashleigh sitting there with her hands folded, waiting patiently.

"I don't know if I should try to put the turkey in the oven by myself," Ashleigh said hesitatingly as if Miss Sørensson's approval might be a rite of passage. "Mom sometimes lets me cook things when she's around, but I don't know if I should try to—"

"I shouldn't worry about that, my dear," Marlene Sørensson broke in with, seeming in command of the situation. "If she isn't home in an hour or so, you and I will see to the dinner, rest assured."

The two of them sat there quietly, both knowing that they were filling time rather than using it to their advantage.

"Is it still snowing out?" Marlene Sørensson asked, disguising the rhetorical nature of her question. Both rose out of their chairs, glad of a simple motion relieving them of the burden of a topic of conversation, then peering out of a window ringed with fir boughs.

"It sure looks like it," Ashleigh said. "But the snow down there in the street is starting to get some black puddles in it where the cars have been. I love the flakes floating down, though."

"They are quite pretty, aren't they, dear?" Miss Sørensson answered nonsensically. As she did so she reached out her slender hand to pat the girl's head. Physical contact was a missing element in Marlene's life; however, it was one that was unusually unfamiliar. Just as Marlene's hand paused, Ashleigh began to turn back from the window. The hand receded back behind the black dress. The pair walked back to their chairs.

Ashleigh Wharton began to look around in the nervous fashion of a child, not knowing what to say. Marlene Sørensson remained preoccupied with what must be done if the hospital decided to hold Caroline Wharton overnight.

"Did you get my card?" Ashleigh asked, the foot of one crossed leg bobbing almost undetectably and her face brightening.

"Sorry?" temporized Marlene as she brought herself back to reality. "Oh...*yes*," she then replied effusively, wondering if it had been the one on the door or one of the ones on the table. "It was very kind of you to have thought of me at Christmas."

"I hope you liked the poem. I hoped it would bring you some cheer—I mean, if you didn't get many cards," Ashleigh said with the ingenuousness of one who has no idea of their words' import upon the listener.

"It must have taken some thought," Marlene responded with a smile to disguise her lack of composure after the realization that her cheerlessness had been evident. "And your words were quite beautiful. I'm sorry if I appear too serious to you. I suppose it comes from living alone and being unaware of appearances."

Ashleigh just nodded, unsure if she had caused Miss Sørensson embarrassment. The snowflakes outside were still falling, and the two sat wondering what should transpire next. Collecting her wits, Marlene Sørensson finally concluded that the best thing would be to go back to her apartment to call the hospital.

"I think I'll just pop back to my apartment for a moment to get my glasses," Marlene said after Ashleigh had bounded over to the tree to readjust an ornament.

On her way back to her somber abode, Marlene contemplated what she would face should Caroline Wharton be held overnight in the hospital. There seemed to be no easy answer.

Minutes later, she reached Miss Paddock. "I was wondering if you can tell me anything regarding the disposition of Caroline Wharton?" she inquired after identifying herself.

There was a pause. One of those passages of time that presage extremely bad news. Marlene perceived what was coming next.

"I'm afraid the news is not good," Miss Paddock replied with gravity. "Apparently, there was more damage internally than expected; substantial hemorrhaging was revealed in the CT scan. Unfortunately, Caroline Wharton died at 10:12 a.m."

A feeling of emptiness pervaded Marlene Sørensson. "Oh, dear," was all she could utter.

"It is a terrible shock, especially on Christmas…" Miss Paddock said, a long pause ensuing. "I know this is a terrible burden for anyone, especially on Christmas Day, but if you could just stay with her daughter for several more hours, it would be a great help…"

Marlene Sørensson remained nonplussed.

"Aa…we have finally reached Caroline Wharton's ex-husband, and he is flying up immediately. He should be here by late afternoon. I know it will be difficult, but do you think you could look in again on her daughter?"

"Yes," answered Marlene softly, remaining dazed but quite affected by strange maternal instincts. "Certainly."

When she reached the foyer table, Marlene came out of her shocked trance just long enough to glance down at the colorful card pinned to her door. Mindlessly, she reached down and opened it, then began to read the poem framed by fir needles and holly.

My neighbor is a nice woman named Miss Sørensson,
Who has made many people happy under the bright sun.
Not just on Christmas but on other days, too.
From cinema screens, she has pleased me and you.

Now she is alone with just her TV.
We hope to change that, Mom and me.
To make her happy and make her gay,
To bring her good cheer on Christmas Day.

Marlene Sørensson breathed out a sigh of twenty years. She stood there just for a moment, hearkening back to all the thousands of instances of the rewards of fame. Reminiscences of the throngs that had worshiped her bombarded in a desultory fashion. And yet, all of their power seemed to dissipate like a mirage. The message from Ashleigh had emotionally affected her senses as if the sun was shining between storm clouds. Marlene picked up her glasses case and then pulled her apartment door open.

"Do you think we should put the turkey in the oven?" Ashleigh nervously inquired when Marlene had finished expressing her appreciation for the thoughtful poem in detail.

"Yes, dear," Marlene answered. "It might be a good idea, so your mother doesn't have to face up to it after serving so many meals."

As the pair began to work together to put the stuffing in the turkey, Ashleigh dropped a utensil. Marlene couldn't help but notice how her fingers trembled before she could pick it up. "Are you all right, my dear?"

"Oh, yes, thank you, Miss Sørensson," Ashleigh replied. Marlene, just for a moment, observed the child with fondness as if she had been her own, then inexplicably found herself placing a steadying hand on the child's shoulder. The turkey went into the oven.

"I think we can cook the vegetables later," Marlene said while motioning that they should proceed back to the living room.

When the pair settled back into their respective chairs, Ashleigh's lower lip began to quiver. Marlene Sørensson experienced, without warning, another wave of human compassion she had been missing for decades.

Ashleigh's eyes became moist. "Mom's not coming home," the ten-year-old said softly, fighting back tears. "My dad called, but I didn't want you to know. I thought it might spoil your Christmas—and I thought Mom and I were going to make it special for you."

"That's all right, my dear," responded Marlene Sørensson, moving to sit on the edge of Ashleigh's chair and putting her arm around the girl's slender shoulders. Ashleigh turned her face into Marlene's black dress and clasped her sleeves. Marlene Sørensson trembled slightly. "It's still Christmas Day, my dear, and you've made it a very special one for me."

Shattered

CRISTINA BROWNE

She had only gotten the courage to unpack the crystal object a few months ago. This one piece was discreet enough not to get any questions on how or where she got it. Being able to display it again was a symbolic step and a reminder of how far she'd come.

So, when it came crashing down and flew into a million pieces across the tile floor, she just had to cry. A few minutes later, she paused since the glass debris unknowingly depicted how her heart felt a few years ago, for one particular moment.

As she wept and swept, all those glass nuggets started sparkling, reminding her of all the beautiful memories still present in her heart. The dazzling pile kept growing and growing as she also imagined all the new memories to be made in years to come! Somehow, that shattered piece had exposed the abundance of love within her.

Poor old guy, my ass

SUE BRYAN

Me an' Jimmy crouched in the wheatfield that ran right into our backyards. We were hoping to see the ghost of the wife he had killed.

"He stabbed her eighteen times!" Jimmy punched me in the chest like he had a knife in his fist. I imagined the cold blade in my gut and pushed him.

He pushed back. I stumbled out of the wheat and onto Old Dapper's scruffy lawn. The old guy stood in the middle of the yard with a hunting knife dangling by his side.

I dove back into the wheatfield, breathing hard. I knocked into Jimmy; we fell to the ground. I heard the moms on the block whistling for their kids to come in.

Now Old Dapper was standing over us. The sun glinted on the knife at his side. We ran until we thought we were clear. But there he was again. Wherever we turned, Old Dapper got there before us, though he never seemed to move a muscle. We twisted through the crispy stalks until it was hard to determine where we were.

Jimmy got his bearings and pulled me toward the houses in the distance. We fell, gasping at the edge of his backyard. Red and white lights were flashing through the dusk. Ambulance. Jimmy's mom was standing outside. "It's Old Man Dapper," she said, nodding toward the lights. "He died, don't know when, and no one knew 'til his daughter showed up today. Poor old guy."

FLIPPING

ELAINE KOYAMA

In the 1960s, my family was one of the larger sheep-breeding operations in Montana. We raised registered Suffolk sheep (the ones with the black face and black legs) and a few Columbias (all white).

Every fall, we would clean up the uncut males and some of the ewes and prep them for the annual ram sales held throughout the area. We went to the Montana Ram Sale, the Casper and Buffalo Wyoming sales, and a few times we went to the Newell, South Dakota Show and Sale. These sales were where folks could buy breeding stock, and our award-winning herd was a key staple for these sales.

One fall, when my brother Robert was about thirteen, and I was around ten, the two of us and our dad were heading to the Montana Ram Sale in Miles City. We had a stock rack on our single-axle turquoise Ford truck. It was a newer truck for us, maybe ten years old, with a standard four-on-the-floor transmission and a truck bed hoist that would allow the bed to raise for dumping a load off the back. Our family did a lot of do-it-yourself projects, as all farmers do—and in this case, we had built a second-level deck on the truck bed so we could haul twice as many sheep on a load. The stock rack, built for cattle and horses, was the perfect height for a double-decker sheep truck.

The three of us were heading out with a load of sheep first, and my mom and two sisters were going to follow in the car. Since our reputation was built in our home state, we took our best livestock to the Montana Ram Sale. We loaded championship ewes and rams onto the truck. We put the ewes on the bottom deck, the rams on the top.

It was a party atmosphere for us; this sale was a big revenue-generating event for the farm. The sale was also a big social event for the men and their wives, with dinners and speakers before the sale. We would always go to the 600 Café, and the adults would end up at the Montana Bar a few doors down on Main Street.

That day, we headed out with a truckload of sheep—Robert driving, me in the middle straddling the gear shift, and Daddy on my right. Back in those days, there was no Interstate 94; it was all two-lane winding roads through the coulees and bench land following the Yellowstone River.

Yes, Robert was driving. He was maybe two or three years away from getting a driver's license, but it was normal protocol for us to drive at an early age in our family. Every farm kid drove early. And he had a lot of experience driving already. The trip was uneventful. We stopped in Forsyth for gas, where Daddy bought me red licorice, some chocolates, and gum. We continued, climbing out of the river valley and driving on top of the bench for fifteen to twenty miles. The coulees that drained the semi-arid land cut rough valleys along the way. The road would wind down into the draws and then wend its way back out. We were lulled by the hum of the truck tires on the blacktop, the low roar of the engine.

As we entered another of those draws, the road descended, curving to the left. It was a beautiful fall day, the leaves turning, the sage pale blue-green and grasses yellow-gold. I could feel the centrifugal force pulling on the truck, my body beginning to lean into my dad's side. Robert and Daddy began talking to each other over my head about the pull on the truck, what to do. It felt like being on a merry-go-round, going fast but feeling sickeningly slow.

I looked down at the candy in my lap, the red licorice open, the candy bars intact as was the spearmint gum. I closed my eyes and told myself, "When I open my eyes, we'll be on the road at the bottom of the draw."

Well, I was right. When I opened my eyes, we were at the bottom of the draw. But not on the road.

I was under the steering wheel on top of Robert, his face covered in blood. *He's dying,* I thought. The truck engine was still running.

Robert looked at me with a frown and said, "Get off of me. You're bleeding all over." I had a bloody nose, and the blood on Robert was my own.

The next thing I knew, my dad was there, pulling me off, flipping the key so the engine shut off. The three of us did a quick check. Aside from a cut on Daddy's arm, we were miraculously unscathed. I got bloody noses all the time as a kid, so we weren't worried about that. We were at the bottom of the gully, and as we looked back up the road, we could see sheep and 2x12 boards strewn across the hillside—the bucks on the top deck had flown off first, and many of them died on impact. Some of the ewes that had been on the lower deck were running around the open ground—a few of the sheep had broken legs, one had a broken jaw, but those running were relatively unharmed.

Robert had walked back, checking some of the sheep lying on the ground. By this time, cars were stopping. I stood on a rise with my dad, surveying the battlefield. I thought, *What am I supposed to do? Maybe cry?*

So I began to cry. And my dad looked at me and asked, "Are you hurt?"

I said, "No."

He said, "Then don't cry. You have nothing to cry about."

I stopped. And I stood there, not even realizing at the time how lucky we had been.

The highway patrol came, and my dad said he had been driving. We rounded up the surviving sheep. Someone had a gun, and they shot a few that were too injured to save. One of the prize rams was dead, but out of about sixty heads, maybe twenty were still alive, huddling as sheep do.

Someone called a local farmer who came and loaded the living sheep on their truck and took them to Miles City. I don't know who came and picked up the dead ones. Another Good Samaritan gave the three of us a ride to the Miles City Hospital, where they put a bandage on Daddy's arm and claimed Robert had a contusion—which I thought was life-threatening but turned out to be a bump on his head. I was unharmed.

Later, we found out that when Mom and the girls drove through Forsyth, they saw the truck that had been towed to the gas station. They immediately stopped, sure that we must have been hurt or killed. They found out we were all okay. They looked inside the cab and saw my candy on the floor. The center of the cab roof was peeled back where a guard rail post had come through, right about where my head would have been.

Turns out that while I had my eyes closed, pretending everything was going to be alright, Robert and Daddy were talking about what to do. Daddy said he was going to bail out. He told Robert to grab me and go under the steering wheel. They had only seconds to do this. We think the top-heavy load began tipping the truck, and then the hydraulic hoist gave out, letting the bed lift, exacerbating the situation. The truck rolled to the passenger side. Daddy was lucky not to have been crushed. And Robert, in spite of the teasing and torturing older brothers do to their little sisters, had grabbed me as planned and held me down.

This is what happened, as I remember it. I never knew how many dollars were lost, never knew if my dad could collect insurance, never even wondered how this might have impacted the family or the farm's economic success. We talked a little bit about how lucky we had been that no one was badly hurt. There was never any blame on anyone for anything. I joked that I had lost all my candy. We all knew that was the least of our losses. But in truth, we lost nothing because the three of us walked away that fine autumn afternoon with barely a scratch on us.

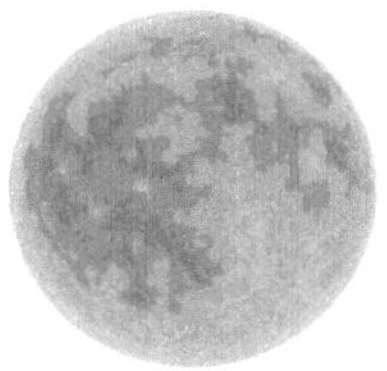

MADONNA OF THE LADYBUGS

VICTORIA GREGG

Robbie and me were in line at the Price Cutter when the Madonna of the Ladybugs pulled up. She set up her trailer in the far corner of the parking lot, where people could see as they drove past on Oak.

"Should we go check it out?" Robbie asked.

He was fifteen that winter, and his voice had changed as much as his clothing. Every once in a great while, he'd say or do something that caught me off guard, made me wonder at how he could live both as a man and a child, all wrapped up in the same lanky body. I could hear the excitement in his voice just underneath the indifference he put on.

"Suppose we could," I said.

Robbie hid a smile behind a stoic nod. "Might be interesting, is all," he said. "Of course, it might be a rip-off, too, so…"

"I've got cash, son, don't worry about it."

A freezing drizzle hit us as the automatic supermarket door slid open. I zipped my jacket to my chin, shivering as the rain hit my face. Robbie was already five steps ahead of me, practically bounding toward the trailer only just set up. I was half-afraid he'd fall and break something.

"I'm going to drop this bag off at the truck," I yelled to his back. He raised a hand in acknowledgment and disappeared around the front of the trailer. I shook my head at his excitement. It'd been a while since I'd seen him that way. He was too conscious of himself to let anything genuine come through. Or at least it felt that way most of the time.

He was still standing at the trailer door when I walked up, face twisted in irritation.

"It costs twenty bucks," he said, gesturing to the laminated sign posted to the door.

"Well," I said, "guess how much cash I've got on me."

Robbie turned to me, brow furrowed.

"Dad, that's only enough for one of us."

I nodded.

Robbie sighed and rubbed the wispy hair along his jaw.

"I don't want to go without you."

His voice was soft and a little fearful, a tremor that he couldn't quite hide. It rubbed me the wrong way.

"Well, now I don't know that I even wanted to go in. I've got enough for you if you want. If not, we'll go home."

"It's just crazy expensive, you know? Like, why do they need to charge so much for some crappy circus attraction?" The softness had gone from Robbie's voice, replaced by the anger I'd gotten to know so well in the last months.

"It's high, for sure," I said. The drizzle was coming down harder now, turning the world around us gray.

"It's stupid. I never wanted to go in anyway."

There was a slump in Robbie's shoulders and a cloud over his face. I couldn't tell if he wanted me to talk him into or out of the trailer.

"Go on in, Robbie. I'll wait out here for you."

I pulled the crumpled twenty from my pocket and pushed it toward him. Robbie stared at me hard, for longer than I normally would have tolerated, before pushing my hand away.

"I don't want it. I just want to go home," he muttered, turning away so that I nearly couldn't hear him. "It's just stupid it's so expensive."

I clenched my jaw. "We can afford it. It's twenty dollars, and you want to go. Go."

Robbie's nostrils flared. So that was what was going to happen? We were going to have it out in the middle of the parking lot, standing in front of some pass-through sideshow attraction. I pictured it, Robbie sullen and prickly the rest of the day, maybe the rest of the week, and me getting madder by the minute because of it. I took a deep breath. Lead by example, Robbie's mother always said.

"Robbie, I want you to go. Have fun. I'll wait out here and see you in a few minutes." I kept my voice measured and calm. Even threw in a smile at the end there.

"Fine," Robbie said, snatching the bill from my hand.

I clenched my jaw and nodded at him as he turned and walked up the metal steps to the trailer door. His shoulders were still tense, knotted up to his ears, as he stepped inside without looking back.

I rubbed the back of my neck and walked to the truck. I had half a mind to sit and wait for Robbie in the cab, but instead, I pulled it up along the trailer and sat on the tailgate to watch for him.

I pulled my hood against the ice and took my first good look at the trailer. From where I sat, I was face to face with the Madonna of the Ladybugs. It wasn't faded as I expected, as the cheap paint and the years of interstate travel usually rendered those sideshow trailers. Her eyes were all you could see painted on the side, amber with dark lashes and thick black liner. Her face was completely obscured by hundreds of painted orange and black beetles, so bright and detailed that they might have flown right off the side. I shuddered. That's what Robbie was in there with. I never really understood what attracted the boy.

I shrank into my jacket, out of the wind whipping across the parking lot. The grocery store was empty this time of morning. Likely, everyone was in church, or at least home, so they couldn't be accused of not being in church. The cold from the unlined tailgate seeped through my jeans, setting me to shivering. Time dragged, minute by minute. I thought of sitting on a deer stand, quiet and still, for the hours it took for a buck to wander into view. Patience for patience's sake, my own father would say at the end of every unsuccessful hunt. As if he could undo all the disappointment by wishing it away. Turn it into some kind of life lesson. Rich from a man who'd as soon smack you in the head as wait out his moods.

A woman in a Carhartt jacket stepped out from behind the trailer, frowning at the weather. She was big, taller, and brawnier than most men I'd come across. I supposed you'd have to get that way, traveling around from scummy town to scummy town, as she most likely did. Keep people from starting anything.

She pulled out a cigarette and threw the empty pack on the ground. She shot a look my way, and when I didn't say anything, she relaxed against the side of the trailer. Her hands fumbled through the pockets in her jacket.

"Need a light?" I asked.

She nodded and grumbled a thanks.

"Got someone in there?" she asked, hitching her thumb back to the trailer.

That surprised me. Shouldn't she know whether someone was inside? I figured she was just making small talk and played along.

"My boy."

She grunted and nodded, and we stood there in silence while she puffed on her cigarette. There was something about her that threw me off. Not that I'm a big talker myself. The quiet never bothered me so long as it was companionable. But with her, I had a compulsion to fill it up with something.

"Why ladybugs?" I asked.

The woman wrinkled her forehead as if I'd asked her to solve a math problem.

"What do you mean, why ladybugs?"

"Just that," I said. "Why not something with a bigger draw? Spiders or scorpions, or those big hissing roaches they got in Africa?"

"Oh," the woman replied, relief seeping into the edges of her voice. "Ladybugs are predictable. They all flock to the highest place they can. She sits up high on that throne, and the ladybugs, they follow, you know? Not everything acts like you'd expect. A lot of animals are unpredictable."

I nodded. Nature disguised as a parlor trick. Everything had a trick hidden beneath it. I thought it'd be good to talk to Robbie about that when he got out. Something he ought to know. He was already mad about the money; it'd be a good lesson.

I looked down at my watch.

"Sure is taking a while," I said, low enough that the strange woman might think I was talking to myself if she didn't feel like answering.

"It's a process," she said.

I grunted an agreement, though she knew as well as I did that I didn't really follow her. The woman gave me a single curt nod before snuffing her cigarette out on the wet pavement. She disappeared back into the trailer through a door I couldn't see on the other side.

By the time half an hour had gone by, my patience was wearing thin. Robbie had surely seen whatever the Madonna of the Ladybugs had in store for him. The more I sat and thought it through, the more irritated I got. I could see it all in my mind, him taking his sweet time just to prove some kind of point. Make me wish I didn't give him the money to go. I could remember a time when things weren't always a game.

I tramped over to the trailer and gave the door a solid knock.

"Come on now, Robbie. I think you've got your money's worth."

I put my ear against the cold metal door and listened. There was nothing. No sound, no movement. I wrenched the door open and stepped inside.

The woman in the Carhartt jacket sat behind a little metal desk next to a thick black curtain. She was scribbling in an accounting book and barely glanced up at me.

"Is he done yet?" I asked.

She shrugged. "I don't have any control over what happens inside."

I rolled my eyes and walked through the curtain, pushing past the hand-painted sign that hung in front of me: "Admission: $20. No exceptions."

The smell hit me first before my eyes could adjust to the darkness. Incense and dead crickets. It was bolstered by the heat, a sort of dry, stripping wave that made the back of my neck prickle. Felt like I was under a heat lamp. The whole inside of the trailer was covered in the same black fabric: floors, ceiling, and walls all black and fuzzy, like the inside of a portrait studio. In the middle was a pedestal, covered likewise in the black fabric. It was the only form in the room. On the center sat a single ladybug.

I felt my way along the wall, pushing against the heavy black fabric for any sign of something behind it. Everywhere I pushed, I only felt the solid walls of the trailer.

"Robbie!" I yelled at the empty room, my voice dampened by the velvet walls. "Robert!"

Nothing. I staggered back through the curtains to the entrance. The woman at the desk didn't even look up at me.

"What the fuck was that?"

"You didn't pay," she said, pointing to the sign hanging above the door. "You don't get to see if you don't pay."

I gaped at her.

"So what, you won't raise those curtains? My boy's in there."

"Curtains don't move," she said. "You pay, you see."

I slammed my palm against the metal desk, but the woman didn't flinch.

"You let him outta there! I swear to God."

"He'll come out when he's ready. Meantime, if you want to experience the Madonna of the Ladybugs, the price is twenty dollars. No exceptions."

I clenched my jaw and let the heavy metal door clang behind me as I walked back to the truck. I dug through the glove box for the stash of money I had there, looking in the side mirror at the trailer. I told myself it was to watch out for Robbie. Reality was, it was as much because of those painted-on eyes as anything. I couldn't shake the idea that they were watching me. Kind of thought kids have.

Once I'd come up with the money, I turned to look once more at the painting and those deeply shaded ladybugs. The wind blew the ice sideways, and the pavement had turned slick. That's why I shuddered so fiercely and why it took all my momentum to get moving toward it.

I stepped inside and shoved the money toward the woman.

"I don't appreciate the scam you're running here. Ransoming kids, basically, and you'd better believe that's how I'll tell it to the cops."

The woman took my money and gestured to the curtain with a smile.

"Thank you, and enjoy your time with the Madonna of the Ladybugs."

If she weren't a woman, I'd have hauled off and hit her. Instead, I snarled and pushed my way through the black curtain. I heard her say something faintly as I walked through, but I didn't stop to ask her to repeat herself.

There was no adjusting to the darkness this time. It was the light, blazing and warm, that I had to shield my eyes against. As my eyes adjusted, the smell hit me—waves of dust and mildew and the faintly rotten smell that comes from fallen logs: halfway through the transition that breeds life from decay.

A kaleidoscope of reds and oranges and yellows surrounded me, all lit from within, as if every little bug had its own power source, humming all at once until that was all I could hear. Individual paper lanterns crawled over every inch of the ceiling, walls, and floors, shifting beneath me and climbing up my legs. I swatted at my ears, even though they hadn't yet made it that far. Millions of them. And in the middle, glowing brighter than the lot, was the Madonna.

I shouldn't have been surprised by the look of her sitting up there on her tall throne. She was just as she was on the outside of the trailer—a pair of amber eyes looking out from a mass of ladybugs. They moved over one another, clumping up across her skin and lining every strand of her hair. Where they left a gap, no matter how small, light came bursting out. It hurt to look, but my eyes wouldn't move from her figure.

"Where's Robbie?" I shouted. The beating thrum of ladybug wings drowned me out as they skittered across the walls.

I repeated my question, yelling so loud my throat closed up. The Madonna didn't respond, didn't so much as move. I walked toward her across the writhing floor. Those shelled bodies crunched beneath my boots with every step. Bile settled into the sore spot in the back of my throat, and I felt sweat running down my hairline. Or maybe it was the ladybugs finally reaching the top.

"Where's Robbie? What'd you do with him?"

I was in front of the Madonna, inches from where she sat. Her eyes followed me, peered down into mine, but the rest of her was still. A pain burned somewhere inside of me, radiating out and almost overtaking my rage. But I didn't let it.

"Tell me, goddamnit!" I screamed, reaching up to grab her arm.

My fingers slid through a swarm of bugs where flesh should be, scattering several away. The light that spilled out blinded me, and I fell to my knees, smearing crushed ladybugs across the soft black floor.

The figure in front of me spread her arms wide and exploded in ladybugs and light, coating my body with layers of insects. I beat at myself like I was putting out a fire. Where my skin was exposed, their sharp alien wings scraped me, leaving microscopic cuts on my hands and face. I shook and walloped myself until the insects had retreated back to the walls and ceiling.

Once they'd stopped flying and I could hear again over the sound of my own heavy breathing, I stood still and listened. A mound of ladybugs in the corner heaved and sobbed.

"Robbie," I said. "Robbie!"

His response was almost too soft to make out, like he was farther away than just across the room. I ran toward him, ignoring the godawful sound of snapping beneath my feet. When I pulled him up, the ladybugs that covered him alighted, flying as one to the dark corners of the trailer. Robbie was pale, shaky, and his bloodshot eyes looked a million miles away.

"It's okay, son. It's all right now."

He shook his head and furrowed his brow. "Dad, I…"

I grabbed his hand, ignoring the tiny cuts that covered it, ignoring the same on my own, and hauled him toward the curtain. My head was filled with questions, but I didn't want to pull them out of Robbie, as much for my own sake as his.

The light beyond the curtain was too gray, too fluorescent to make sense of after the red-orange glow of the inner trailer. The woman was gone, her ledger still open on the metal desk. The ordinariness of the little office made my stomach turn. I squeezed on Robbie's hand, trying my best to ignore how limp and clammy it was.

"We'll get you home," I said, maybe to him and maybe to myself.

He nodded and let go of my grip, walking out of the metal door and disappearing into the drizzle of the grocery store parking lot. I gave the room one last look and followed him out.

Robbie was already in the truck when I climbed inside. He pressed his forehead against the window, eyes closed tightly. A ladybug crawled across his collar, and I swatted it away with more force than I should have. Robbie didn't flinch.

I turned the ignition and started to say something before stopping myself. Nothing would have been right.

"Dad…" Robbie said, voice cracked and soft.

From the corner of my eye, I saw the tears staining his cheeks. His body folded against the door, made him half his size. I clenched my jaw and nodded in his direction. In the rearview mirror, the painted eyes of the Madonna of the Ladybugs watched us pull away.

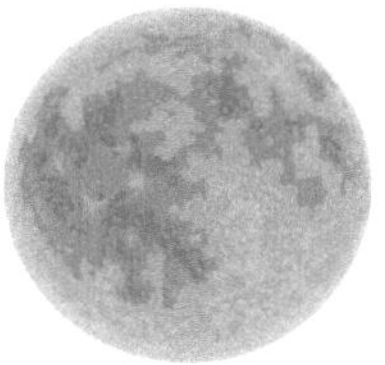

"HALLOWEEN" PARTY

PATRICK X.L. LEE

I'm at my friend's Halloween house party. It's me and a bunch of other horror movie geeks. I don't know most of them. People are wearing costumes of horror icons: Freddy Krueger, Jason Voorhees.

I'm standing by the drink table, doing my best to be silent and scary in my own costume. Not sure it's working.

It's raining outside. Lightning flashes in the windows, followed by a loud clap of thunder. Folks jump, then giggle nervously.

One woman is wearing a sari and an Indian blouse. "I'm a yogini," she says, whatever that is. She's at a small table using a kitchen knife to cut a cake shaped like a jack-o'-lantern.

On the TV, John Carpenter's "Halloween" movie plays. Even with the sound muted, I know the line voiced by one of the characters.

Dr. Loomis: "I met this six-year-old child, with this blank, pale, emotionless face, and the blackest eyes ... the devil's eyes. I spent eight years trying to reach him, and then another seven trying to keep him locked up because I realized that what was living behind that boy's eyes was purely and simply ... evil."

Haha, such a perfect line.

"Nice costume!" a short guy says.

He's standing in front of me. His compliment sounds like a condescending lie. But I nod in thanks. I'm not an asshole.

"Michael Myers from 'Halloween,'" he says. "The original film, amirite? Based on the Shatner mask?"

The guy is persistent and knows his horror films. Guess I have to be friendly.

"Right," I say. "So you know about the mask?"

He's dressed as Art the Clown from "Terrifier," a horror movie from a few years back. His black and white costume is spot on. Except for the part where Art never says a word. I won't say I'm impressed. After all, he's too short.

"Of course, who doesn't know about the Shatner mask? Where'd you find it?" Art says.

It's a good thing he can't see me blush. I can't tell this dork that I bought a cheap Chinese-made repro mask from some fan site. I'm not rich enough to buy the high-end prop replicas, after all.

"Oh, from this collector I know. He let me borrow it."

"Coolcool," Art says. "I love that movie."

So obvious.

"Yeah," I say.

"So what's your favorite of the 'Halloween' sequels?" he asks, popping a candy corn into his mouth. I guess he's not going away.

"I'm partial to the Rob Zombie ones," I say. "I dug the psychological backstory."

Art ponders this. Takes a pull from his beer. He leaves black lipstick marks on the bottle.

"Hmm."

"You don't agree?" I say. I'm kinda defensive about my critical judgment.

"Oh, they were great," he allows. "It's just … "

Now I'm irritated. He clearly doesn't know I write movie reviews for *Bloody Disgusting*.

"You just …?" I goad him.

He scrunches up his Art face. "Well, Michael Myers isn't really about psychology, is he?"

"Whaddaya mean?" I say. "He's fixated on his sister Laurie!"

Art nods. "Sure. In 'Halloween II,' for sure. But in the original 1978 movie, Laurie's not his sister, is she? I mean, she's just some random babysitter he comes across."

I'm enraged. How can a horror geek be so dim?

"It's the tag in the original movie!" I say. "Dr. Loomis goes back to the sanitarium and finds the word 'Sister' scratched into Michael's door!"

Art nods. "Yeah, well, sure," he says. "Yeah, in the broadcast version of the film."

I tilt my head like Michael did.

"By the way, that was something NBC asked Carpenter to do," Art says. "Carpenter disavows that. He actually said he never liked the idea of Laurie being Michael's sister."

"Where'd you get that from?" I ask.

Art nods. "Yeah, John told me that himself. When I interviewed him for ComicBook.com a couple of years ago. After David Gordon Green's 2018 sequel came out. You saw that, right?"

I'm stunned. I nod.

Art takes another sip from his beer. "Yeah, that was why Green removed that part of the canon from his movie and picked up directly from Carpenter's original movie, where Laurie was not related to Michael," he says.

I need to sit down. I walk over to the kitchen and take a chair at the table next to the jack-o'-lantern cake.

Art follows me. He sits next to me.

"Here's my take on Michael," Art says, leaning forward. "He

has no psychology. Dr. Loomis doesn't have a bead on him because he never talks. Michael has no trauma, no backstory, no subtext. He just *is*. He's like a falling rock. Like thunder. Like a lightning bolt."

I'm not listening anymore. Just go away, Art.

But he continues. "He's not even evil like Dr. Loomis says." Art rests his arm on the table.

"Evil is a funny word," Art says. "It's how humans frame things they can't make sense of, like natural disasters or serial killers. But something like Michael: He just shows up, and if you're in his path, he just kills you. And death can happen to anyone, anytime, amirite?"

Art looks at me when he says this. I look at him. He picks up the knife from the cake and plunges it deep into my neck.

The pain is excruciating. I try to scream but only gurgle. I stand up, I grab the knife with my right hand, pull it out. I feel the warm blood pulse out of my neck.

I start to get woozy. I sit down hard, my head light. My vision gets fuzzy. I hear a voice in the distance.

"That's a shitty mask, by the way," Art says as he walks away before everything goes white.

THE SOUND BARRIER

DANIEL HUANTES JR.

Without sitting on his hands, Greg didn't know what to do with them. He sat at the circular dining room table and watched his mother in the kitchen. She rushed from station to station, stirring and sipping and salting as she moved. It was chaos to Greg but clear to his mother, who never stopped for more than a moment. Greg understood why his dad had jumped at the opportunity to run out for last-minute groceries. Within the kitchen, his mother readied herself for war.

The tamales were stockpiled, the avocado was mashed, the limes were cut, ready to be put on nearly everything. Greg winced as he saw the salsa hit the sarten, the fumes from the chiles lifting into the air, a step away from chemical warfare. Greg knew from experience how unforgiving that gas could be. Greg once tried to explain the feeling to a friend, but the closest thing his friend could conjure was the smell of frying pickles. Greg felt something was lost in the transition from pepper to pickle. A burning something was lost.

Food was a double-edged sword. Every time his family gathered, they asked for seconds. Every time they left, they asked for antacids.

Greg turned from the kitchen toward his little cousins as they tiptoed across the living room. The oldest of the troupe at nine years old, Diego was demonstrating to the youngest, Noah, how to sneak polvorones out of the kitchen and eat them, hiding behind the couch. Sitting on the couch, seven-year-old Brandon ate his cookies in the open, brave or unaware. Greg couldn't quite see what Diego was saying but imagined it was sage advice regarding obfuscating the number of cookies the adults thought they had eaten. Each sugary pebble was a boulder to the small brown hands that gripped them. Greg remembered his seniority, stood up from the circular dinner table, marched toward the counter, grabbed a cookie, and only made a small effort to hide it. He turned his back on the kitchen, leaning on the white counter, and started to eat.

Greg felt a sharp tap on his shoulder and jumped, coughing up sugar. He turned around to see his mom repeating his name.

"What?" Greg signed.

"I've been waving my arms at you, but you don't listen!" His mom signed, punching the air. Greg was silent, unsure if a response was what she wanted.

"Go change. Your Welo and Wela are almost here. Everyone else won't be too far behind." She turned him around and pushed him out of the dining room to go get ready.

. . .

Greg walked in and was startled to see the house full. How had they all gotten there so quickly? His mother turned and motioned for him to come.

Greg's heart beat hard as he approached his family. He could barely lip-read Spanish and knew he needed to practice more. All at once, three of his uncles detached themselves from the family and pushed away from the small circular table they sat around. A wall of grins formed, and Greg felt his heart rate ease. The three of them standing together looked more like larger versions of Diego, Noah, and Brandon, equally as likely to be caught stealing polvorones.

"What's up!" Tony signed, speaking along in English.

"Nothing much," Greg replied, shrugging but unable to hide his smile. Carlos shoved Tony aside, attempting to sign himself, but before Greg could figure what he meant, Tony had rammed back into him. The pair struggled shoulder to shoulder, trying to knock the other down.

Gustavo stepped in front and signed in front of his stomach so only Greg could see.

"My brothers are idiots."

Greg laughed.

"Happy Birthday, Greg. We're all glad to see you."

With Gustavo now tasked with making the final decision as to the winner of the shoving match, Greg walked past them and began greeting his family.

Greg smiled at his Tio Lalo, who slapped him on the back, shaking his hand and pulling him into the crowd of his relatives. Each tight-packed family member pulled him around the table with a mixture of signing, smiling, and words that Greg tried his best to discern. Tia Alma hugged him, her squat frame previously hidden behind his two towering cousins, Edgar and Marcello, who both nodded at Greg. Edgar and Marcello knew how to sign, but at sixteen, they were far too cool to say anything, signed or otherwise. The top of Tia Alma's gray hair barely reached his chest, but her grip was strong, and she held him tight before letting go. She said something to Greg in Spanish, but he couldn't make out any of it. Greg smiled and nodded.

"Si, gracias," he mouthed. He turned, unsure if Alma could read lips.

Greg continued around the table until he arrived in front of his grandparents. He looked down at his Wela, even shorter than her sister Alma. His Wela beamed and stood up, wrapping Greg in a soft hug. He felt warm and decided he had to try to say something. He pulled back from the hug and cleared his throat.

"Temo," he spoke slowly. Greg looked at his grandmother, hoping that this was good enough. Her head tilted, confused, and she turned to Greg's mother.

Shit, Greg thought. He cleared his throat and tried to ignore the stubborn toad sitting in his mouth.

"Te. Amo," Greg spoke. He was embarrassed but felt his second attempt was good. His Wela turned back to him, beaming again. Greg could see her lips begin to fly as she spoke in a rapid stream of Spanish. He tried to make out a word or a phrase on her slight lips before giving up. He hugged her again, and when his Wela finally let go, Greg saw her turn to him clearly and mouth "Te amo." Greg felt warm.

Greg turned to his Welo, now beaming himself, sturdy in his black leather cowboy boots. Greg reached out to shake his hand, but his Welo knocked it away, laughing and embracing him before pulling back and signing.

"Happy birthday, Mijo. Congratulations, you are fourteen."

Greg smiled wide and mouthed, "Thank you," stunned. When had Welo learned to sign? Greg turned toward his grinning mother.

"He took a class last week!" his mother signed with exuberance, her pride in her own father radiating out from her. As if on cue, Greg's father emerged from the garage holding two tall, cold, blue cans of beer. He feigned handing one to Greg, laughing hard at his joke, before handing the can to his grandfather.

Greg sat down and was handed a plate. The fiesta had begun.

• • •

The family ate together. Some nodded and smiled, engaged in a half-dozen disjointed conversations, stopping and starting between bites of food. Some told stories about work or kids, and some called to pass along more salsa, rice, or tortillas. Carlos waved from across the table, catching Greg's eye.

"My diet is RUINED!" Carlos signed, laughing before piling more tamales onto his plate.

"Blown to pieces," Greg signed back, grinning.

Greg noticed the small side conversations peter out, absorbed into the escalating conversation between Tony and Gustavo. Tony leaned forward and brushed off Gustavo, directing his words toward the rest of the family. His Wela rolled her eyes but was engaged like the rest of them. Greg tried to watch his lips, but Tony spoke in quick Spanish, turning to engage the whole table.

Tony's story became more animated as he began acting out scenes. Tony began making faces, imitating some character in the story. Greg chuckled at the theatrics as he tried to make out what the story was about, staring at Tony, hoping a familiar phrase would give him something to anchor onto.

So far, Greg had caught that the story was about Gustavo, more from body language than anything. Trying to find the thread, Greg became caught in the energy. He laughed, watching Gustavo's head in his hands as Tony aired his dirty laundry. He saw a few clues. He saw "hermano" delivered with rolled eyes and laughed harder as he caught Gustavo growing red at "novia" and "bailar." Although many words missed him, Greg laughed harder and harder, his whole family doing the same, wrapped up in Tony's energy.

Greg watched as his Welo wheezed, trying to catch his breath, and the family laughed even harder in response to the story. Greg wiped tears out of his eyes as he tried to return his focus to the story. Tony slowed the story almost to a halt, and from the climax, with

Gustavo as red as the pozole in front of him, Greg caught a single word: "chones."

The family exploded, and Greg started to wheeze just as his grandfather had a moment ago. Together, the family laughed themselves out of breath, only catching it long enough to begin to laugh again. Like crashing waves that kept returning to knock them down, the family seemed stuck. Gasping for air, Greg looked around the table, and even Gustavo had begun laughing, wiping tears from his eyes. Tony sat back, proud of himself.

The table finally began to quiet down when everybody turned at once. Following their faces, Greg looked toward his father, facing him. Smiling, making clear, deliberate signs, and articulating each syllable, his father addressed Greg only.

"Did you understand that?" his father asked. The family turned to Greg, who wished he could disappear. He felt like a squashed bug. For a moment, he had been a part of the family; for a moment, they laughed together. Now they all knew that he wasn't one of them. Greg was on the outside looking in.

"Some," Greg signed back. He felt the eyes of his family boring into him, and he knew he, too, was turning bright red. He was dying. There was no coming back. Greg looked down and hoped his father would have the decency to leave him to die in peace.

His father began to sign, and Greg got ready for everyone to watch as the story was explained again in excruciating detail. But with his father only a few words in, Gustavo stood up to get the table's attention.

"Now!" he signed and spoke, winking at Greg. "I think if it's all the same with y'all, it's my turn to tell the REAL story."

Levity returned to the table, and Greg began to laugh. They were a unit once again.

Lessons Unlearned

GREGORY L. WAGNER

Jonah stares at the answer to problem twenty-one in the back of his organic chemistry book. Staring doesn't change the answer. He looks at the notebook page to his right. His conclusion doesn't agree with the book. Calculations litter the page like confetti after a homecoming parade. Jonah cannot follow his own attempts at logic. Paper crinkles in the stillness of the library as he turns his wire-bound notebook to a fresh page.

Jonah hears the pine-snake hiss of a nylon windbreaker being shrugged off, the telltale snap of metallic zippers hitting the tile floor of the main library hall. He writes down the basic equation and the information from problem twenty-one for the fourth time. The dark gray strokes from the pencil are clean and precise on the ruled page. He begins again.

"How's it going?" The voice is hushed. It's Saturday early afternoon. Anyone in the campus library today is here to work.

Adrenaline surges through Jonah's chest. His hand twitches in a move to cover his notebook. He succeeds in keeping his hand still.

Claire leans over his arm to look at the notebook page. "Problem twenty-one? That one's not too bad. Problem forty-three sucks."

She slides out of the chair next to him and sits down. The wood chair legs screech on the tile as she shuffles up to the thick slab table.

"Great." Jonah cringes. He looks at Claire out of the corner of his eye. A ray of sun from the overhead cupola's windows highlights her blonde hair. "Problem twenty-one is kicking my ass."

She leans sideways to look at his notebook. Her left shoulder comes to rest against his upper arm. "May I?"

The crinkling paper is conspicuous as she turns back to his previous attempt. He feels the blush surge over his cheeks.

"Okay," she nods quietly, "I can see what you were doing." The weight from her shoulder increases as she reaches over with her right hand to point at the beginning of the messy page. "This is right. You totally had it. But," her finger traces down to the next line on the page, and she twists her head to look at him. Her shoulder remains in contact. "Why did you go here?"

He doesn't meet her gaze. He shrugs.

"Silly," Claire nudges him. "You need to trust yourself."

She sits up straight. Jonah feels the loss of contact. His back slumps slightly.

Claire opens her math book. "You keep making the same mistake, Jonah. You get it; you know how to do it right. You just need to trust in yourself."

Jonah takes a deep breath and starts back in on the problem. He finishes in less than five minutes. The answer agrees with the book. He stares at the notebook page and the clear, obvious solution.

Claire turns, settles her arm over the back of his chair, and leans in close, looking at his calculation. She smells of flowers and autumn leaves. She turns her face to his, only inches away.

"Told you." She smiles.

He meets her gaze. Claire's powder blue eyes sparkle in the sunlight. His smile is shy. "Thanks."

She sits up straight and pulls her math book and her own wire-bound notebook closer to the edge of the table. "God, I hate differential equations."

Jonah shakes his head and chuckles lightly. A student at the table next to theirs turns and glares at him. Jonah cringes dramatically and mouths SORRY. The student looks at Claire, rolls his eyes, and returns to his work.

He leans in close to Claire. "How can you breeze through organic chem and have trouble with diffy Q?"

Clair tilts her head in his direction, her eyes on the math book. "How can someone breeze through diffy Q and stumble on organic chem?"

"Touché." He sits up straight.

Out of the corner of his eye, he sees Claire smile. "Good study buddies," she says softly. "That's why I came here today. Figured you'd be hunkered down."

A wave of warmth washes over Jonah. "Was hoping you'd stop by." He feels the blush redden his cheeks. "I needed some organic chem help," he says in a hurry.

Claire's smile widens. The space between them narrows.

They work quietly next to each other.

• • •

"Okay, members of the Robert Owen Housing Co-Op, it's that time again."

The room quiets. Metal folding chairs groan and scrape on the cement floor as everyone turns to face Meredith.

Meredith grins. "Starting off this week's rotation is, by popular demand, bathroom detail." She looks at her clipboard. "Mathew K, Sierra, Malik, and Jackie."

"Seriously?" Mathew groans. "It's Burrito Monday and Spicy Asian Thursday this week!"

Cheers greet the complaint.

Meredith's expression hardens. "Stop your bitching. We all share all the tasks."

"We work together for the betterment of all," Georgia says by rote.

Georgia sits to Jonah's left. He turns and gives her two thumbs up. She bows in her chair.

Mathew turns around and glares at Georgia. "Your gastrointestinal peculiarities are definitely *not* to my betterment."

Georgia shrugs. "Hey, I'm unique. I relish my personal, distinctive characteristics."

"Enough," Meredith shouts. She reads from her clipboard. "Georgia, you and Jonah have grounds detail."

Georgia grimaces. "Leaf season," she says quietly. "Serves me right."

Jonah reaches over and pats her arm. "It's okay, Peaches."

She rolls her eyes at him.

Meredith continues to hand out assignments.

Jonah leans over to Georgia and speaks quietly. "How's the foundry project coming? You make any progress today?"

"Great progress," she says. She leans her head on his shoulder. "Right up to the end. I was trying to smooth the wax on my mold and totally miffed it. Have to start over tomorrow." She sighs. "That sculpture is forty percent of my grade. There goes my Sunday."

"Sorry. That sucks."

"Thanks, Goober."

Jonah smiles. Things aren't too bad if Georgia calls him Goober. She gave him the moniker their freshman year. He and Georgia were in the same group touring the campus as random high schoolers. When they saw each other in Intro to Sociology, they started talking. Georgia is the best friend Jonah's ever had. And vice versa. But then, her taste in boys is questionable.

Meredith raises her voice. "Lastly!" Jonah and Georgia turn back to Meredith. She glares at them. "This evening is the Nu Mu Psi Fall Social."

Georgia swears loudly. Her profanity is lost in a cacophony of boos and groans.

"Now, now, people," Meredith claps her hands. The room quiets slowly. "They are our neighbors and schoolmates." A mask of disdain and annoyance settles over her face. "Even if they *are* Greeks."

Georgia sits up straight in her chair. "Our entitled, do whatever they want to ensure their entitlement, neighbors," she says loudly.

Jeers and catcalls echo around the room.

"Everything they do is for themselves," Ben, an architecture junior, yells. "They can't be bothered with the welfare of other people."

"Unless you have money," Georgia responds. "The dues to live in their entitled, self-promoting little enclave is more than our tuition!"

"People! People!" Meredith takes back control of the meeting. "They have their philosophies, and we have ours. And," she raises her voice as the grumbling grows louder, "we will hold to our beliefs and conduct ourselves accordingly."

• • •

The rusted, steel wheelbarrow clangs as the two leaf rakes strike the bottom. Jonah grasps the worn wood handles and pushes it out of the small gardening shed. He wheels it around the side of the co-op and to the front lawn that borders College Street. The pungent fragrance of dry fall leaves fills the crisp, late afternoon air. Maple and oak leaves crunch under the wheelbarrow's front tire. Jonah sets the wheelbarrow down on its wooden legs and extracts one of the rakes.

"Work from the street backward?"

He turns and smiles at Georgia, sauntering toward him. A motorcycle accelerating in the distance briefly drowns out the swish and crinkle her hiking boots make in the leaves.

"Sure," he says. "I brought the fifty-gallon garbage bags the kitchen uses for recycling."

Georgia tugs on the ends of her long-sleeve shirt in demonstration. "Ready for stuffing."

They begin raking backward from the street toward the co-op. The muscles in Jonah's forearms start to burn. His upper back begins to ache. It feels good. They work as a team from the edge of the block to the wrought iron fence that marks the boundary with their neighbor. The iron chimes as the rake's tines strike the bars.

"Are you going to jump in the leaf piles? How fun!"

Jonah looks through the iron fence at the sorority girl. She is wearing a black minidress and holding a steaming cup of Starbucks coffee. Their lawn is green and perfectly trimmed. The hired gardeners finished earlier today. Three more girls get out of the car behind her.

Jonah's stomach turns to lead.

"We're not out here raking for fun!" Georgia's voice drips with sarcasm and disdain. "It's called work." She points to the poured-cement housing complex behind her. "It's a co-op?"

The three girls join their sister. A tall brunette steps to the front. She stares at Georgia. Her expression is calm and serene. "C'mon, Britany, we have over a hundred guests to prepare for."

"Right," Georgia says, "your fall soiree of the *have's and want to keep's*. What's the entrance fee for that?"

"One hundred dollars," the brunette says. She is composed in the face of Georgia's disdain.

Georgia shakes her head slowly. "You really do believe your little sorority is the pinnacle of society!"

"The sisters of Nu Mu Psi have among the highest placement rates of any order in this country. We support each other in pursuing women's advancement into professional, well-paying careers."

The brunette turns on her heel and walks away. Two of the girls join her. One remains. She steps up to the iron bars.

Jonah can feel her proximity. Gravity strains to pull him into the earth.

"The Fall Social is a fundraiser, Jonah," Claire says. "All proceeds are donated to the city's food shelf." Her eyes lock with his.

"Oh?" Georgia's eyebrows raise, her face contorts in disbelief. "You two are friends?"

Jonah breaks from Claire's gaze. He looks at his rake. The tines have brushed the soil. Isolated blades of green grass mix with the dried leaves. He begins raking.

"Always the same mistake, Jonah," Claire says. She turns and walks away.

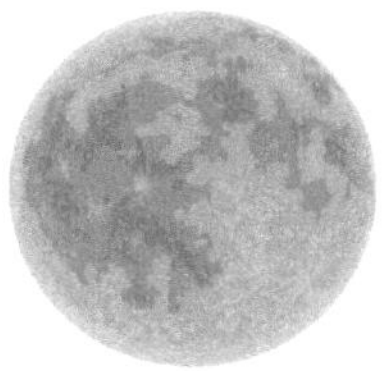

EXISTENTIAL LOVE STORY

JENNIFER EDELSON

The cedar sauna is pitch black inside, like an ink stain that never dries despite the heat. To navigate, I keep one hand on planks of blistering grooved wood until I find a flat surface directly in front of me. Evan plops down and pulls me up against his body, and the jolt loosens a little air bubble from between my lips.

"Do you love me?" he asks.

I want to say *I think so,* but don't answer.

He kisses my neck, and my mind wanders from song lyric to song lyric, following a chain of associations. I sing, "Love, love will tear us apart again . . ." until Evan kisses me quiet. His hands explore fleshy planes of fat and skin. And though I feel him tangibly in the hot, dark sauna, I can't help wondering if he's a figment of my imagination.

My pounding heart fills the boxy room. The space feels like it's expanding, but my skin still puckers in anticipation. Evan's touch is electrifying, and as he lays me back against the hot bench and rests his weight on top of me, my body arches up to meet him.

Evan says my heart is like a motel vacancy sign, sometimes the lights are on, sometimes nothing. That I should care more about who or what occupies each room. It's soul-crushing to think he questions my commitment. He's more a part of me than anyone.

"What are you thinking about?" he asks.

"You're not just some transient lodger," I whisper.

"You sure?"

"Yes. Plus, the 'motel' is in ruins. Maybe now it'll shut down permanently."

I want Evan to know he's the only person who makes sense of life in a way I understand. That we may not agree on things like God or children, but that he exists in a way I respect, and because of it, I admire him. But it's late, and knowing I may never be able to tell him makes me want to run as far away as possible.

Evan kisses me again. His kisses travel down my neck along with his hand, which scrunches up my t-shirt above my stomach. I really need him to know how I feel, so though I only mean to take off my shirt, somehow, he manages to get me naked beneath him. He takes off his own clothes, then takes my hand and shows me his soft spots until all sorts of agreeable emotions come flooding out of me.

In the dark, Evan's body makes no sense. Muscle and bone push against tight skin like well-placed padding, defining long limbs and slender torso. Under my fingers, they're like guideposts staking boundaries between voyage-worthy destinations.

"Don't worry," he says, "I know you're not into it tonight. I just want to touch you."

"You think I'm empty?" I whisper.

"No, baby. I think you're amazing."

Evan closes my eyes with his fingertips and traces a pattern across my upper chest with his index finger, back and forth between the hollows above my collarbone. He recites travel facts from

National Geographic as he walks his fingers over my stomach, and it's so sexy.

For a moment, we are one. The ghost in Evan is the ghost in me, if ghost is what it is. Evan knows my ghosts better than anyone.

We move against each other, but my mind goes into hyperdrive. Instead of focusing on Evan's touch, I think about my dinner earlier, about the life my cod probably lived—swimming thousands of miles, chasing Russian submarines. It's upsetting knowing I snuffed out those memories. Just like that, I destroyed another unique, irreplaceable thing.

I think about the difference between me and Jupiter. How she's composed of the same electrical impulses that travel through my body, how I'm made up of the same iron, and oxygen, and energy. It makes me sad. Four-billion years of inertia would drive me crazy.

I think about snowmen. How futile it must feel to sit paralyzed while your body melts away, and just when you've started living. I think about petrified trees and the millions of years' worth of experiences they'll never share with me. I think about how small I am, about how little space must care that I'm out here. I obsess about relativity, and it screws with my head because knowing I'm so inconsequential sometimes makes it hard to endure.

I think about ghosts, and aliens, and ESP. How thousands of people can't all be liars, how my inner skeptic excels at canceling out belief. I think about Jack the Ripper and the Zodiac Killer. Did they believe in *anything*?

I think about how every day, someone dies in a car accident, or drowns in the shallow end of their pool, or chokes on a carrot. How it's all completely random. I worry about people dying from yellow fever and foodborne germs. I worry about environmental diseases. I think about earthquakes destroying California and a thirty-mile-wide asteroid hitting Earth while I sleep. I wonder if a tidal wave can make it all the way from the beach to the city. Then I realize

I really should quit thinking. I'm more likely to worry myself to death, which would be its own catastrophe.

"Maybe we should stop," Evan says softly, interrupting my ruminating. "I can tell you're somewhere else."

"I'm trying," I whisper. "I'm just anxious tonight."

"Try for *you*," he says sort of thoughtfully, "I'll be here no matter what as long as you're honest with me." He props himself up and rests rigidly on his elbows, feeling around my body for a box of cigarettes. "Open your heart, babe," he says as he sits up, "whatever it is you're looking for, you'll find it eventually."

"What if I die in a car crash before I do?"

"That's what you're thinking about?"

Evan lights a cigarette. Orange flecking glows in the pitch room, leaving a stubborn imprint. We sit and stare at it in silence for a minute until his hand searches for me on the wooden ledge, finding a space for his thumb right between two of my ribs.

"What if?" he asks. "You're looking for absolutes that don't exist. Statistically speaking, ninety-four percent unlikely may be the best you ever get. And I'd take those odds, honestly."

"Statistics are meaningless when it comes to humans. That four percent still represents flesh-and-blood people. And given all the horrible things out there, there's a whole lot of numerically improbable slots to fill."

"That's partly what makes life exciting, don't you think?'

"No, it's too uncertain. What if there really is a right path, and I never find it? I need a guidebook," I tell him.

Evan laughs. "Guess you're out of luck, babe. But it's not okay to wait and do nothing until you figure it out. You have to play to win. Meaning is a romantic notion, but it's also pretty academic when it's still just a word."

"I'm going to screw up, Evan."

"If you didn't screw up, I'd worry about you."

I hesitate because I know I shouldn't say it. "Maybe I'm not the kind of person who can love someone."

"*Do* you love me?"

Wiping little beads of sweat off my chin, I say, "I love the way saltwater feels when it's tacky and foul after it dries on my skin. And how sunburned skin feels snug, like it's holding everything inside me together. I love peeing when I've waited for an eternity. I love the smell of hot tar on a hot day. And the way the airport smells all the time, but especially airplane exhaust in winter. I love the way orange and blue look together. I love the words 'discipline' and 'debris.' And I really love Taco Bell tacos. But I honestly don't know what it feels like to love a human."

"This." He grasps my arm gently. "This is what it feels like."

I frown again, then sigh. It's Evan all the way for the win.

"What's really in that head of yours, sandwiched between all your fear and uncertainty? What's so important you can't just lie back and stop thinking?"

The stubby end of my cigarette burns all the way down to the filter. I take another one out of its box and then scoot away from him because I don't want to be close enough to feel it when I hurt his feelings.

"I don't think I know *how* to love you, Evan."

I flick my lighter to see his face better. Tainted by an orange glow, it looks strange and distant—like he sees through me and doesn't exactly like what's behind the veil.

"Do you regret anything?" he asks.

"I regret lots of things," I say softly.

"Marrying me?"

"No." I shrug. "I don't think so."

"You won't at all, one day," he whispers.

"How do you know?"

"Because I do. One day, we'll be an epic story. I'll be that enigmatic boy who played the guitar and won your heart over a pool table. Tonight, right here, will be the first time you looked outside yourself and saw it all clearly. The thing is, babe, everyone has to lose it a little to move forward. Someday, I promise you, you'll understand there isn't a thing in this world you'd rather do than live in it with me."

In the dark, as he grasps my hand and uses it to stroke his cheek, I already know in this amorphous way that though the road ahead is my own, I really don't mind sharing. We may be opposites. But we can love each other differently. I just have to find a way to show him I want it to work.

I flick my lighter again and hold it up, meeting his eyes.

If I remember anything about tonight, it will be this moment. The way Evan looks in the glow of my flame. I will remember he looks happy. I will remember that I love his smell—a mix of cigarettes, leather, sweat, and wood—and what it does to me. We exchange gazes void of awkward pauses or paralyzing insecurity. It's all there in his eyes. Evan already knows I believe we're an epic story. He's just waiting for me to voice the ending.

Ms. Esther's Cottonwood

AMBER TRAIN

Mornings were always frantic, with getting all of the residents out of bed, cleaned, dressed, and, where necessary, diapered before getting them to the dining room. So, it could be understood how Ms. Esther was forgotten in the dining room that morning. Kayla had already worked a twelve-hour night shift and had to stay through the day shift to cover for several other nursing assistants who had not shown up that morning. And Ms. Esther needed less watching as she was one of the easier residents. She was not yet suffering from any terribly debilitating physical ailments, had no signs of dementia, and was free from any bitter resentment regarding her current living arrangements, a resentment that plagued the minds of so many other residents of High Desert Retirement Home. Ms. Esther, it seemed, was simply alone in this world and had reached that stage of life where she could no longer quite live by herself, so here she was at High Desert.

Esther stayed in her chair in the dining room for some time, patiently waiting for Kayla or some other nursing assistant to help her back to her room. She was of a generation of women imprinted with the qualities of patience and quiet fortitude, even at the expense of her own comfort. However, at some point, Esther began to wonder if she might become a nuisance to the ladies trying to clean up around her and decided to try and make her own way. Esther's limbs had become gnarled with arthritis in her old age, but she had her cane and could still move her own body, just much more slowly and with much more effort than she used to. As she rose, her eye caught the view of the garden through the dining room window. Since it was still morning, the sun was tilting diagonally through the aspens and cottonwoods outside. Autumn was in full swing, and the leaves in their golden glory seemed almost promiscuously beautiful to Esther. The trees were so alluring that Esther considered trying to go outside. The residents were certainly allowed to do so; High Desert was no prison, after all. But it was not encouraged either—the fear of a resident falling never far from anyone's mind. Esther looked down at her feet, confirming that Kayla had put her in sensible sneakers that morning. She glanced around, feeling oddly devious, and noticed nobody noticing her. So, Esther took up her cane and shuffled down the hall toward the door to the garden terrace. And she simply opened the door. The air outside was spiced with the smell of fallen leaves, sharply contrasting with the soft, persistent smells of oatmeal, disinfectant, and bodily fluids on the inside of the door. Esther stepped through to the outside, raised her face to receive the sun's beams, and inhaled. Her deeply mottled skin, gray and dulled with age, luminesced to a silvery shade in the sun. Esther glanced behind her once more, the sensuality arising in her causing her to reflexively check if she was being observed in such a state. Finding herself still alone, she went forward. The path, though dirt, was scraped smooth, designed to accommodate elderly gaits. The beguiling trees Esther had spied from indoors clapped their drying leaves at her, and she followed their call.

For a moment, Esther considered that Kayla might find her gone and worry. But Kayla had so many other things on her mind she likely wouldn't even notice. The young nursing assistants often chatted mindlessly to the residents, knowing the residents had no one to pass their confidences on to. As a result, Esther knew that Kayla had two young girls she raised without their father. And that she struggled to find childcare on her night shifts. Sometimes, Kayla's mother would watch the girls, but Kayla worried about that since Kayla's mother was usually passed out from drinking by 8:00 most nights. Sometimes, Kayla had to leave the girls home alone all night, and she would be especially rushed and stressed as she got the residents ready those mornings, anxiety and exhaustion etching premature lines into her pretty face. Once, when she was in such a state, Kayla had brushed Esther's hair so vigorously that white cottony puffs of it had drifted down around Esther's face. Her scalp had ached for the rest of the day. But Esther had not complained. She understood the sorrows of the young mother. Long ago, she had been a lonely young mother herself.

So, Esther continued on the path. House finches bathed in a fountain set off in a small courtyard to the right. Esther watched their flapping wings spray water droplets over their own bodies, a self-baptism in the stone-pooled water. Esther had her girls baptized at St. Vincent de Paul's in Baltimore. Esther's main memories of those baptisms were so much white and a glut of happiness. The immaculate white of the christening gown, first worn by Charlotte, then a year later by Charlotte's younger sister, Hope. And the voluminous, flowing white robe of Father Angelo. Back then, there was still a whole family—Esther and the children's father, and both maternal and paternal grandparents—in attendance. And some aunts and cousins, too. Esther had been a math major in college before becoming pregnant with Charlotte, and the memories caused her to imagine her family as a formula of exponential decay written out on some dark blackboard of the universe, in which she was the sole remaining factor. Such visions made her suddenly tired, and she stopped to rest beside a large cottonwood tree.

The tree was gray and aged, but where Esther had become slighter in her years, this tree was spacious. Three Esthers could not link their arms together around its girth. While its limbs, like Esther's, were gnarled, their twists and angles suggested stores of strength rather than frailty. Esther rested her hand on the rough bark and closed her eyes in communion. The sun was moving overhead now and warming. Esther dropped her cane, allowed her weight to be held by the tree, and came to rest on the ground, her back against the trunk. It had been a long time since Esther had been embraced. Certainly, Kayla, or one of the other nursing assistants, held her in the sense of supporting her in dressing her or sometimes helping her into the shower or off the toilet. But not this kind of embracement. The way her mother had once embraced her and she had once embraced her children. It was beatific, and blessed, and restful.

It was eighteen hours into Kayla's double shift when she finally noticed Ms. Esther missing. It was long before Kayla forgave herself that fact, not understanding she sought penance for an offense Ms. Esther would not recognize as such. It was John, the groundskeeper, who found Ms. Esther—fallen faceup next to one of the cottonwood trees. Her body splayed on the leaf-gilded ground, arms spread as if in *Hallelujah*. The cottonwood filtered hallowed light on Ms. Esther, leaves chattering some ancient prayer.

THE FAMILY LETTER

JOHN SELF

Hello Family,

I know that our once-close family is now scattered all over the country and even the world. Even in this age of the Internet, it is tough to stay close. I remember so well getting together each year with tons of food, laughter, interesting discussions, swapping recipes, catching up on life's trials and tribulations, and arguing about the best football team. Who can forget when Uncle Bubba tripped over a boulder and went sprawling into the pool in his underwear? He always claimed that he was drinking Diet Coke. Sure. I believed him, but thousands wouldn't.

Unfortunately, those days are gone. Some of us have even become estranged for various reasons, some serious, some trivial, but nevertheless, causing pain and separation.

I would really like us to return to the "good old days" of food, football, great conversations, and just the warm feeling that comes with being around family. As everyone knows, I am a giver. So, I will take the first step in bringing us back together by writing a heartfelt letter with a little about us to start the ball rolling in the hope that you can relate, feel more connected, and be inclined to take steps to reconnect, and maybe, just maybe, become a little closer.

So, with that said, I'll start with the hope that the past year was very, very good for everyone.

Okay, enough about you. On to the heartfelt, warm family letter about us.

As you know or have heard, Babette and I usually travel a great deal each year. Unfortunately, this was a year of limited travel as Babette and I just didn't have much time. So, to make up for quantity, we went for quality, going to Tuvalu, Kiribati, and Montserrat. I know you know, but if you've forgotten, all those countries get less than 10,000 visitors each year. Personally, I'm not surprised there were so few visitors since all were only mildly interesting. Thankfully, we did go to two fairly interesting places: the Hobbit village in New Zealand and a quick visit to Antarctica.

To the South Pole.

By dog sled.

See it on the *National Geographic* channel.

We did have one splurge. We went a little crazy and rented a sixty-foot boat. We looked at each other and spontaneously decided to sail it around the world. I mean, why not? Besides being terrified, it turned out to be a great experience. (See attached 1,264 digital pictures).

Since we had a lot of time onboard, Babette and I explored the boat and found a trunk that had some Dollar Store parts, a roll of duct tape, and an old 8-track player. Quite by accident, we put together a device that made it possible to talk with dolphins (patent pending).

Boy, were we surprised when we heard from one of the dolphins whose name, we came to find out, was Yul. I know, it surprised us, too. I mean, who names anyone Yul these days?

Turns out Yul is two years old and single (but looking). Babette and I took turns videoing him with our phones. Yul was so full of exuberance! He just loved being filmed. After a few hours of editing, we were pleasantly surprised when the Discovery Channel optioned it for a special coming out next year.

As a side note, we discovered a new region of deep-water volcanoes; the United States is giving us credit, but to be completely transparent, Yul told us where they were. The government has stated that it will be officially named the BabetteJohn Volcanic Range. I know, awkward, but it was their idea, not ours, and we do appreciate the courtesy. Probably should really be the Yul Volcanic Range, but life isn't always fair.

John wrote a wildly successful eBook titled *Being Successful; Keeping Humble* that was on the *New York Times* Best Seller list. (But just for three weeks. I mean, does that even count?) John was very active in charity work at the local elementary school, teaching Texas Hold 'em poker to the kids after school, which, to be honest, had mixed results.

Babette had a relatively slow year. In between her work as an artist and life coach to the stars, she introduced a line of casual furniture that will be shown exclusively at Neiman Marcus and Walmart. Babette has also been dabbling in real estate. She found a wonderful fixer-upper starter home on Craig's List for only $18,000. Babette has such a good decorating eye that with just a few "cheap and cheerful" additions, she was able to flip it for $1.5 million just three weeks later.

Almost forgot, we were invited to visit North Korea. It was okay, as the food was a bit drab for our taste, but the premier of North Korea, Kim Jong-Un, was a hoot. Should have seen Bippy (he made us call him that. Who knew?) and John trade jokes while drinking Bud Lights. But the real highlight was singing karaoke in his fabulous studio. Jong-Un (to his lesser friends) had a videographer film the karaoke in IMAX 3D. (We PROMISE to get each of you a copy). Yes, there were the annoying guards with AK-47s in the videos, but we'll edit them out. Before we could leave, Bippy made us promise to visit next year. I had to say no, but, as you can probably imagine, I had to let him down easily since he is known to have a bit of a temper.

I know everyone will be excited to know I've almost completed my memoirs or, as I call it, 'Opus Maximus' (too much?). I've heard from many tens of my loyal Facebook followers demanding more details of my life. Therefore, I will not disappoint them. I have decided to model my memoir after Karl Ove Knausgård's six-book autobiographical series, *My Struggle*. The difference is that mine will be limited to only three volumes as modesty limits even me, but I promise it will be more colorful.

We know you will look forward to (and let's be honest, you'll come to rely on) our recommended movie and book lists so you'll know exactly what you should see and read in the coming year. (Please see Appendix B of this letter for a complete list of the 432 movies and 623 books we saw and read this year). We have cross-listed each by title, length, nationality, actor, director, screenwriter, genre, and, of course, our rating.

Ahh, now for the kids. What true family letter wouldn't be complete without hearing all about kids you don't know and quite possibly don't even like?

Two daughters, Tiffany and Talia, and one son, Taylor. Four grandchildren: Tristan, Tiana, Tyson, and Travis. All doing pretty well, considering, but of course, I'm so proud of each anyway. One positive note: Feeling particularly magnanimous and loving, I got each grandkid a preapproved Capitol One credit card that comes with six hundred points. Six hundred points!

Chili, our cat, normally a constant underachiever, surprised us by learning to speak Spanish. Granted, she's not fluent (yet), only conversational, but it has helped her deepen her friendships with other cats and negotiate with the dogs when we take her for walks around the neighborhood.

I know this was just a short note, more of an appetizer, but Babette insisted I keep it short. I know that most of you will want more (I don't blame you!). For this reason, we have created a website detailing our modest adventures, plus three blogs, Instagram, Twitter, (I mean X), Facebook, YouTube, and LinkedIn. There's also our app for only $12.99 available on iTunes, Android, and Windows. But for my dear family, I have included a code for a five-percent discount.

After reading this, I know you probably have a million questions. Let's get one out of the way first, even if it is a bit personal; I understand how the little details make a person real rather than remain so unattainable. The first question that inevitably will come up is "Boxers or briefs?" Well, I have to say… boxers.

Other than the above, it was a very quiet year. So, from our family to yours, may your New Year be prosperous and healthy. I am hopeful that this letter will be a catalyst in bringing us all a little bit closer and that you feel that you can candidly share bits of your life as we did. We sincerely hope to see everyone real soon.

I know I feel good about letting you see behind our glamorous façade to the reality of our life; some of it, by first-world standards, might seem pretty grim. I hope that taking this bold first step to get us back together will help us reconnect once again and bring us closer together in this time of turmoil. There really is nothing like family to keep us all grounded and feeling good.

Babette and I can't wait to hear from all of you.

Really. We mean it.

With love, affection, and hope,

John

NEWS HEADLINES FROM MY APARTMENT

STEF WILLEN

WOMAN, 44, GOES BACK TO BED JUST HOURS AFTER WAKING UP

LEADING SMARTPHONE UNDER PILE OF DIRTY CLOTHES, PERHAPS

PLOT TO KILL SPIDER WITH COWBOY BOOT FOILED BY THOUGHT OF SPIDER GUTS ON BOOTS

SPANISH DICTIONARY SET ON BACK OF TOILET TO IMPRESS PLUMBER

FRUIT ARRANGED BEAUTIFULLY IN BOWL, NO WITNESSES

GUMMY BEAR POPULATION HITS TEN-YEAR HIGH

30 MAYFLIES FOUND DEAD IN GLASS LIGHT FIXTURE; NO PLANS TO REMOVE BODIES ANYTIME SOON

DUST UP

GAS BILL SLATED TO BE OPENED WITH TEETH

SHE STOPPED BRUSHING HER HAIR. HERE'S WHAT HAPPENED.

SHE STOPPED USING UTENSILS. HERE'S WHAT HAPPENED.

MAC USER DIDN'T KNOW THIS ONE SIMPLE TRICK, AND SHE REFUSES TO LEARN IT

THE FELLOWSHIP OF THE DRUM

ANDRÉ FLEUETTE

Detective McNealy leaned in and handed a paper cup to her partner before easing into the warm car and closing the door on the December rain. "One black coffee," she said. "Sorta hot. Extra nothin'."

"I wanted a latte," Kinsey said, scowl partially hidden beneath his hipster beard. "Vanilla. Two-and-a-half pumps. Extra hot, extra foam. I get the same order every time. You know this."

"And I wanted to retire last year to Hawaii, but here I am in south Philadelphia, muckin' around with you." The kid set the cup in the center console with a pair of little creamers and a handful of sugar packets. McNealy was certain that Kinsey wouldn't drink the coffee. *Whatever.* More for her. She carefully removed the lid from her own cup and inhaled the steam coming off it. She loved the smell of hot coffee on a cold night.

"I always get what you want," he whined.

"That's because I take mine black and straight from the pot, two dollars at the bodega. But the bodega isn't good enough for you. Every night, you insist on coming down here for your fix. Nine dollars for your bougie coffees, Tim. Every time. I'm goddamn tired of subsidizing your caffeine habits."

They sat, watching the traffic pass on Broad Street while Kelly McNealy enjoyed her coffee. She was nearing retirement and felt every minute of a long career in her gut and the terrible diet in the gout that plagued her joints. Next to her, Timothy Kinsey stewed, offering little more than an occasional huff of discontent, tattooed hands clutching the steering wheel, his breath fogging the window to his left as he pointedly avoided looking at his older partner.

"C'mon, let's go for a drive," she said sometime later, finishing her drink.

"Whatever," Kinsey's answer to seemingly everything. But he put the sedan in gear and eased into traffic, making his way north. The wipers clacked as they swept the windshield clean.

McNealy crumpled the paper cup and put it into the plastic bag at her feet that she used for trash, then took the cup that Kinsey had rejected. Why let it go to waste? Kinsey took turns randomly, picking his way through city streets festooned with silver tinsel and colored lights, blinking festivity from nearly every window they passed. Christmas was only a few days away, and the mood in the city was warm despite the freezing rain. Eventually, Kinsey pulled over to a curb outside a market in Strawberry Mansion.

"Gotta piss." He ran into the building, leaving the engine running. Across the street, near the corner, a trio of obviously homeless men stood around a barrel where a small fire burned. They were covered in plastic sheets, like trash bags, and passed a bottle of clear booze between them. Despite the rain and the chill they must have felt in their bones, they laughed, enjoying the banter between them. They shared a warmth in company despite the frigidity of the night. McNealy shivered sympathetically, eyeing their feeble fire.

The car door flew open, and Kinsey flopped heavily into his seat. He shook water from his head and wiped his face with a pile of napkins he'd liberated from the store. "Pfft," he huffed and pointed at the homeless men. "Look at that. You know that fire's illegal," he said. "They need a burn permit."

"They're cold," McNealy said without taking her eyes away from the fellowship of the drum.

"The city should clear them all out. They're everywhere anymore."

McNealy grinned and turned to look at Kinsey. "Tell me, Timmy. Where do you live?"

"What does that have to do with anything?"

It was clear that she'd touched a nerve. "You're in your parents' house, aren't you?"

He rolled the window down and spat into the street. "That's different. I got a divorce and just needed a place to go for a minute."

"Uh-huh," McNealy said, now fully smiling. "Maybe that's what happened to some of these guys, except that maybe they didn't have a parents' house to go to." The cell phone buzzed in McNealy's pocket.

"That's not a fair comparison."

She held up a finger commanding quiet and pressed the answer button. "McNealy," she said by way of greeting. She listened silently for a minute, then hung up the phone.

"What you got?" Kinsey asked, the previous conversation forgotten.

"Do you remember that body that Dickerson talked about last month? The old one that got dug up at that bar in Feltonville? The Proudstone Beer Garden?"

"The one that came gift-wrapped in plastic? Like, crazy neat? The staff found it during a cellar rehab?"

"Yeah, that's the one."

"Sure, yeah." Kinsey shrugged. "Wasn't a lot to go on, if I remember. Just some liquified dude in a tidy-ass bag."

"Yeah, well." She pointed at the street. "Doctor Lonergan wants to see me about Mr. Liquid."

"Lonergan wants to see *you*? Not Dickerson?"

"Yeah."

"Why?"

It was McNealy's turn to shrug. "Dunno. Let's go find out."

Once more, Kinsey eased the car into traffic, this time heading toward the morgue.

• • •

It had been some time since McNealy had been in the morgue—a blessing, she thought—and she found the addition of brightly colored Christmas decorations, the tinseled cardboard ho-ho-ho draped over the sink and ornamented tree in the corner somewhat off-putting. Dr. Lonergan, who had summoned McNealy to her den, appeared from a door in the far corner, drying her elfish hands on a paper towel.

"Hey, Kelly," Dr. Lonergan said cheerfully, the tassel on her green Eagles-themed Santa hat bobbing festively. She popped onto her toes to give McNealy a brief, familiar hug that smelled faintly of nutmeg and ginger.

"Naomi, you're looking fine," McNealy said, cringing inwardly at the familiarity. "Sorry, we've had a busy night," she shot Kinsey a look, telling him to play along. "You got something for me?"

"Oh, yeah," Lonergan smiled. "This one took a little bit to put together thanks to the extensive formation of adipocere…"

"Of what?" Kinsey interrupted.

"Grave wax," Dr. Lonergan interjected. "Under the right conditions, a body can transform during the putrefaction process into adipocere through saponification."

Kinsey's face screwed up in confusion. "Through what-ification?"

"Our frozen buddy is a big bar of soap," McNealy said. "Stinky, stinky soap."

"In his own bathwater." Lonergan laughed. "Basically, yes, that's right. Between that and the fact that our subject is missing his teeth and fingers, and there was no DNA match available, made him kind of hard to identify."

"That's kind of nasty," Kinsey said, a disgusted look on his face.

"It's *really* nasty," Lonergan admitted, hopping up to sit on one of the long, metal exam tables. "Stinky, like Kelly said. Because it's Christmas, I've spared you the full sensory experience and left him nestled all snug in his bed."

"Thank you," McNealy and Kinsey said in unison.

"There's not much to see anyway." Lonergan's legs kicked like those of a small child. "We pinged the body as a Caucasian male between the ages of twenty-five and thirty-five. He's been dead for at least fifteen years. Cause of death was a single gunshot wound to the heart. Nine-millimeter Beretta 92."

McNealy huffed. "That's a pretty specific determination."

Lonergan laughed. "It's easy when the killer leaves the murder weapon with the vic. Clean, of course, serial filed off, but we were able to pull the last three digits. Five-two-niner. Ballistics is chasing a match."

"Okay," McNealy said, leaning against a tiled pillar. "Anything else on the body?"

"Well, first, he was packaged beautifully. Whoever killed him wrapped him for the long term. Never seen such a neat job before. Professional quality. But, for the body itself, he had a few unique tattoos. And that's where we got lucky." Lonergan nodded at Kinsey. "Timmy here knows, right? Each artist is unique. Has their own style, their own way of tattooing."

Kinsey nodded. "The good ones do, anyway."

"Right. So, we got some shots of an angel our boy had on his back. It was messy, but thanks to the nerds downtown, we were able to resolve a few clear images."

Something tickled McNealy's memory. A perp with an angel tattoo. Someone terrible. "I'm not going to like where this is going, I think," she said. Her stomach fell as thoughts trickled into her head.

"Maybe. Maybe not." Lonergan hopped down from the exam table and walked over to her desk, immaculately organized like the rest of her morgue. She picked up a thin brown folder and walked back, holding the bundle out to McNealy. Kinsey leaned in close from the side to have a look of his own. "There's only so many tattoo artists in Philadelphia. But the suits only had to go to three or four places before someone recognized the work. And, yeah. They found the artist, and he was able to identify his own design, even years later. And, what's more remarkable was that he had pictures of the work in his portfolio, along with the name of the person he'd inked."

McNealy opened the file and saw a face that she recognized. One that she hoped she would have never seen again, in this life or the next. "Toussaint Denis," she whispered.

Lonergan nodded. "Auguste Toussaint Denis, to be accurate."

"Who's that?" Kinsey asked, picking the image of the dead man from the folder in McNealy's hand.

"Two-cent Dennis," McNealy said, her voice a whisper and hands shaking. "The Devil's shitty stepson."

"Oh, damn," Kinsey said. "Even I've heard of Two-Cent."

"I'm getting too old for this shit."

• • •

An hour later, after an awkward goodbye with Lonergan involving promises to meet for drinks over the holiday, McNealy once again

134

sat in the sedan with Kinsey as non-traditional Christmas music played softly on the radio. A thick folder sat open on her lap as she flipped through pages, re-familiarizing herself with one of the worst perps she'd ever been associated with.

"Why an angel?" Kinsey asked, a smaller pile of McNealy's rejected pages in his own lap. She bristled at the interruption but swallowed her words. He did stop for coffee after the morgue. A bodega this time and his treat. The cups still steamed in the center console between them.

"Hmm?" She arched an eyebrow, turning away from a case write-up.

"On his back. The angel tattoo. I was wondering why an angel?"

"Why not an angel?"

Kinsey put his forearm into the light and rolled up his sleeve. "For most people, tattoos are something important. A narrative of their life. Not including the drunken idiots who roll into a tattoo parlor ripped up on tequila shots and have a Celtic knot or Chinese characters that read *General Tso's Chicken* inked on them. People think about them. They have meaning." He pointed at one of his own tattoos, a female warrior waving a Norwegian flag. "My tattoos have meaning. They tell my story."

"I thought they said your mother didn't hug you enough."

"Fun." He pointed at the warrior woman. "This is for my great-grandmother's sister Agnetha, who gathered intelligence for the resistance in Norway during World War Two. She was still a college student when the Gestapo killed her."

"Sorry," McNealy said. "I shouldn't have made fun."

Kinsey nodded. "It's okay. I was just wondering why this guy had an angel." He shrugged. "Maybe it had meaning."

McNealy set the page in her hand down and flattened it on her lap. "Denis thought that he was sent by God, somehow. That he was some kind of an agent of the divine. I guess the angel was God's mark upon him or something." She sighed. "I really don't know. One of the profilers had some thoughts on it, but I never paid much attention."

"So what happened with this guy?"

"In a nutshell? Toussaint was a rapist who graduated to murder. Children, mostly. Very ritualized. What the brains called a process killer."

"Ah, he was in it for the kill itself. Didn't collect trophies as a necessity of the kill."

McNealy nodded appreciatively. "Okay, Kinsey. Points for you."

"I listen to a lot of true crime podcasts."

"Take the points." McNealy went on. "Denis was smart. Tough. Disciplined. Former military. He didn't make a ton of mistakes. Didn't leave witnesses, either. There were a few killings that we thought were random that were later connected to Denis. Cleaning up his loose ends, as it were. People who might have connected him to one of his other crimes."

"Yikes," Kinsey said. "I mean, looking back, I think I heard of this guy at the time, but I was just in grade school."

"Who didn't back then?" McNealy sighed loudly. "One of his 'loose ends' was an old partner of mine. We had stopped working together after a dust-up, but Nichols was a good man." She returned her attention to the file in her lap. Leafing through the pages until she found the one she was looking for. Her own handwriting scribbled at the top listed an address, a home she remembered from almost two decades earlier. "Margo Lockett was only eight years old at the time, but she was the one who got away. He stabbed her in the back and slashed her face with a razor, but she still fought her way out of a window. She was crazy lucky. She managed to run all the way home to her parents, who called the police. The kid was even able to bring us straight back to Denis's house." She held the page out to Kinsey. "It was a damn abattoir."

"Hell of a kid," Kinsey said, taking the report and looking at the photograph stapled to it.

"No kidding. She was a legit badass kid. Unfortunately, we were too late. By the time we got there, Denis had cleared out, and we never saw him again. We assumed he left the city because of the heat and started again somewhere else. For years, I watched the wire, looking for similar MOs, hoping I could help someone else, some other department, but nothing ever came up. After a while, for my own sanity, I stopped."

"Looks like someone found him first."

"Yeah," McNealy said, her head swimming. "Do me a favor and see if you can get an updated address for the Lockett family." She turned her attention back to the documents of horror in her lap.

• • •

"Stay here," McNealy said. Commanded. It had taken little time to find the home of Warren and Rita Lockett, parents of now twenty-five-year-old Margo. Their car idled in front of an old snow-covered, two-story pale blue bungalow. It even had a white picket fence, with Christmas lights twinkling in the windows and on the bushes in the front yard. McNealy sighed, hearing her own words and tone, then leaned into the car to look Kinsey in the eye. "Please."

The argument on his face stopped and melted away. "Sure."

"I've got some history here. And…well, she was just a baby."

"I get it," Kinsey said, pulling out his cell phone. He turned the music up on *Fairytale of New York.* "I'll just hang here with the Pogues."

"Great song," McNealy smiled at him, then stopped. "Hey. Maybe you could dig into Mr. Lockett while I'm in there. Warren Lockett, age about…fifty or so. See if he has a history."

"Sure," Kinsey appeared pleased to be given a task and smiled back. "Anything in particular?"

"Nope." She closed the door. There were four cars in a driveway built for two. No garage. Light smoke whispered from the chimney. Family get-together for the holiday. And here she was, the harbinger of…what? Good news? Would they celebrate the fact that the monster who surely haunted their nightmares was long dead? Or… something else.

"What do you do for a living, Mr. Lockett?"

"I'm a bookbinder. Mostly, I do restorative work for libraries, universities, and museums."

"You make a lot of money doing that?"

He laughed. "When the work is there, it pays well."

"And when it's not?"

"I do a little carpentry. Some bartending on the side. Paint houses. Whatever I can get."

Why did she remember that conversation so clearly? Warren Lockett was a warm man. A provider. The kind of man who would starve before he'd see his only child go hungry. Rita was an…accountant? Bookkeeper of some kind?

She knocked on the door. The smiling face of a man she recognized almost instantly opened it as if he was waiting for the intrusion. He had lines in his face now and gray hair under a pair of fuzzy antlers, but it was him. He was still laughing from some joke or comment, his face falling when he saw the unexpected person before him.

"Hi, uh…" He clutched the door. "Merry Christmas. Can I help you?"

"Mister Lockett?" McNealy asked, though she knew that it was. "Warren Lockett?" In the family room beyond, a fire blazed in a brick fireplace traced with silver tinsel. A half-dozen candles burned on a mantel lined with monogrammed stockings, and a trio of faces looked toward the door in confusion. "Uh, Merry Christmas."

"Yes, that's me. And you are…" Recognition filled his eyes, and his face fell. Was it dread? Fear? How could you blame him either way? "Detective…?"

"McNealy, yes. It's been quite some time since we've spoken, but there's been a…development. Is there someplace where we could talk privately?"

• • •

Warren apologized to his family for the interruption but didn't introduce McNealy to them. He quickly ushered her through the living room to a sliding door that led to an enclosed porch behind the kitchen. A thankfully heated addition off the back of the house that had been appropriated as a workshop. He offered McNealy a stool, but there was only one. She took it, and he leaned against a heavy table cluttered with unfamiliar tools.

"I'm sorry to bother you this close to the holidays," McNealy said. "But, as I mentioned, there's been a development."

Warren glanced through the door into the kitchen and into the living room beyond. Young Margo stared back, though she was looking at McNealy, not her father, her eyes watering.

"Huh. A development," Warren said, looking back. It wasn't a question. He held a mug of what might have been eggnog in both of his hands. "How have you been, Detective?"

"For the last…what, seventeen years? Good. Well, you know how that story goes, right? Divorce. Surgery. Foreclosure. All the wins." Suddenly McNealy wanted a drink, even if it was some of that nasty eggnog. "So, why am I here?"

"Yeah."

"There's no way to sugarcoat this. We recovered a body a few weeks ago in the basement of the Proudstone in Feltonville. An *old* body."

Warren didn't meet her gaze. Instead, his eyes flicked back to the living room. Toward what was important to him. His daughter. His family. His grandchild. "Yeah?" It barely registered as a question.

"Yeah. You don't seem surprised, Mr. Lockett. Do I need to tell you who it was that we dug up in that basement?"

Warren stared at the ground.

"Tell me, Warren. Do you still bartend?"

He shook his head. "Not for a long time now." His voice was not more than a whisper.

"Let me guess. About seventeen years, right?" She sighed. "If I dig into it, I'm going to find out that you used to fill in at the Proudstone from time to time, aren't I?"

Warren nodded.

"And, let me guess. You used to own a nine-millimeter Beretta, but I'm guessing that disappeared right about the time you stopped bartending?"

Warren was silent for three long breaths, then raised the mug and took a long sip, his fingers trembling. "She was so scared. So tiny, covered in blood and screaming. Rita was beside herself. I didn't know what else to do."

"So your daughter told you where to find him. And you… what?" She surprised herself by laughing. "Don't take this the wrong way, Warren. But if anyone had told me that you, the mild-mannered bookbinder from Lancaster County, would take out a piece of trash like Two-Cent Dennis, well…I just wouldn't have believed them."

"I'm not…proud of what I did," he said. "I know it was wrong. But he hurt my baby."

McNealy should have arrested him right then and there, but something stopped her. She shook her head and excused herself, telling Warren she'd call him in the morning.

"I've got some thinking to do," she said from the stoop before Warren closed the door behind her. "Don't go anywhere. Please."

The last thing she saw in the house was the crying face of pretty young Margo Lockett, tears glistening along her razor-scarred cheek, a baby sleeping peacefully in her arms.

• • •

"Anything?"

Kinsey coughed. "You weren't gone long enough to do a thorough search, but there wasn't much to find anyway. This guy is *clean*. Like, stupid clean. I'm not that clean, and I'm a cop."

"Not surprised," McNealy said, gathering the papers and organizing them in the overstuffed folder.

"The wife had a speeding ticket about four years ago. Forty-two in a thirty-five zone."

"Lock her up," McNealy said, sniffing what was left of her coffee. It had grown cold.

"I did a little digging there as well. And guess what? It was the same night her grandson was born."

McNealy laughed. "All you could find on this family…"

"Aside from the connection to our stiff."

"Right. All you could find was that grandma went a little fast on her way to the hospital?"

"That's about it."

"Alert the media." McNealy debated telling Kinsey everything, but stalled. There would be time for that tomorrow. "Thanks for looking. Now I want a sandwich," she said. "A cheesesteak."

"Good. I gotta piss again," Kinsey said, driving away from the curb.

• • •

The trio around the barrel fire had grown to a quartet when Kinsey eased the sedan to a halt outside the Strawberry Mansion market.

McNealy glanced at her watch. Almost six o'clock, the night before Christmas Eve.

"Overmorrow," she said out loud. "I just learned that one this morning, on my 'word of the day' calendar. The word for the day after tomorrow is *overmorrow*."

"Well, that's interesting and useless."

"Christmas is overmorrow."

"Less than overmorrow, now. Three-quartermorrow."

McNealy snorted. "I'm done, Timmy. Just done."

"Cool. I'll drop you back at the station."

She smiled, her head bent as she stared at her lap. "Nah. I'll walk from here. I could use some fresh air." She could feel her partner's eyes on her and turned to face him. "This thing with Two-Cent. I don't know, Tim. I've had this…fear of him. For almost two decades, he's been in my head. Haunting my nightmares. The thing that had me checking my closet before I went to bed every night, and why I sleep with a loaded piece under my pillow. And now, just today, I find out…" She exhaled slowly and shook her head. "It was all for no reason."

"Sounds to me like you had a great reason," Kinsey said softly. "Two-Cent Dennis scared a lot of people. *Me* included."

"Thanks for understanding, partner." She smiled and slapped his arm with the back of her hand. "I'll be okay. I think I just want to walk and clear my head."

"Sure," Kinsey said. "Last chance. You sure you don't want a ride?"

McNealy glanced across the street at the three men and one woman who laughed around the burning barrel. "Nah. I'm gonna wander. I haven't done that in a while."

Kinsey promised to pick her up in the morning if she needed a ride and drove off, leaving McNealy alone on the sidewalk. She went into the market, ordered a half-dozen cheesesteak sandwiches and select pint bottles of various spirits, paid, and walked with her bag across the street. The quartet looked up at her, surprised, as she approached them.

"Mind if I join you?"

They muttered to themselves for a minute until McNealy held up the bag. "I brought treats," she said.

"You a cop?" the woman asked, her face lined with wrinkles.

"Used to be a detective," McNealy said. "But I'm just Kelly now."

Two of the men shuffled aside to make room for her, and she stepped up to the barrel, the warmth of it delightful against the chill wet of the winter night. "Here," she said, handing the bag to one of the men before she lost the thick folder under her arm. "Go ahead," she said with a smile when he hesitated.

"For reals?" he asked, looking into the bag.

"Why not? It's Christmas."

The man passed sandwiches around, making sure to start with McNealy herself. She accepted one, sliding it into her coat pocket for later as her new friends dove into their sandwiches.

"You couldn't bring me a Geno's?" The man across the barrel from her said to a round of laughter.

"Pat's next time," McNealy said. "Never Geno's."

When they finished, the wrappers went into the fire, and the pints came out, passed around the circle. They introduced themselves as Elmo, Gardner, Jimmy, and Elaine.

"Let me ask you all a question," McNealy said. "Is it always important to punish someone for their sins?"

"Depends on the sins," Elmo said. He was the oldest of the group, a wizened man with short silver hair and piercing black eyes. The rest deferred to him as their de facto leader.

"Explain," McNealy said, accepting a bottle of vodka from Jimmy.

"The way I see it, the righteousness of an act depends on why someone does a thing. If I broke your window to steal a pie, that's a sin. But if I broke the same window to tell you your house was on fire, that's a righteous act. The same act. I broke your window. But why did I break your window? That's what counts."

"And if you stole my pie, you should be punished."

"Well, now. I think that depends on the pie," Elaine said with a wink.

"Sure," McNealy said with a laugh. She pulled the folder from under her arm and held it in front of her. "This is all the evidence in the world that connects a good man to a bad act. But as I'm standing here, I don't know if he was wrong."

"So, you *are* a cop."

"Technically," McNealy said. "But like I said…I think I *used* to be." She stared at the fire, picturing the cozy scene of the Lockett home, the tears in Margo's eyes. The defeat in Warren's, a man who had spent almost two decades fearing her visit, and the resignation of will when she appeared like a frumpy Dickens ghost to make him pay for his sins. The folder in her hand suddenly felt very heavy.

"Fuck it." McNealy dropped the folder into the barrel. The fire blazed as papers ignited in the middle of five glowing, smiling faces. No one would cry at the side of Two-Cent's grave. Aside from the relief of knowing he was dead, no one would feel anything at all. Least of all her. His death would be a blip. A drop of rain wiped away on a windshield. A fart in the wind. All those hours of casework, the interviews, the nightmares, and the dread, all gone in a whiff of smoke that dissipated in the rain. Everything that connected Warren Locket to the devil's stepson, Two-Cent Dennis.

It was a hell of a way to end a career.

"Okay to open up the rest?" Gardner asked, pointing at the bag they'd set on the ground near the barrel.

"Absolutely," McNealy said. "That's what it's for. Just save me some." She stepped away from the fire, slid her phone from her pocket, and called Kinsey.

"Change your mind? I stopped for some phò a few blocks away. I don't mind coming back."

"Nah, I'm good. For tonight anyway. But I will take you up on that ride in the morning."

He laughed. "I figured you would. I was planning on it."

"Cool. Oh, and coffee's on me. Let's stop by your bougie place before the station, and you can get whatever you want." After agreeing on a time, McNealy asked him to find a number for her. After thanking him and promising to call in the morning, she dialed the number. Just one last thread left for her to trim.

"Hello?" A tired voice on the phone. By her voice, young Margo Lockett had aged twenty years in the past couple of hours. McNealy couldn't imagine the hell her visit had put the family through.

"Margo. Hi, it's Detective McNealy," she began.

"No," Margo pleaded before breaking into sobs. "Please, no. Don't…"

"I won't, Margo. I promise," McNealy said. "And I've fixed it, so no one ever will." She smiled, her heart filled to bursting though the world blurred in tears and the rain. "Merry Christmas."

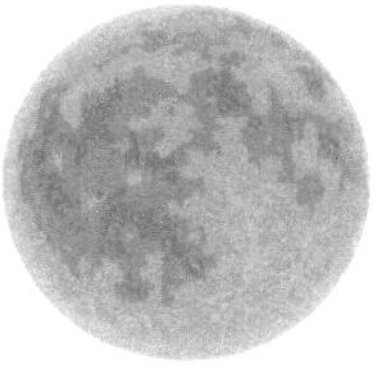

THE SIGN OF THE MULE

MELINDA CROSS

’ve never been one to take any omens of bad luck seriously. A black cat scampering in front of me, the strange hoot of an owl, or a menacing crow on a telephone pole behind my house never faze me. So why would I pay attention to a mule refusing to budge over a ten-foot patch of dirty snow?

Mules bear the brunt of disparaging comments, starting, of course, with "stubborn as a mule." There's a Simpson meme where Homer's dad says to him, "You're as dumb as a mule and twice as ugly!" And then there are the bad jokes, such as "mules are a half-assed attempt to make a stronger horse." I had no opinion of mules nor recollection of meeting any until I arrived for a hiking trip in the Eastern Sierras near Bishop, California, one August. I was soon to find out that Homer Simpson's dad had it all wrong—well-bred mules are very smart and are thinkers, not just haulers. Their stubbornness is really their cautiousness in not wanting to put themselves or the people they lead in danger.

There are a dozen or so mule pack outfitters in Bishop offering hikers a rugged and remote wilderness experience. You can sign up for anything from an "appetizer" of a five-day backcountry trip to a thirty-day trip that takes you the entire 211-mile length of the John Muir Trail. A pack of mules carries your group's camping gear and food and is led by guides on horseback while you walk behind with a lighter daypack. It's like re-enacting the first pioneers' journey to cross the Sierras, except there are coolers and ice with fresh food for gourmet meals prepared three times a day.

I'm an urbanite always looking for a way to get my cowgirl on and was willing to trade a few days of hot showers to immerse my-self in Eastern Sierra's historical romance and ruggedness to traipse along the same trails as did Kit Carson, Mark Twain, John Muir, and Ansel Adams.

My five-day trip was organized by Diane, a native Californian raised in the 1960s by parents who made the six-hour drive from San Diego to Bishop every summer to escape the crowds and heat and teach their children outdoor skills. I was spontaneously invited just a few weeks before the trip began by our mutual friend Bonnie. I jumped at the chance partly to prove to myself yet again that I wasn't the twig-like weakling of my youth. For Diane, I imagine this trip was her way of reconnecting to the glory days of her youthful, athletic self. She had recently retired from her job as a healthcare ex-ecutive managing hundreds of employees and complex projects and now devoted her days to kayaking, surfing, and long-distance biking.

Bonnie was a self-employed writer who would pivot her sched-ule on a dime if a new adventure presented itself. She was as cre-ative and spontaneous as Diane was disciplined and focused. "Diane sometimes gets impatient with my free-spirited ways," Bonnie said. I figured this trip would be the best of both worlds. Diane would bring the wilderness expertise, and Bonnie would bring the fun.

On our first meet-and-greet phone call, I sensed Diane didn't want to deal with a second Bonnie on the trip and was annoyed at this last-minute addition to her hand-picked group. Getting to basecamp would be an eleven-mile, eight-hour trek over Mono Pass at twelve-thousand feet and then down rocky trails into the backcountry mountain lakes and valleys known as the Recesses. The last thing Diane wanted was a hiker with unproven skills who could slow the group down or, worse yet, get injured and require some protracted evacuation plan. I dropped mention of my hiking in Patagonia and attempting a fourteener in Colorado. That seemed to assuage her fears of being stuck with a novice.

The other hikers in the group were three of Diane's long-time friends from southern California—a couple in their late sixties and a work colleague in her early fifties—along with her twenty-six-year-old niece from San Francisco. We met up the night before the trip at Tom's Place Resort, perched on the edge of the Inyo National Forest, where we could sleep in a real bed one last time and pick up any last-minute supplies before our pack life began. The store was a wonderland of outdoor fishing, hunting, and hiking supplies. Billed as "a step back in time," Tom's hasn't updated a cash register or a bedspread since the 1950s, at least.

My first face-to-face with Diane immediately stirred up my insecurity about my athletic abilities. She was taller than I had imagined—close to six feet— giving her a long gait that measured about one step to my every three. There was a tomboyish look to her with gray hair cropped close and Army green clothes that were baggy and loose. Her style choices made her friendship with Bonnie seem even more unlikely—Bonnie, who accentuated her petite figure with brightly colored, form-fitting athletic clothing and wore trendy French mountaineering sunglasses. Over a pork chop and mashed potato dinner, Diane quickly assumed her leadership role by giving us tips on what to bring in our daypack and coaching us on the grueling four-thousand-foot elevation climb over Mono Pass. She regaled us with stories of her seventy-five-mile-a-day bike rides with her husband and their whitewater kayaking feats. I felt my muscles weaken by the minute, not to mention my stomach.

I was out of Diane's athletic league and had been so for most of my life. I still feel the pain of being picked last for kickball teams in grade school, and who can blame the captains? I never managed to kick a ball past the pitcher. In third-grade gym class, I lived in fear of those thick, rough climbing ropes that dropped for miles from the ceiling to the floor. Get to the top? My arms were so feeble I couldn't wiggle myself two feet off the ground. I received a D in seventh-grade physical education because I failed the basketball free throw exam by making zero shots out of four.

My dad was the athletic parent of my two who coaxed me into learning to ski and golf, even though he knew I'd rather be reading or practicing my violin and piano. Our two-week summer vacations were camping trips in northern Minnesota, where I spent most of the days with my nose in a book under a tree or in the tent. I begged to bring my violin along, and my parents explained that no one goes into the wilderness to hear a fledgling violinist in the next campsite practice her scales every day. I once slipped and fell getting into a canoe, my arm becoming wedged between the metal seat and its side. It took an hour and a stick of butter to free it.

After college, I reluctantly agreed to play in the office summer softball teams. The guys organizing the teams were always in need of more female players, and I have a lifelong affliction of not being able to say no. They assigned me to play left field, of course, since it's rare that a sixteen-inch softball makes it that far. The one time it did, I misjudged my glove's placement, and the ball landed smack in the middle of my forehead. I fell to the ground more in shock than pain.

In my early forties, one of my close friends in Chicago put together a women's hiking trip to New Mexico. I immediately fell in love with the forested beauty of the Pecos mountains outside of

Santa Fe. Epiphany! Hiking was one athletic activity I could succeed at. I didn't have to compete on time or speed. No one was keeping score. All I had to do was simply put one foot in front of the other and go at my own pace. It had taken half my life, but I had finally found a sport that didn't shake my physical confidence.

At the packing station the next morning, the reality of the day's arduous endeavor ahead hit me. I quickly assessed where I might fall in the order of hikers on the trail. Robin and Norm, who were in their late sixties, looked to be at the same fitness level, even though I was ten years younger. Laura was in her early fifties and looked like she could keep a pretty good pace. Diane's niece Andrea was super athletic and had the legs of a gymnast and the agility of a mountain goat. Based on what seemed to be everyone's ability, I guessed the order would be Diane, Andrea, Bonnie, Laura, and a rotating combination of Robin, Norm, and myself at the end of the pack.

After handing over our small duffels of clothes to the guides for packing, our group huddled around a picnic table eating breakfast while Dale, the pack station owner, pointed out on a large map our day's trek on the Mono trail. Everything about Dale seemed as rugged and unforgiving as the granite peaks surrounding us. His voice was raspy, his sentences terse, and his frame and personality towered over everyone else at the camp. Dale did not suffer fools, nor should he—he took his responsibility very seriously to keep his animals, staff, and guests safe in the remote backcountry. He explained to us that the snow melt in the passes was very late this year because of the huge volume of precipitation from the previous winter. We were one of the first groups to hike into the Recesses this season, even though it was already early August.

He looked up from the map directly at Diane and asked, "You have a topo map, don't you?" A topographic map is a highly detailed and accurate illustration of the geography, and shows the specific contours of the terrain, helpful especially with elevation changes. I remember seeing a whole rack of them back at Tom's Place.

"Ah, no, I…I…we…we didn't bring one."

"You shouldn't head in without one. That's plain foolish."

Diane didn't seem to be fazed by this blunt chastening. I glanced around at the rest of the group, and no one seemed willing to suggest to her that perhaps we shouldn't start up the trail without getting our hands on a topo map. Cell phone service would be lost less than a mile from the trailhead, so the topo apps on our phones wouldn't work either. We were on our own on the way up as the three guides had gone ahead on horseback, along with six-pack mules carrying all our food and gear to set up camp before we arrived.

Dale handed each of us a copy of a primitive black-and-white map of the Mono Trail that was nothing more than hand-drawn scribbly lines of the winding trail with a few of the surrounding lakes and taller peaks added. There was no indication of mileage or elevation.

"How about a compass?" Dale asked. "No…no…we don't," Diane replied.

We? "We" were never informed that we needed to carry these backcountry essentials with us.

"Well, your guides don't carry satellite radios, and if you get separated or lost, it's going to be tough for them to get help if you can't find you," Dale explained. He then pushed his massive frame up and away from the picnic table and walked back into his office.

There was an uncomfortable silence, clearing of throats, and last-minute adjustments to daypacks among our group. I noticed water leaking from my new Camelback inside my daypack. I had not screwed it on tightly enough to the tube connecting it to the mouthpiece. I prayed Dale didn't see that. I didn't need to add any more doubt to his perception of us as an ill-prepared lot.

I was barely a mile into the hike, and I could already feel the altitude starting to make each breath more difficult. As I predicted,

I took up the rear of the hikers. I was disappointed in myself that I didn't feel in better shape. I knew the only way up was one step at a time, not waste energy on conversation, keep my head down, watch for rocks that might cause a twisted ankle.

The weather started getting cloudier and cooler as we got closer to the pass itself. Now, at twelve thousand feet, we had left the green of the trees behind, and everything seemed a dull gray hue at this point—the sky, the lake off to our right, and my mood. Dale didn't exactly send us off with a vote of confidence. I wondered how much that got to Diane, who had now stopped the group for water and a snack before the final push over Mono Pass. Up ahead of her was a guide standing alone with a mule, pulling the reins in all directions to get the guy moving. He wouldn't budge. A ten-foot patch of thin snow covered the trail, and the mule had no intention of setting even one hoof on it.

I was now seeing firsthand how stubborn a mule can be. I assumed he was a young mule without much experience walking at altitude. I felt sorry for the guide who had his day upended by this opinionated fellow and would end up having to take him back down to the pack station. As we started our ascent, I turned back to check on the mule one last time. I swear our eyes met, and he gave me a look of warning. Did he have some intuition about our group's safety?

● ● ●

Even though it was high season in the Eastern Sierras, we saw no more than five or six other hikers and only one other mule pack during our four days of camping. Our mornings were spent hiking to spectacular vistas and afternoons napping and reading by the pristine lakes. It was hard to believe there was such a remote area in a state of forty million people.

On the morning of our hike out, it was the typical scramble of tearing down tents, packing gear, filling daypacks with water, lunches, and snacks. The guides had the time-consuming job of carefully packing the mules with all the tents, duffels, campstools, stoves, bear-proof food boxes, and coolers. Diane made the decision that the hikers would strike out before the guides and mules to get a jump on the eight or nine-hour hike back down. Her niece, Andrea, who had probably had enough of hanging with fifty- and sixty-year-olds by this time, announced she was going to speed hike out in hopes of making it back to her car and drive back to San Francisco later that day.

To get back on the Mono Trail from our campsite, we had to cross a twelve-foot-wide stream by balancing precariously across a fallen tree that provided a footbridge. Diane failed to notice a thin coat of early-morning dew on the tree's rotting wood. She quickly lost her footing and landed boots-first in the stream. Soaking feet were not a great way to start a long day of hiking. Cleary shaken by her first small faltering of the trip, Diane asked Bonnie and me to take lead of the group.

We could easily pick out the trail for the first couple of miles as it snaked between large boulders and along small ridges. The trail became much less distinct when we hit the grassier areas near streams and low-lying marsh areas. There hadn't been enough hikers this early in the season to stomp down the grasses and create an obvious trail. I recognized little of this area from the hiking day in—I had been too tired at that point and had my head down, coaxing my feet to keep moving.

By this time, Diane had regained some composure and had taken over the decision-making when we met a big fork in the trail. It was unclear to all of us whether left or right at the fork was the right choice. I looked back, praying the guides had caught up with us to lead us out. No luck; the other choice would be to wait for the guides, but that would require Diane to admit she was unsure which way to go. She pulled out the primitive map Dale had given her and decided to take the trail to the left.

Two miles and forty-five minutes later, we saw a lake ahead. Great, I thought, this must be the lake I noticed on the way over Mono Pass. Except when we arrived at the shore, the trail ended. Not a slender path in sight. This is not how we got into the Recesses, and it would not be our way out either.

If one of Dale's smart mules had guided us, we would have turned around and retraced our steps back to the fork. The mule's survival instincts would have kicked in, and the mule would have wasted no time in deliberately getting us back on the right trail and into the pack station by sundown.

"Well, looks like the only way out is to turn around," suggested Norm.

"We just need to get back to the fork and take the other trail to the right," Robin added.

Diane would hear none of it. Despite having no topo map, she was convinced we could hack our way out without backtracking.

"Let's climb up to the top of that ridge." She pointed in the distance across what seemed like a football field of boulders and chunks of snow between us and the promised escape route. "From there, we should be able to see our trail and meet up with it."

My instincts told me this was a bad idea. We had no way of telling what was on the other side of the ridge. I sensed the others felt the same, but no one spoke up. Common sense didn't seek to work on Diane's stubbornness.

I like trails with even footing for many reasons, but primarily to keep my bones in one piece. The boulders were as tall as me, and while Diane's long legs made scrambling from one to another possible, the rest of us had to pick our way between them gingerly. I began to doubt that no one would leave this trip without a broken appendage. Sure enough, I slipped and jammed my ring finger between two boulders. It began to swell and bruise instantly, but I would not let myself sit down and cry over the pain and frustration of the situation, despite how much I wanted to.

We were on the eastern side of the slope, and there wasn't enough morning sun to melt the winter snowpack. Traversing the ridge at different points required us to butt surf down on the snow to find a clearer path. The scene would have been very funny if it had been in a movie, a bunch of middle-aged adventure wannabes set loose in the wilds of the Sierras. But it felt more like a tragedy waiting to happen. I could see the headline now: "Six elderly hikers perish in self-inflicted boulder slide."

Diane's decision to off-road from any marked trail began to look downright stupid and a dangerous way to protect her ego. She had to realize we were wasting precious daylight on her ridge-scaling scheme, which was getting us nowhere. Finally, her thinking brain seemed to kick back on, and she announced we would head back to the lake. My relief in this saner plan matched my joy in meeting two fishermen casting on the shore. They confirmed we took the wrong fork two miles back. Time was not on our side, however. It was now early afternoon, and our group had six or so grueling miles to go before sundown.

When we reached the fork, the pressure of beating the clock weighed heavily on us all. We agreed to split up—Diane and Bonnie would hike as fast as possible to catch up to either the guides and mules ahead or down to the trailhead, where someone from the pack station would be waiting. The remaining four of us—Robin, Norm, Laura, and myself—would stick together until either horses or mules could pick us up.

By this time, my adrenaline had run high for several hours. Intense-flowing adrenaline in stressful situations cuts off proper oxygen flow to the brain. I felt dizzy. I could barely focus on the trail. My fuel tank and spirits were getting lower and lower. None of us could gauge how much farther we had to go. Crossing Mono Pass the second time around looked even worse than the first—like a Tatooine desert in *Star Wars,* and its barrenness left me with a chill despite the warm afternoon sun.

As the hours ticked by, we still couldn't see any markings that gave us a clue on how close we were to the trailhead. The sun dipped below the mountains, and dusk was settling in fast. Where was the rescue party? I suggested we start looking for a place to camp for the night. I knew hiking in the dark was about as foolish as off-trail bouldering to a mountain ridge. The four of us discussed the merits of throwing our remaining food way off into the woods. This was bear country, and the smell of food could attract an unwanted midnight guest.

Just as the trail started a steeper decline, two cowboys riding horses appeared, each holding the reins for two other horses—one for each of us.

"Can you help us? We've been hiking down for hours. We can't find the trailhead." My voice carried an unusual combination of desperation and relief.

"Ma'am, we're here from the pack station to take you back down."

He informed us we were less than a mile from the trailhead. Despite our exhaustion, the four of us decided we had made it this far; we could tough it out and keep a little pride by walking the rest of the way. We piled into the pickup truck waiting at the trailhead to take us to our cars at the pack station. My hands were shaking so badly I could barely hold the hot tea and cookies the mess staff gave us when we reunited with Diane and Bonnie at the station.

"Thanks for staying calm out there," Diane said to me in passing. What she really meant was thanks for not pointing out the folly of her ways out on the ridge.

I could see Dale sitting in his office doing paperwork under a library desk lamp. He didn't look up at us or say goodbye. Who knows if he worried that he had a pack of lost hikers on his hands? He had warned us he wasn't to blame.

I didn't sleep a wink that night in the motel in Bishop. I felt like my entire body had been given an injection of uppers. The adrenaline wouldn't stop flowing. My mind was racing and retracing the day. Then I went back to that mule on that first day of our ascent and his look of warning. Did he sense something I chose to ignore in our group leader?

Heck, if dogs can sense things like illness in humans and bad weather on the horizon, maybe mules can detect foolish behavior coming, too.

WORTH A THOUSAND WORDS

ANDEE BAKER

My sister and I aren't exactly close. I guess we never were too chummy, except when she was little, and I was her older sister by seven-and-a-half years, so happy to finally have a sibling. I remember us hugging goodnight, giggling, and holding hands across the small space between our beds. My mom told me that, no, you two didn't get along, not after she started talking. Huh. I thought it was a little longer than that, maybe much longer, although I do recall placing some kind of physical barrier down the middle of our room later on. Her name is Elizabeth, but she goes by Liz, just Liz, not Lizzie or Liza, not Beth or Betty. My brother and I named her "the Lizard." Compared to other non-humans, she does have a few lizard-like qualities. She has a rather small head, carrying most of her weight below the waist. Her hair is curly, cut in layers, resembling a lizard's scales, each row laid in a pattern over the others below.

Flashing back aways to a family photo of the five of us, standing together in two rows, Mom, Dad, and three kids, my brother born a few years after the second girl, I wonder who took that shot or if it was a delayed-action camera. Such photos didn't appear often in our albums, probably because we most commonly all gathered collectively only for meals. Here was this decent one, all smiling faces, from after my sister and I had left home. Our mom had tacked it up on her bulletin board. I commented to Liz, as we passed it in the hallway, "Good photo, huh," to which she responded in an annoyed tone, through clenched teeth, "Good of you, you mean," unleashing the hissing, lizard-like sounds of sibling resentment of which I was only dimly aware at the time. She added later on that she thought she "looked fat" in it, something I had not noticed at all.

I innocently assumed a general spirit of goodwill between us, big sister and little sister, until well into adulthood. Once, after my dad died, I took a funny photo of my niece and nephew, my brother's kids, when they were about four and six. Listening to them tell me a story of one of their more colorful schoolmates and his drunken father, I wanted to take their picture. They were imitating the classmate's facial expressions, facing the camera, standing close, both with their heads tilted in the same direction. My nephew, the older one on the right, wore a gray and navy-blue Dallas Cowboys shirt, given to him by an aunt in Texas, while my niece had on a white alphabet tee, all twenty-six letters arranged into five rows. He looked happy, with an off-kilter, closed-mouth smile, his lips in a slightly curved line spread across his face, whereas she sported a sad smirk, with one half of her mouth tilted downward, the two of them in an improvised pose. They both have thick brown hair, his waving just below the tops of his ears, hers several inches longer and curlier. Together, they completed the clownish tableau, like a child's version of the comedy/tragedy masks. For the holidays, I made four-by-six prints for the immediate family, putting them into wooden frames of different colors and textures, a floral cutout design for my mom, blue and green stripes for my brother, and a faux reptile-skin frame for my sister.

When sister Lizard unwrapped her gift on Christmas Day, we were all standing nervously around the table in my mom's condo dining room, unaccustomed to communal gifting. I could almost see her cold-bloodedness surfacing as her tongue peeked out of her mouth, upper teeth showing. As she unwrapped the gift, an inch and then another two inches of tongue appeared, flicking back and forth, ready to lash out. On seeing the photo, she asked, in a shrill voice, "Did everyone get this?" with emphasis on the word "everyone." I started chuckling, a grim laugh. I felt stupid to have expected "Thank you" or a statement about the photo's content, such as "How cute!" Even a question about what the little kids were doing in the photo would have been nice, about what had prompted their unusual expressions.

Another photo op came after the three of us planned a 75th birthday party for our mom, somehow not knowing how much she hated surprises. About fifteen minutes into the party, attended by local friends and relatives from in and out of state, she turned to me and said, "Please don't give me a party for my 80th." I told her not to worry, thinking, okay, whew, I hope we get through this one. The party progressed with each of us three offspring doing our own form of tribute to our mother, ending with a gift of a framed art piece we had no idea if she would like or not. I asked people to cluster together for a group picture, and they obligingly followed my request, except for one person: my sister. She stood several feet in front of everyone. So commanding was her stance that no one had the guts to verbally insist that she move back to join the group, much less to change her position physically. I politely asked her to move, an awkward request. Pause. Nothing. With the camera in my right hand, I waved with my left hand, a feeble backing-up motion, saying her name. Pause. Still nothing, no movement, not counting the Lizard's alligator grin, slowly widening from the center to the far edges of her lower face. Sneaking a look at the few other attendees I could see, I noticed their eyes opened wide, and their jaws dropped to create the round O of shocked surprise.

I took the photo anyway, entirely ruined, since over two-thirds of the partygoers were blocked from view. In full lizard form now, I imagined how her thick, spiked tail curving upward, rising full-length behind her body, slowly waving left to right, right to left, prevented anyone nearby from moving forward. That was an epiphany, the point in time I understood how far my sister would go to sabotage something I wanted, even while demolishing the permanent record of a celebration for us all. She probably counted on people forgetting her action, remembering only that they never saw a photo of the event.

Liz's profile picture on Facebook shows heavy eyelids half down, much like certain species of her namesake animal, pupils angled off to the side, away from the camera.

Okay, I guess our mom was right: "You two never did get along."

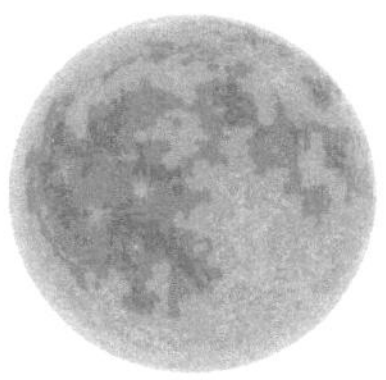

TENANT #23: COUPLE WITH CAT

SUE BRYAN

Note to the living: a bathtub is a stupid place to hide from a large knife and malevolent intent. My blood still stains the grout behind the cheerful caulking.

Tenant 23 is a shower shaver with delicious Speedo tan lines. I flick the soap out of his hand.

"Shit!"

Again.

"Fuck!"

He lathers and draws the cheap-o BIC along his jawline. I boost the hot.

"Yow! Honey, stop using the water!" No answer from her.

I watch a rivulet of blood trail down his neck.

The cat is growling and spitting maniacally.

They'll be gone in a week.

THE CUP

CRISTINA BROWNE

I awoke as usual and went to the kitchen to make some coffee.

I opened the cupboard and then the dishwasher…but my cup wasn't there.

I rushed outside, still in my pajamas, but it wasn't there.

My heart sank, and I felt a pit in my stomach…I <u>have to</u> find that cup!

I dressed, telling myself, "Don't panic; it's here somewhere. It's not like it vanished into the multiverse or was taken by aliens. I will find it!"

I asked Gemma and Kasper to help me look for it, and when we went to the backyard, they started sniffing around.

We followed our usual route, and I checked near every branch and bush…but it wasn't there.

My heart sank some more. I *have to* find that cup!

Then I started thinking about how we put value on things.

It's not like I don't have any other cups to use, and some probably cost more than that one cup.

But I only wanted the cup that wasn't there.

It's the perfect size, not too big and not too small.

But more importantly, someone thought of me when I wasn't with them and brought that cup back for me!

It's the idea and thought of how that cup came to me.

It has loving energy that nourishes me every day I use it, and *that* is beyond priceless!

We continued our morning walk, then came back in through the garage, and then I saw it.

There was the cup!

It was safely sitting on the shelf, smiling back at me.

A huge wave of relief and gratitude washed over me.

I found my loving energy cup again and could finally have my morning coffee!

THE HANKIES

ELAINE KOYAMA

For as long as I can remember, I've had a connection to the Imer family. Sheri Imer was my first friend in first grade. Her dad, Dick Imer, was the football and wrestling coach at Hardin High School, and my oldest brother Tom was one of his first star athletes. Dick Imer's roots were in Chicago, a mysterious and distant city I only knew of because every Christmas the Imer family would drive to Chicago, depriving me of my best friend during the long holiday break.

But Betty Imer's roots were in the hills of eastern Montana near Lame Deer. At the time, it might as well have been as far away as Chicago—Lame Deer was seventy miles from Hardin, and their ranch was probably another fifteen miles from there. Betty's maiden name was Broadus—related to the founders of Broadus, Montana, another fifty miles beyond Lame Deer to the east, and I was always so impressed to know someone who was connected to the founder of a town.

Betty grew up a cowgirl on the family ranch. There are pictures of her in cowboy boots, spurs, chaps, and plaid shirts that epitomize her life growing up. It is iconic. Ranching on Rosebud Creek was every bit a struggle as a person could imagine—semi-arid land that's measured in sections rather than acres; range fires, water shortages, fights over mineral rights, winters that would blow in with nary a tree to break the blasts of cold.

Behind all that was Betty's mom, Margaret Broadus. Margaret lived in an era where the family trip to Yellowstone Park was in a horse-drawn wagon. She was a rancher's wife, no stranger to hard work and isolation, living miles from civilization. Sheri and her family referred to Margaret as Gram, so that was how I knew her. She was a tall, long-faced, weathered woman, a little bit scary and always a mystery to me. I wondered what her life must have been like on that ranch. Wondered what it was like when a person couldn't just "run" to the grocery store for milk or eggs. What life was like for someone so old they rode a wagon to the park, yet still alive to drive a Buick sedan.

As Margaret got older and after her husband died, she moved into town—Hardin—and volunteered at the Catholic church. Father Fabian was the priest in charge. I didn't know exactly what she did there, but she lived or stayed at the rectory and did church things. She drove her own car for years, and then later, she caught rides with people in town. My mom, who would have been in her mid-seventies at the time, gave Margaret rides to Billings to shop and run errands.

At one point, Margaret lived in some apartments near the church. She stayed active for all that time. Finally, in 1998, she ended up at the hospital and then probably the nursing home. It was around Christmas, and her health was failing. We were home from Minnesota, and my mom hadn't put up Christmas lights, so my husband Scot was up on the ladder stringing lights on the house when he fell. He caught himself and ended up at the hospital with a minor fracture in his hand. I was away from the house, probably spending time with my own mom. So, while Scot was at the hospital, he went to see Margaret and sat visiting her. I meant to go in to see her later but never had the chance. She died on New Year's Eve, 1998. She was ninety-one years old.

Her funeral was in Colstrip, which was not that far out of the way for us heading back to Minnesota. It was a cold and windy January day. The place was packed with family and friends—mostly Betty's generation since Margaret's friends had passed on already. The rooms were warm and crowded. My daughter, Maiya, who was nine years old and close to Margaret's great-granddaughters, ran and played with these cousins. One of the aunties found a box of Margaret's hankies and began giving them to the girls. They gave one to Maiya, too.

The hanky was grayish lavender with a flower pattern of leaves and vines. It was soft, soft cotton, probably resulting from being washed countless times in the wringer washer and then later in the automatic spin washer. It was folded neatly, the fold lines evident, even as the girls unfurled the hankies and ran about the room. The girls were oblivious to the sad occasion, vaguely aware that the hankies were symbolic of their grandmother, unaware Gram was gone forever.

But there is comfort in laughter, and the laughter of children is even more consoling. The girls chased each other, pausing only to let a younger cousin catch up, reminding us all that Gram lived on in the little girls at play.

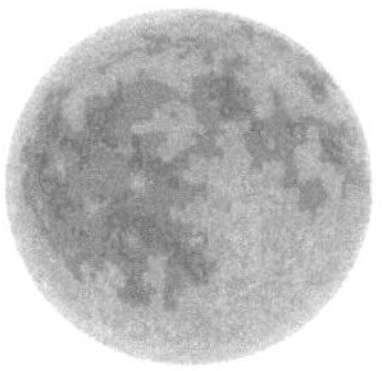

PARANORMAL ACTIVITY

STEF WILLEN

When the Trinity River Lumber Mill burned down, I had reached a new summit in my romantic life. The view was painfully obvious: My attraction to older, unavailable women was not a good strategy. Crushing on women with crow's feet who walk away from me shortly after I engage them in conversation and being smitten by ladies who show signs of graying and of being in a committed relationship was leaving me lonely. I plunged a flag into my newly crested epiphany: Life is short. Go after what you want; stop staring at it and wishing it would talk to you. Go! Go! Go!

But the only place I went was Weaverville, California, home of Trinity River Lumber Mill. Husked in flannel, capped with a hard hat, I sat with similarly clad millwrights who helped me sort bushings into A, B, and Q hubs. I didn't learn to overcome my fears and walk up to available women in bars, slosh some bourbon on them, and say, "Nice pants." I learned to tell the difference between 120, 140, and 78 chains and that Nipples look nothing like nipples.

When I heard that the fire was estimated to cause over ten million dollars' worth of damage, I booked a room at a local B&B for the entire month. The bonhomie was a nice counterpart to spend-ing my days untangling every last coupler, every last anything that looked like something, from a Mobius strip of electrical wiring and pulley chain. I could lounge in the parlor on a Victorian medal-lion-back sofa and flop my hand into one of several nearby bowls of bonbons, pop two into my mouth at once. Things were fine—boringly fine—until Nicole, the owner of the inn, softly rapped her knuckles on the entryway and informed me that I was sharing the sofa with a ghost, and that's why the cat had been acting so strange.

"Do you see it?" I asked.

"No, I can't see them," she said, looking all around the room. "But Bob does. He told me this morning that our place has ghosts. Then he pointed in here and said she was on the couch with you."

She?

That's when Bob, her boyfriend, slunk in, wearing some kind of duster. Bob was cute in an Alan Jackson sort of way, and I wanted to like him. But he lacked boundaries. Every evening, he'd sit across from me in the parlor and watch me type. I'd hear him uncross and re-cross his legs. If I glanced up, he'd start talking about the rodeo, and *gawl*, how he missed ridin' bulls. When Bob was ignored for long stretches of time, he'd make a noisy ordeal out of leaving, but not without stopping in front of me and pulling out his last card—even if it was "Did you know I have a special power?"

Yesterday, I learned that Bob's special power was guessing the gender of unborn things (his cousin, his nephew, Nicole's baby colt). Now, where I saw empty chairs and throw pillows, he claimed to see the souls of people who were not of this world.

Bob explained that three other ghosts hung out in the parlor: a young couple and an older fellow named James, who once threw a pen at him. He said the girl was a middle-aged woman, probably from the 1800s. Then, he added that she liked to watch me work. I tried to shoot Bob a look that said *Bullshit. It's you who likes to watch me work*, but he told me to come see Princess.

Princess is Bob's orange cat, and it was true; she was acting strange. She hadn't joined me in the parlor like usual for the past few mornings, and now she was wedged between an Apple computer monitor and the kitchen wall.

I don't believe in ghosts. I chalk their sightings up to gas leaks, tricks of light, the electromagnetic field, or a dire need for attention. I was once hired to inventory the famous haunted Mt. Lassen Hotel after it caught fire, and I became a temporary hero for being the only person who would go into "the murder room" and record what had been left untouched since a man was brutally stabbed forty times two decades ago. I was supposed to have felt a cold draft, sensed someone watching me, heard something go bang, gotten pushed. Of course, the scariest thing that happened was that I forgot to turn my Dictaphone on and had to start over after fifteen minutes of talking to myself.

But, when I looked at Princess and saw her hair bristling as her dilated pupils slowly tracked the movements of something behind us, I got scared. Bob may be full of shit, but Princess was the only living thing in the house that didn't need to see something that wasn't there to make life more interesting—and the cat *was* seeing something.

For nearly five minutes, the three of us huddled around that cat. I hadn't told Nicole anything personal, and I would never tell Bob anything personal. Yet, somehow, right then, they could not misunderstand me or me them. Like an earthquake brings you close to strangers, the "ghost" in the parlor made my world fall down around me a little, just enough to make me feel like hugging them. Nicole's long, silvery hair was pulled over her left breast, and some of Bob's salt-and-peppered chest hair poked out where he'd buttoned his flannel; he was older than I thought. It was the sweetest thing about him. I almost touched them both. Then, Nicole said, "Well, I've got to go to Costco."

They asked if I was okay alone because Bob had to go mend a fence. I said sure and something about not really believing in ghosts anyway. But I was beginning to think I was not okay alone; that despite my many smug pronouncements, I'd never been okay alone—that life was one long trick of deceiving yourself, figuring yourself out, then deceiving yourself better. On that note, I summoned the courage to go to the parlor and stare at the couch.

I tried to look through it as if the couch was one of those 3D stereogram images, and some transparent, middle-aged woman giving me a lustful look would flow forth from the cushion pattern. Nothing manifested, but across the room, Nicole's dried grass and flower bunch moved ever so slightly. The baseboard heater? A ghost from the 1800s who liked me? I had an incredible urge to go gussy up.

In the shower, I became slightly afraid of the other three disembodied souls. Who had this James guy been? Maybe the kind of guy who always wished he could slip through walls to see naked girls showering. Perhaps the young married couple spiced up their afterlife by writing things on steamed-up mirrors, like "We're here" or "Boo-yah!" I had locked the door, which was kind of quaint. But, it made me feel safer, able to really do a good job washing my hair and then blow-drying it with a big round brush so it had volume and curl. I put my makeup on slow and careful, so I looked like I wasn't wearing any. Except for lipstick. I put on red. Then I walked down the stairs feeling sexy and decided the woman waiting for me in the parlor looked just like Catherine Keener. An ectoplasmic Catherine Keener in some kind of 19th-century dress.

The parlor was still empty, but entering it felt thick and warm and scary, like walking into a blind date. I sat myself down on the middle of the rug so as not to be too forward and accidentally sit on her. I could feel the air in the room moving around, even through the hairs on my bare arms. I was aware of everything. I grabbed a book off the coffee table called *Fifty Places to Fly Fish Before You Die* and pretended to read.

About two minutes had passed when something gently covered my hand. It felt like a warm electric blanket if you could feel the electric part. I had been leaning most of my weight on that hand, which could explain the weird sensation, but maybe this is my problem—I never let anyone close; I always explain them away. So, I raised an eyebrow and looked over my shoulder. I saw my hand on an oriental rug. As I stared at it, the florid patterns seemed to rise and float in the air. This could be my astigmatism, or it could be my chance to believe a ghost had taken my hand, a ghost who looked like Catherine Keener.

I leaned into her a little, and She didn't do anything haunting like make me feel alone after I already believed in her, and I didn't do anything heartbreaking like act like She didn't exist when we were in the same room. I closed my eyes and felt myself fall further into a warmth, and it was exactly like falling into the dress of a beautiful woman, all the way to the buttons. The warmth was real. It was maybe really happening; her arms wrapping around my waist, her breasts against my back, her face nuzzling into my neck so our cheeks were about to graze, her thick, splendid dark hair about to slide over my shoulder.

Then, there was a hollow knock. I opened my eyes, and She was gone, but on the porch, there was a soul still trapped inside a body, and it was carrying some sort of jug.

"Pear wine?" Bob asked as I let him in. I told him no, and then no again when he winked and asked if anyone had bothered me while he was gone. It was just too humbling to maybe have something in common with Bob. Or to be trying to. But I tried again that night. It was my last chance as Nicole was closing the inn for a month, and I had to book a room at the Motel 8 where there would be no creaks, no framed black-and-white photos of grainy faces long departed. I would probably just come back from the mill, toss my dirty clothes in a corner, order a small pizza, and sit on the bed winking at girls on match.com. Then those girls would write some unforgivable thing back like, "What up, gurl?" or "LOL!" Or, maybe they'd just write back too soon, and it'd be over for me. I deserved someone who wasn't so easy, someone who took her sweet time revealing herself to me.

I opened my bedroom door a crack, changed into sexy underwear, put on tinted lip balm, and got into bed and waited. Maybe I'd fall asleep and slowly awaken to her weight on the mattress and then her weight rolling on top of me, cloaking me in a careful and sweet way. I would be scared, but I would not be afraid of intimacy and ask, "Who are you, and what do you want with me?" I would say nothing and just lie there, unable to move.

In the morning, I awoke with no sign my life had changed. If I wanted to, I could argue that I didn't remember putting the pillow exactly where it was, but that wasn't nearly as exciting as what Bob had discovered. As I stood in the kitchen, waiting for Nicole to get my bill, he pointed to the laundry room door and told me all about the squeak he heard at 5 a.m., how the doorknob slowly turned, and an old, old woman carrying a laundry basket came out, didn't acknowledge him, and vanished into the dining room.

I stared at the brass doorknob and thought about the tedious mountain of metal I had to inventory at the mill. Part of me was jealous of Bob. I wished I could hear a squeak and believe humans can transcend earthly existence. But I could feel that I was going back to being myself: someone who doesn't believe in making bigger mysteries to solve smaller ones. I knew that at some point, perhaps under the popcorn ceiling of that night's Motel 8, I would have to admit that the simplest explanation for my brief, unrequited romance wasn't that She existed and I had fallen into her arms but that I had found yet another way to start falling for someone who wasn't really there. I mean, who is more unavailable than a ghost from the last century whom you only sort of convinced yourself you felt and don't really believe in? No one. Not even Catherine Keener.

I resolved to call the US Geological Survey when I got home to see if there was any seismic activity in the area that only cats could feel. I would research whether it's possible some mechanical unit produces a sound that wigs out felines but is inaudible to humans. I would consider the possibility of finding older, available women attractive.

I hugged Nicole goodbye and gave Bob a couple quick pats on the shoulder. Then I put on lipstick and took the long way to my car, past the parlor, so I could imagine, just once more, that someone who wasn't a possibility might rise up from the couch, think I'm beautiful, then float away from me.

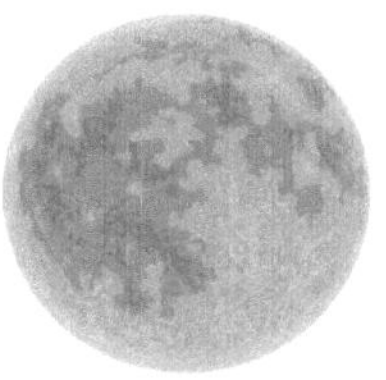

Siempre Contigo

SUE BRYAN

Mindy and I were tooling along a dusty two-lane surrounded by rolling hills of brown grasses baking in the climate-changed sun. It was hot for mid-Autumn, and my back and legs were sweating against the plastic seat of the Rent-A-Wreck.

"So, what do ya' think? Was it worth the trip?"

I could barely hear her over the sound of the wind rushing through our four open windows; the air conditioning had given out before we left our little hometown hamlet. I thought about it. We had come back to our roots from the city we had escaped to—together—a dozen years ago.

"I guess." I raised my sunglasses to look over at her. She kept her eyes on the road and her hands at ten and two. "I hate to say it, but Mrs. Perkins's pies are still really good."

We laughed, and I went back to dipping and plowing my hand through the wind outside the window.

"I don't know," she said. "I couldn't wait to shake off this dust back then, and I can't wait to shake it off now."

We had at least an hour before we reached our motel near the airport. An hour of scorched desert and breathing dust.

"It was good to come, though," I continued as if there had been no break in our conversation. "We haven't been back since…" I couldn't go on.

She took her eyes off the road for a few seconds to look in my direction. "Justin."

"Yeah." I was surprised that his name could still wrench my belly the way it always had. I used to fly down this road on the back of his motorcycle, my hair tangling out behind, my body tucked up to his like a bespoke glove. Safe in the knowledge that whatever we had to face, we would face it together.

The three of us had been tight back in school before Mindy and I escaped. Clowning around. Bowling on Saturdays. Drinking too much and driving too fast. He never saw an escape route for himself. For him, it would be the oil fields or the military and more drinking to ease the boredom. He always knew I wouldn't stick around for that, and he loved me enough to give me the escape route I needed. He drove that cycle right into a tree. On purpose? No one ever asked.

It was after the funeral that Mindy and I scrounged up enough airfare to get the hell away.

I sighed. Here we were on that same road. A hay truck thundered past, going the other direction. My eyes itched under my sunglasses, and Mindy sneezed.

"You gonna tell me about that dream?" she asked. I regretted mentioning it to her this morning. It hadn't been a dream, more like a vision, and it was hard for me to look at it straight.

I gazed over at her, words stuck in my throat for a moment. Mindy was a rare friend. She would never push me; she always let me take my own damn time. Maybe it would help me understand the dream if I told it to someone like her.

"Yeah." I nodded resolutely, stretched out my shoulder belt, and turned toward her.

"Me an' Justin were in an arroyo, tucked between little hills. Like this." I gestured toward the sandy landscape, covered in browning grasses and peppered with chamiso and piñon on either side of the road. "Don't know how we got there, but this church was right there in the middle of the arroyo."

Mindy raised her eyebrows. I could tell because her sunglasses bobbed up and down.

"Yeah, I know. But there we were standing in front of this church. A cute thing, painted white with a little, whachamacallit," I pointed my fingers upward.

"A steeple?"

"Yeah, a steeple pointing right up into the blue, blue sky." I closed my eyes. "The sky was so freakin' blue, little clouds hangin' there."

Mindy leaned forward and looked up at the sky through the windshield. "Like today."

I hadn't noticed, but yeah. "Yeah, like today. Anyway, the church doors were open, and we stepped up the front stairs and went right in. It was cool inside and dark, except for rays of sunshine catching dust, you know the way they do…"

Without taking her eyes off the road, Mindy nodded but stayed silent, letting me do this my way. I loved her more than ever for that.

"Here's where it gets kinda hard to explain," I said, watching a mile marker whiz past. We still had forty-five miles 'til civilization. Mindy just waited.

"Inside the church, there were these little rows of benches, no backs like a regular church. And off to the side was a shelf with hymnals or prayer books or something. They looked a hundred years old. Justin picked one up and opened it. It was so weird, you know.

Like you knew Justin. He was never religious or anything. I'm not sure he ever went into a church, even as a little kid."

Mindy sneezed again, and I took a good breath, looking out the window. "So, Justin handed me the open book, but I couldn't read the words. I could see that something was written there, but it looked all blurry or like it was in a different language. Then we were sitting on one of the benches. He had his arm around me, and, oh, Mindy. I felt so safe there. Like everything was the way it used to be."

My eyes were fighting back tears, and I saw Mindy swipe under her sunglasses, so I guess she was feeling it, too. We had each loved him in our own way. When he died, the bottom fell out, and Mindy and I—left behind—clung to each other like lichen on rocks.

"Anyway, that was about it. The important part was that feeling. It was so real. As real as holding onto him on the bike. I could smell him, you know, like his leather jacket, his dirty hair. I don't know." I ran out of steam and shrugged it off, trying to tell about it. "It's been twelve years since he died." I grabbed at Mindy's arm. "How could I possibly smell his dirty hair?" Now I couldn't stop the tears.

It wasn't a sloppy cry, more like a meandering stream that flowed off into the distance and left us both quiet, the wind filling up the space.

There were no other cars on the road. I tried the radio again but only found fire and brimstone or the occasional crackly Christian rock. I gazed out the window at the rolling hills when I saw something.

"Stop!" I put a hand on Mindy's arm. "Stop the car!"

"What the hell? No." Mindy shook off my hand.

"Seriously, Mindy, pull over." I guess she could tell that if she didn't stop, I was going to jump out anyway. "Back up. Just a few hundred feet."

"No."

"C'mon, Mindy. I saw something."

She looked pissed, but she jammed the shift into reverse. As soon as she stopped on the verge, I opened the door and jumped out. "There," I called over my shoulder, but I didn't care if she heard me. I ran up the sandy hill, sidestepping cholla and other low spiny things. My sneakers slipped on shale as I topped one rolling hill and started down into a sandy arroyo.

I couldn't believe my eyes. It was the church from my dream. Sitting there in the middle of nowhere. Nothing but desert for miles around. The little steeple pointing up to heaven or whatever in the bright sky. A part of my brain told me that this couldn't be true. I stopped and closed my eyes. But when I opened them again, the cheery white church was still there, its doors invitingly open.

I gulped a few breaths to calm my heart from beating out of my chest, then took a few steps toward the building. The steps were whitewashed but felt spongy under my feet. It was cool in the church's shadow. I was vaguely aware of Mindy crunching in the sand up behind me.

I stopped in the doorway, letting my eyes adjust to the dimness. Just like in my dream, rows of backless benches and sunlight filtered through windows or openings high up in the steeple. I smelled rotten wood and dust and then…leather. What? "Justin?" I whispered into the darkness, then stepped inside.

The aged floorboards creaked ominously under me. The benches were splintery, but I tugged down the legs of my shorts and sat down anyway. The minute my butt hit the bench, I was overcome with a sense of being held, kind of like when you step into a sauna, how the heat envelops you. "Justin?" I pleaded again. "Is that you?"

I sat there being hugged for I don't know how long. My body recalled snuggling up behind Justin on the back of his bike. I breathed him in as visions floated through my mind. Lazy Sundays, hungover, and lying on a blanket with him in my backyard. Him and me and Mindy laughing our heads off over breakfast at Denny's. The three of us sitting on his front porch watching the sun sink behind the mountains. I was in a time warp, and it kept me paralyzed on that rough bench, feeling like his arms were around me, my head resting on his shoulder. It seemed as if the silence was trying to tell me something, but I couldn't make it out.

Suddenly, in the distance, I heard Mindy calling my name, and I stood up quickly and turned to leave. My hand brushed against the splintery bench, and a sliver impaled my palm. I shook my hand. The light was too dim to see anything. Again, I heard Mindy outside calling.

A cool breeze blew in from the open doorway. It ruffled the thin pages of a book, which was now lying open on the bench. I would swear that there had been no book there when I sat down. I recalled the hymnals and their murky words from my dream. This time, the words were clear. The book was open to a hymn, *Siempre Contigo*.

"Look, Mindy," I picked up the book. As I turned toward the door, the little hymnal disintegrated into dust that spilled through my fingers. "No!" I spun wildly around. "Justin! Come back."

I stumbled down the creaking steps, and Mindy ran toward me. "What the hell are you doing?" She grabbed my shoulders.

I squinted in the sunlight, and she handed me my sunglasses. "You dropped these over there." She waved her hand back toward the road. "Seriously, what are you thinking? That old place could've crashed in on top of you."

"Mindy, it was Justin. He was there, like in my dream."

She yanked my arm. "Let's go." She started off back to the car, and I stumbled along after her.

"Really," I tried again. "It was just like my dream. The steeple, the benches, the hymnals, the light through the windows. Everything. Justin."

With a rough jerk on my arm, Mindy turned and glared at me. "I don't know what you're talking about. You scared the shit out of me. Now let's go. We're getting in the car, and we're driving into the city." With that, Mindy marched up the embankment, dragging me behind her.

We didn't speak as the dusty length of road spilled out behind us. I spent the time digging at the splinter in my hand. We didn't speak as we checked into our motel. We didn't speak as we each took a shower and changed.

Only at the diner we found for dinner, over burgers and beers, did I finally break the silence. "I'm sorry if I scared you."

"So, what the hell happened?"

"I got a glimpse of the church from my dream. And then, when we stopped, and I ran over there, it was just like I told you. The doors were open, and when I went in, I could smell Justin, his jacket, his hair. Him. It was all there, just like in my dream."

Mindy snorted and rolled her eyes.

"Mindy, I felt him holding me. I breathed him in. The only difference was that this time, I could read the words in the book. It said *Siempre Contigo*." I felt tears dripping from my eyes.

"Siempre contigo? Yeah?" Mindy pulled her phone out of her back pocket. "Here," she scrolled the screen. "Here is your church. Here is the ruin you stepped into this afternoon."

I grabbed at her phone, but she pulled it away. "I don't know what went on in that brain of yours, but you should probably get it checked out. There was no church, no shining white steeple, no little books of hymns. And no Justin in that arroyo today. Here, look." She handed the phone to me.

I scrolled from photo to photo. She had taken a lot of them. Each one showed only a ramshackle lean-to, decrepit with age. A crumbling structure of graying wood.

"I couldn't find you anywhere. I was screaming my head off, calling for you. I took the photos so I could identify the place for friggin' search teams. When you walked out of that…thing…I was freaking out. I couldn't imagine what you might have been doing in there. It could have fallen in and killed you. It could have been an old mineshaft. And there you were, prancing down the rotten steps like you were on a catwalk, all dreamy-eyed. I could have killed you, I was so scared."

I stared at photo after photo, trying to see what I thought I had seen in it. It didn't make sense. But then, loving Justin had never made sense either.

"It doesn't matter now." I gulped my beer. I got what the dream had been trying to tell me. That Justin knows where I am and that, somehow, he's with me. And he's with you, too. We're still a team."

Mindy raised her glass and tapped mine with it. "You are out of your mind, girl. But we'll just go with that. Siempre Contigo."

I grabbed her hand and gave it a kiss.

A SINGLE MOMENT IN TIME

GREGORY L. WAGNER

"I don't understand what's wrong!" Edward slams his fist into the tabletop, knuckles first. The beat-up wood table vibrates from the impact. Loose papers, creased and warped from repeated trauma, scatter from the surface onto the floor of the sub-basement laboratory. Battle-steel gray epoxy paint has chipped away from the abused floor in random patches, exposing the lighter gray of naked concrete.

Dr. Calvin Campbell bends down and begins to gather the papers with fastidious care.

Edward glares at the offending table. Frustration drags his cheeks down. Dark circles ring his reddened eyes.

Calvin straightens up and hands Edward the recovered papers. "The table is old," he says. "Perhaps a bit gentler treatment is called for?"

"Sorry, Professor."

Calvin smiles reassuringly. "I realize we haven't encountered each other among the Physics faculty, Edward, but I've known Dr. Kuzack for many years. She's a close, personal friend. As I said, she asked me to stop by and talk with you about the trouble you're having."

"Right." Edward reaches up and runs both hands through his unkempt, long brown hair. Intense, crystal blue eyes focus on Calvin. "Are you familiar with the temporal aspects of quantum field theory?"

Metal screeches on concrete as Calvin pulls one of the two decrepit lab chairs out from the table. A patina of rust covers most of the chair's square, tube-steel legs. The faded mint green vinyl seat cushion is cracked along the front edge in multiple places. He sits, crosses his legs, and removes his worn black fedora. He sets the cap in his lap and aligns the front to his right knee. "The temporal aspects of quantum field theory," he says. He looks up at Edward. A rueful smile pulls his lips sideways. "No, not as such. My research has been slightly afield of that."

"Okay, well," Edward turns and rifles through the papers on the tabletop, scattering them into further disarray. Two sheets creep partially over the edge and threaten to plunge into the concrete floor. "The details are a bit involved, but …" He stops in midsentence and holds up a piece of paper to inspect. He turns and thrusts the crinkled page of calculations at Calvin. "This should make it obvious, Professor."

Calvin takes the page and tilts his head back to read the writing. He squints down the length of his thick nose. Mathematical equations march in tight formation across the page, the rows stacked immediately atop one another. The letters and symbols are crisp and distinct, the writing clean and fluid.

Edward quick-steps around the table and up next to Calvin's chair. "You see, if you limit the spatial extent to which entropy applies to a region, effectively close it off, then temporal solutions to the field equations are valid for both positive and negative values!" He leans over Calvin's shoulder and points excitedly at the paper with a long, slender finger. The fingernail is chipped and impacted with grime. "Right here! See?"

Calvin skews his eyes sideways and up to look at Edward. A blend of unpleasant odors hangs in the stagnant air. Edward hasn't left the laboratory in a bit too long. "Negative solutions to time?" Calvin asks.

Edward pops up straight, pivots, and quickly steps back, both hands raised, palms out. "I know," he says in a rush. "I know it sounds crazy. But Dr. Alena Kuzack herself looked over the calculations. And she was nominated for a Nobel Prize!" He drops his hands and takes a deep breath. Exhausted eyes struggle to focus. "And I'm right. It is possible, given the right conditions, to travel through time. Theoretically both forward and backward." He pauses, eyes flicking left and right before migrating back to Calvin. "Well, we always travel forward, so that's a known solution."

Calvin sets the page of calculations back atop the table with explicit reverence. Alena Kuzack had been very clear when she talked with Calvin and asked him to stop by; The work of Edward Maitley, PhD candidate extraordinaire, went far beyond the mundane classification of Advanced. Alena was convinced Edward was the next great revolutionary. She was personally invested in the brilliant young man and took her duties as a mentor seriously.

"Then let's start with that assumption," Calvin says. He turns and looks at the construct in the corner of the small lab: a spherical shell, eight feet in diameter, apparently assembled from every spare and cast-off piece of wire Edward could find. Thick wire, thin wire, bare wire, and wire clad in every color of the rainbow were wound together to form that shell. It had not been done neatly or with any discernable forethought. In style, it resembles a ball of yarn, constructed from a multitude of cast-offs, played with by a drunken cat, and wound back up by a three-year-old. A dirty sleeping bag lay crumpled up next to the shell of wire. Calvin raises a bushy eyebrow as he turns back to Edward.

"It works," Edward says quickly. "I didn't have a budget for this; it's a little off-topic for my thesis." He shrugs, embarrassed. "I had to scrounge for everything. And I put it together in kind of a hurry."

Calvin nods slowly. He tilts his head to indicate the mound of paper covering the desk. "How long did the calculations take you? From start to finish?"

Edward looks down at his feet and begins to sway side to side with a small oscillation. "Four days." His lips pull into a grimace. He doesn't look at Calvin. "The calculations took me four days. I got a little confused with the dimensional transformations."

Calvin's expression remains as close to neutral as training and a great deal of practice afford him. "That's perfectly understandable," he says. "And how long to build it?"

"Eleven days." Edward looks at Calvin. The edges of shame ring his eyes. "I'm more a theoretical physicist than experimental. I had a little trouble with the power supply."

The chair squeaks as Calvin adjusts his seat. He speaks with a soft, even cadence. "Eleven days is very respectable, Edward."

Some of the tension leaves Edward's shoulders. The side-to-side oscillation ebbs to a halt.

Calvin looks back to the eight-foot shell of tangled wiring. A lot of bare copper shows in that entwined nest, and three large electrical cables traverse the floor. The cables snake into a rusted electrical box on the wall. He turns back to Edward, both eyebrows raised. "Do you think that's safe?"

Edward turns quickly and looks at the wire structure. "Ah … mostly?" His eyes track back to Calvin before his head follows suit. "You need to be kind of careful getting into the entropy containment sphere."

"Kind of careful?"

"I fixed that problem!" Edward says hurriedly, again with the palm display. "It won't trip the breakers to the buildings on the campus quad again."

Calvin nods slowly. "So that little power outage we had last night at 11:17 p.m. was from your experiment?" He smiles, and Edward's eyes widen in surprise. "You're not the only person at this university who has a proclivity for working odd hours, Mr. Maitley."

"Yeah." Edward's grimace threatens to turn into a shy smile. "That's how Dr. Kuzack found out about my experiment."

"I see. Four days to do the calculations and eleven days to build it. I understand you have been using yourself as a test subject. How long have you been experimenting with it?"

"Eight days. I can go in once every ten hours or so." His eyes track back down to his feet. "It's a little hard on you." He looks up quickly. "Physically, that is. You need to rest after a temporal displacement."

Calvin looks at the crumpled sleeping bag next to Edward's device. "Let's talk about the temporal displacement. Although I confess, I've always considered the logic machinery of time travel to be a bit like Swiss cheese." He turns back with a smile. "Full of holes."

Edward stares at Dr. Calvin Campbell with a blank expression.

"So," Calvin continues, "let's walk through what seems to be going wrong. I'm an excellent sounding board and quite skilled at figuring out the right questions."

"I would really appreciate that, Professor. It's not doing what it should." Edward's shoulders sag, his arms go limp. "I keep ending up at the same exact time, regardless of how I adjust the field parameters." He shrugs, the motion slow and heavy. "I'm certain it's not the entropy containment sphere. There's no leakage, and the temporal displacement would be random if that were the problem. There is no randomness. It's always precisely the same."

Calvin indicates the other metal chair snugged up to the table. "You said the same exact time. Are you traveling to the same place as well?"

Edward pulls out the chair and sits down. The chair wobbles on unlevel feet. "Place?" His face screws up in confusion. "You mean spatial location?"

"Yes."

"But that's irrelevant! I'm at the same precise moment in time, so obviously, I'm at the same precise spatial location!"

Edward notes the confusion on Calvin's face. "Here, Professor." He bends forward and ruffles through the papers on the table. "I can show you what I mean."

Calvin reaches out and touches Edward's forearm lightly.

Edward goes completely still. He looks at Calvin with wild eyes.

"Edward, how about you just explain it to me."

"Right." Edward's eyes flash left and right as he bobs his head. "It's really very simple. The past has happened. The solutions to the equations already exist; they've been fully defined in space and time. Hence, if I go back in time, I can only access the equations relevant to me, not anyone or anything else. That's why spatial questions are irrelevant. If you choose a time, the spatial solution is defined."

Calvin nods in understanding. "Then you can only revisit times and places you have personally experienced." He tilts his head and studies Edward. "And it would be impossible to change that."

"Obviously!" Edward's head turtles back. "Changing your own past contradicts causality, Professor."

"Of course," Calvin nods. "But you are having trouble traveling back to the specific time you are trying to reach?"

"It's worse than that." Edward grabs Calvin's arm across the beat-up table, his grip tight and demanding. "I should be able to surf through time, flow through the sequence and equations at will. But I'm only reaching a single point." He points to the shell of jumbled wires with his free hand. "Regardless of the field settings!"

Calvin ignores the death grip. "*When* are you going, Edward? And how do you know it's the exact same moment?"

Edward lets go of Calvin's arm. "Twenty-three days ago, at 11:54 a.m. I'm near the corner of Fifth Avenue and Divine Street. It's the precise moment I came up with the idea. The sun was beating down on my shoulders. There was no wind at all. It was perfectly still. I was looking at a hole dug in the ground. It had straight walls. I can smell the grass, cut only the day before, and the smell of the freshly turned earth from the hole. Not the sweet, musky smell of loam, but the stale, brittle smell of clay. The hole was deep."

Calvin tilts his head. "I believe I understand. Why do you think you are getting trapped in that single moment in time?"

"Trapped?" Edward recoils as if slapped. "I'm not getting trapped, Professor. I just can't figure out why I'm only accessing a single temporal point." He stands quickly. The chair screeches on the concrete before the legs stick, and it falls backward. It crashes against the floor with a jarring clang of metal. In the echoes, the steel tubes chime lightly. "I'm sufficiently rested to try it again with the new parameters." He thrusts a hand out to Calvin. "Thanks for stopping by, Professor."

Calvin picks up his hat, stands, and shakes the hand proffered. He closes the door quietly as he leaves.

Dr. Alena Kuzack leans against the corridor wall outside the sub-basement lab. The overhead fluorescent bulbs are widely dispersed in the unpainted, concrete hallway. The dim light has a bluish tinge.

"The calculations?" Calvin says to his old friend.

"Brilliant, though convoluted. In my first quick read-through, they appeared to contain no errors and support his conclusions."

Calvin nods once. "I would expect as much." He settles the fedora on his head before clasping her small hand between his. "You were right to come get me, Alena. I'll personally take on Edward and give him the help he needs. It's best we intervene after his next experiment when he's tired and in need of rest." He tilts his head, watching her. "A last question. Fifth and Divine, twenty-three days ago at noon?"

Welling tears bring out the green flecks in Alena's eyes. "It was his Mother's funeral."

He squeezes her hand gently. "It will be a subtle process. We'll need to guide him to the self-realization that his contraption is just a useless tangle of wire."

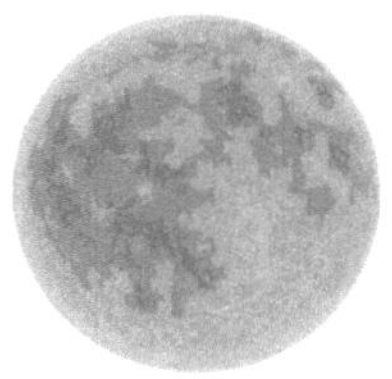

ACE IN THE HOLE

JENNIFER EDELSON

Girls who kiss in cars always get more than they bargain for; that's what Momma always says.

The day I fell off Jimmy Mason's swing set, and Eddie swooped in outta nowhere to save me, lashes fluttering over earnest brown eyes bigger than wheels, I was done for. Kissing in cars? Heck, I would have jumped Eddie on Jimmy's lawn, in front of all the mommas on Milton Street, just to prove I'd be Eddie's forever.

Eddie patched my knee, and that summer, I made it my business to steal his heart, taking up all the space in his bigger-than-life shadow. Every day, I rode down the block past his house on my bike, and to the park whenever he umpired, donning a big old mask that made him look a little like Jason Voorhees, and to Mr. Smith's corner store whenever he helped his daddy stock Mr. Smith's backroom. And later, when his momma got wind of what my momma called 'my little preoccupation,' to Eddie's house, dragging Jimmy along like a too-worn security blanket behind me.

Even at ten, I knew Jimmy was an asset—my ace in the hole—Eddie's competition and the reason Eddie never lost interest in me.

Momma taught me that one. She had an ace in the hole her whole life, too: buttoned-up Vernon Lewin. Polite as a pope, the other mommas called him.

Momma swore Vernon helped her sort the losers from the winners down at the Tipsy Cow whenever she went jonesing for her beer. All she had to do was teeter in on those big, stacked heels with Vernon on her arm, and the men would all drop their pool sticks where they stood and gather 'round her like she'd come to dole out first-class tickets to heaven. The winners, she said, fought for her, sometimes in the dusty parking lot by the dumpsters even, because they knew a good woman when they saw one. The losers walked away with their tail between their legs, like Daddy. And they never needed directions.

Jimmy, Eddie, and I spent that summer exchanging wits over cookies in Eddie's sunny kitchen, beneath frilly worn curtains and his momma's cherished 'Bless Me Jesus' needlepoint. Or when Eddie's daddy went on a bender after work, on Jimmy's creaky backyard seesaw, catching splinters where the sun don't shine. Our jokes were gems that glittered on our tongues, and I swear we even made Jimmy's seesaw weep—its drawn-out squeaking as we battled for solid ground, proof we weren't the only ones listening.

"Why did the ketchup blush?" Eddie would yell at me, planting his feet in the patchy grass before pumping his legs up and down, springy like the coils in my mattress. The one Momma used to yell at me for mistaking for a trampoline.

"Why *did* the ketchup blush?" I'd yell back, giggling as I stared up a slope at his pale face, reduced to a smudgy thumbprint by the sun behind him.

"Because he saw the salad dressing!"

Eddie would whoop then, falling to Earth as my own seat rose high into the air above him, confusing my favorite beat-up Keds for birds as I reached the pinnacle.

Then Jimmy and Eddie and Me, we'd all burst out laughing.

Sometimes, Jimmy got in on the action, too. It's how he tested bad words, padded as innocent declarations.

"Listen up!" he once yelled from the sidelines, watching us soar on separate ends of the same yellow beam. "Two fish swim into a wall, and one of them says. . . *damn*!"

That one especially made me laugh. But not Eddie. He called Jimmy's joke *crass*, repeating this word his momma liked to call the pictures we sometimes drew to make each other snicker after we'd sneak down into Eddie's basement to read his daddy's dirty magazines. Even though I found out later, Eddie got enough of a whooping himself for repeating it at the dinner table that night over a plate full of fried chicken—because *damn* isn't one of Jesus's favorite words.

Jimmy, though, my laughter sealed the deal, elevating his joke so it lived on in infamy for months. He loved the word *damn* so hard that summer he probably repeated it to everyone in town, punctuating it with a shriek like an exclamation mark over and over until all our ears burned.

That was the best summer. The first year before the last year Jimmy and Eddie really got along. The year before the year, Eddie made me pick between them. Eddie, my heart, or Jimmy, my would-be brother. That last year—the 'bad year' I call it—Jimmy stopped being my ace in the hole. That last year was the year when Jimmy turned into a bargaining chip and stopped being my friend. His words.

Those who cast stones should not live in glass houses. It's Momma's favorite saying. And I'll be honest, I never understood it. Except now, Caddy Jenkins is Jimmy's ace-in-the-hole, and he parades her past me at every opportunity. Though, God's honest truth, except for missing his stupid jokes, it doesn't bother me a bit; doesn't even ruffle a single hair on my head. Plus, at least Caddy is someone else's something. Because, as my momma also says, she's just a little bit shy of dumb and just a little bit left of homely.

Maybe, sometimes, I do miss Jimmy. But time don't change it. My *life* is a bargaining chip where Eddie's concerned. And no matter what Momma says, any random minute with Eddie is worth every moment of fire and brimstone that waits for us. Babies, shame, poverty, disease—they pale in the shadow of his kiss.

At least, that's what I've imagined. That's what I'm guessing.

The other thing Momma says? Girls ain't got no right to be kissing when they're only thirteen.

Momma brought me into this world, but Eddie fuels my soul. Momma feeds me meatloaf and green beans, but Eddie is the air I breathe. And unlike Momma, Eddie doesn't ask for anything. He doesn't demand I clean his messy room or help him cook dinner when I'm too tired to do anything but listen to music, or do his stupid, useless homework. Plus, Momma wouldn't steal the keys to Uncle Jessie's Cutlass and risk a beating just to prove how much she loves me. And she definitely wouldn't do it twice, like Eddie did. Especially not after being shoved into the back of polite as Pope Vernon's police mobile and taken down to the station, sirens blaring just to make a show of it.

"What do you call a boomerang that doesn't come back?" Eddie asks, sliding closer across Uncle Jessie's bucket seat.

"What?" I giggle.

He takes off his glasses and places them on the dashboard. "A stick."

Eddie's saucer eyes glimmer under a glint of moonlight reflecting off the rearview mirror.

"I got one." I raise my hand, dying to tell him.

Eddie leans in, hovering so close I almost swallow the part where I tell him it's alright if he officially claims me, as long as he's a gentleman.

"A monk asks a priest if it's okay to kiss a nun," I say, waiting a beat. "The priest replies, just don't get into the habit."

Eddie raises an eyebrow. "Just watch me."

It's black as asphalt out now. Uncle Jessie's worn bench seat shifts again as Eddie moves closer, determined to close the distance between us. I reach for him, ignoring Mamma's voice and the hollow in my heart where Jimmy's face sometimes haunts me.

"What happens when a clock is hungry?"

"Mmmm?"

"It goes back four seconds," I murmur against his lips.

Our mouths meet, and my heart skips, and I think about how Momma might call that last joke a 'mixed message.' Right before she grounded me.

The past, present, and future walk into a bar. It was tense.

That's the joke I'd tell Jimmy if he were here now—

Jimmy.

I know what I want, clear as the glass in Eddie's frames. But now that Jimmy's a ghost, I also know *now* can feel like forever and that until it's at my door, tomorrow doesn't even exist. Time's like that—always confusing people, making us feel like we've been tricked when, really, we just never stop to reckon with it.

Jimmy would love this moment. The uncertainty.

The space between then and later, where nothing yet is final.

Not even Momma's warning.

Ohana

PATRICK X.L. LEE

On the last day of Peter and Maya's Hawaiian vacation, they decided to surrender to the lure of a luau. Peter turned his nose up at the gauche tourist spectacle of the luau, the worst kind of cultural appropriation—exoticized ritual dances and sanitized food to give the mostly *haole* audiences a faux taste of the islands and their history.

But it was Maya's first trip to Hawaii—or *Hawai'i*, as Peter insisted it be called—and she wanted it all. He couldn't refuse her, so he agreed.

The luau went as expected, right down to the loud crowds of mai-tai-soaked mainlanders in their aloha shirts and flower leis. At least the weather was nice, and the multi-hued sunset over the Pacific was spectacular.

The show ended with the overly familiar Hawaiian song *Aloha O'e*, known to mainlanders as a love song, an expression of sentimental longing. Peter knew it differently from the time he was a young boy when his mother would sing it to him while he strummed along

on his child-sized ukulele: The tragic farewell of Princess Liliʻuoka-
lani to her lover—and, by extension, to her people and land as the
Americans took over her island kingdom.

But on this night, as the stars winked on overhead, the song
suddenly and unexpectedly touched Peter somewhere deep inside.

One fond embrace

A hoʻI au

Until we meet again

The refrain triggered a sharp sadness, and the tears welled up.
He quickly wiped them away in confusion.

Maya noticed.

"Babe?" she said, squeezing his arm.

He turned away, embarrassed.

"Thinking of your uncle?"

The question caught Peter off guard at first, until he realized
what she meant, and he nodded in assent.

Their vacation was impromptu: A few days in Honolulu after
attending his uncle's funeral the week before in Hilo. Peter hadn't
spoken with his uncle in nearly forty years; attending was a familial
obligation, a gesture more of respect than affection.

Peter looked at Maya and smiled wanly.

"It's nothing," he said.

She looked at him with concern, squeezed his arm again.

The song ended.

• • •

That night, Peter lay awake in their hotel bed as Maya slumbered
beside him. Memories came unbidden, sparked by the song that
replayed in his mind.

A word.

Ohana.

One of the first Hawaiian words Peter's mother had taught him when he was very young.

Family.

More than family, his mother had explained. "*Ohana* stands for the people you are related to," she had said, caressing his face. "But it's something else as well. It's the people you love, the people who depend on you, the people who love you. It means loyalty. And forgiveness."

Peter closed his eyes, remembering that last bit.

More memories surfaced.

When he was a boy, Peter spent much time with his extended Hawaiian family, even though he was born and grew up in California. His nuclear family often traveled to Honolulu for summers on the beach with his many cousins, and uncles, and aunties, blood and not. He would run along the white sand, his skin darkened by the sun to the color of koa wood, the warm water of the Pacific glistening on him as he laughed and played. Afterward, there would be food, mountains of it, shared with dozens of relatives, his mother and grandmother squatting at the hibachi, grilling ever more meat.

But the summers would end. Hawaii would remain as it was, in the middle of the sea, a promise, a hope. But he would move somewhere else, and things would change, and decades would pass.

Peter turned on his side away from Maya.

He still had family, he thought. An image of his sister, Darlene, came to him. They could have been twins, so close were they in age and temperament. Too close, maybe.

"I hate school," Darlene would tell him. "I always get the teachers you had, and they always compare me to you."

"Not my fault," Peter would say and would punch her in the arm.

Peter felt shame about it now.

Physical violence was common in his small family. His father, a frustrated man, would blame Peter for things, even when he was small. The blame turned to shouting and eventually to hitting. The slap, the sting of a belt. Peter winced at the memory. At the time, it left Peter frightened and confused. Eventually, it would make him angry. Peter took it out on Darlene.

Peter wasn't the only target, not that he or Darlene or his mother ever spoke of it. Eventually, his mother and father divorced. Peter himself went off to school, then to the East Coast, as far away as possible. Darlene moved out first, though. She went to Oregon, where she married and had a son of her own. Nathan. For reasons he could not dredge up, Peter had never met him.

For that, Peter's guilt weighed on him like a boulder on his chest.

• • •

Maybe because of his own family, maybe in spite of it, Peter had never wanted children. Neither did his first wife, Jill.

Unlike Peter, Jill was an only child, but she had her own rocky relationship with her parents. They shared a mutual need, Peter would conclude later. It may be why they found each other. At the moment, it was enough.

Ohana was a myth, Peter came to believe. Jill sympathized.

"What matters is the tribe that finds you," Jill had said. "That's your real family."

Peter and Jill set out to build their own tribe. She called them "the island of misfit toys" after the old TV Christmas special. Each person they found had been cast off in some way. Each had an empty place that maybe they could fill.

Peter and Jill's apartment became the tribe's clubhouse.

"Let's do Sunday dinners, like we did in Hawai'i," Peter said. "We can do them every week. We'll have so much food they won't be able to eat it all." Jill, the only child, loved the idea.

The first dinner, Peter grilled short ribs and made steamed rice. A dozen people filled the apartment. Jill made mai-tais. The alcohol-fueled laughter and jokes and embraces, and the evening lasted until the small hours.

"Love you," Peter said to his tribe as they filed out into the night.

The Sunday dinners went on for a couple of months. Weekly, then biweekly, then monthly.

Eventually, Peter's anger came back.

Jill left.

He didn't hear from his tribe for a while, then at all. He moved back to California and started therapy.

• • •

Darlene called Peter one September a few years later.

"Nathan's gone," she said.

Peter said nothing. He sat heavily on the floor, the phone in his hand.

An overdose. Nathan was twenty-one.

Peter went to the memorial service in Portland, Oregon. He went by himself.

He walked into the church, where the family had gathered at the altar. Darlene and her husband saw him enter. He walked up to Darlene and embraced her. She hugged him fiercely.

After the service, Peter sat alone at a table. Darlene's nieces and nephews drifted over to introduce themselves. Peter found himself sharing drinks with the young people, who wanted to know everything about Nathan's mysterious uncle. Darlene looked over and smiled.

Peter stayed in Portland for a few weeks, sleeping in Darlene's spare bedroom. They spent time with the nieces and nephews. Darlene and Peter sat up late at night, sharing memories of Hawaiian summers long past.

The leaves had gone from the trees by the time Peter packed up his car for the drive back to California.

"If you need anything …" he said.

"Love you, big brother," Darlene said.

• • •

The letter arrived the week after Christmas.

It was from Darlene. Peter had not spoken to her since the month in Oregon.

Peter's hands trembled as he read it. "I will never forgive you," Darlene said.

"You missed out on the life of one of the best people I have ever known. Where were you? How could you have abandoned Nathan? Our family? Now you will never know how wonderful he was. I hope you carry the regret of what you've done for the rest of your life."

Peter crumpled the paper up and threw it in the fireplace.

• • •

The alarm in the Honolulu hotel room went off at 7 a.m., waking Peter from his memory of Darlene's letter.

Maya was already up and in the bathroom brushing her teeth.

"Aloha," she called out. "Did you sleep well?"

It was their last day. They went to Rainbow Drive-In for burgers before heading to the airport.

"Do you want my pickle?" Maya asked. "I know you do."

Peter had met Maya the New Year's Eve after Darlene's letter. She was sitting on the sofa at a friend's house, talking to a tall man Peter did not know. But she kept looking over at Peter, who smiled at her.

They moved in together a year later. Maya talked with her

mother on the phone every day. Peter found this remarkable. He recalled years when he had not spoken with his own mother, as much as he loved her, before her health declined, and he moved close by to look after her before her passing.

Peter had told Maya he would never remarry. "You don't understand how hard marriage is because your parents have been happily married for fifty years," Peter said.

"Maybe you should take a closer look at them," Maya said with a laugh.

They married a year after that.

Now, sitting at the Rainbow Drive-In, Peter looked at Maya as if for the first time. He took Maya's pickle, and they ate in silence for a minute.

"What was up with you at the luau last night?" she asked finally.

Peter took a pull from his Diet Coke. "Just something I remember my mother saying. About ohana. No big," he said.

"Ah, okay," Maya said. "You don't want to talk about it now, that's fine. I forgive you."

Peter looked at her.

"Are you happy?" he said.

She looked perplexed for a minute. Then took his hand.

"Ya big dork," she said with a grin. "You know I'm not going anywhere."

MY WEEKEND

CRISTINA BROWNE

"How was your weekend?" they asked. Seems a simple enough question.

And then my inner voice remarks, "Exactly which weekend?"

The one where I sat in a dark room with strangers, hearing the elderly man next to me quietly sobbing during a poignant scene in the movie…and realizing I was sniffling too? And when the credits rolled, he leans over and thanks me for sharing the movie with him?

Or the one where I went hiking at x, y, or z and was engulfed in the beauty and serenity there? And as I pass a couple just starting the hike, the lady asks, "Was it worth it?" and the man exclaims, "Just look at her smile…I think that says it all, don't you?"

Or the one where I went to a local restaurant and sat at the bar with all the other solo people, and no one made eye contact?

Or the one I spent trying to bicycle the many hills around here and actually did some?

Or the one I spent talking to gallery owners around town and listening to their stories?

Or the one I spent all morning in my pajamas watching Bugs Bunny cartoons and laughing like I was a kid again?

Or the one I got covered in mud from walking the trails and slipping down a hill?

Or the one where I stepped outside at 2 a.m. hoping to watch a meteor shower and burst into tears as I witnessed the splendor of countless stars that reminded me that I was just a speck in this interconnected universe?

So how was my weekend? It was wonderful because I lived it!

WRITING LETTERS AT HOME

ELAINE KOYAMA

I lived on a family farm one mile out of town. My world was one of working on the farm—feeding sheep, driving trucks, and being by myself—taking my horse out on adventures on the ninety-acre home place or riding down to the Big Horn River to explore the tree-lined shores of the fast-moving water.

Our family raised Suffolk sheep and sold the ewes and rams as breeding stock. Part of that process was to compete in livestock shows and sales to promote the herd. For years, we were part of the Big Horn County Fair in Hardin, the Montana Winter Fair held in Bozeman, and the Empire State Fair in Billings. These events took me out of our local community into the wider livestock arena. They allowed me to meet like-minded farm and ranch kids from around the state.

These friends were 4-H club members, as was I. Competing at the fairs became the gateway to participating in statewide 4-H events, which in turn became a rich environment to meet even more kids. But to stay in touch and cultivate friendships in those days required an art form that is rapidly vanishing in today's tech-driven culture.

Many hours a day, I would sit in my room, at first in a wing chair with a 1" x 12" board resting across the armrests as my desk. Later, a second-hand desk appeared, and I had a more comfortable workspace. As the youngest in the family, and with a gap between my sister and me of over seven years, I didn't have to share a bedroom for most of my conscious life. I spent much of my limited disposable income on buying stationery and stamps. And I would write.

Torian Donahoe was one of my best friends growing up. She lived on a fabulous ranch in the Absarokee mountains in a real log home. I wrote to Torian at least weekly. We once traded weekends staying with each other, a huge effort given we had to have our parents drive us to each other's homes, a distance of one hundred twenty-five miles, one way, on two-lane roads. Torian raised and showed Hampshire sheep. When I went to visit her, I found her in a barn about a mile from her home, milking a cow. She was sitting on a stool, her face resting against the cow's flank, her hands automatically and rhythmically squeezing milk into a can.

Marjorie Krause lived outside of Lewistown and showed Columbia sheep. Marjorie's mom had what I remember as flaming red hair with a personality to go with it. Marjorie's sheep had white faces, and Suffolks had black faces. She, too, lived in a mountain-like area. Our letters spanned years, and later, we re-connected in Denver, where we continued our friendship, face to face. When Marjorie was about fourteen and I was about eleven, she painted a picture of Columbia and Suffolk lambs, noses together, like our friendship. I just ran across the painting in my latest move.

Karen Wolfe lived in Stevensville, Montana, in the Bitterroot Valley, a picture-perfect setting in Western Montana. It's over four hundred miles from Hardin, my hometown. She raised Suffolks like me, and we must have come across each other at the Montana Winter Fair. I was always fascinated by where Karen lived, as my brother-in-law also grew up in Stevensville but was over ten years older than us. Karen recently found me on Facebook through an app called Checkmate. Um, it's a little weird since checkmate scans for criminal activity… But she now lives in Hawaii, a far cry from small-town Montana.

Not all my correspondence was with those who lived far away.

Susan Kerrick and I corresponded for many summers. Susan was one of my childhood friends who lived in the town of Hardin, a mile away. Unlike my own kids, whose summers were filled with soccer, tennis, summer classes, and play dates, I never saw my town friends once school ended. I stayed connected by writing letters, mailing the letters by putting them in our mailbox on the highway in front of our house, and raising the red flag that signaled there was outgoing mail.

Cathy Miller went to school in Hardin but lived about twenty miles east of town on Sarpy Creek. Her dad and my dad went to high school together and were good friends, and Cathy and I were best friends, too. Our letters were necessary because she lived so far out of town, but I actually saw Cathy more than most of my town friends, as we had many sleepovers. We would ride horses along the sand rocks across the road from her house, having adventures in the scruffy pines, sagebrush, and rock formations. One night, her mom made pork chops for supper. I remember each of us kids getting one pork chop and a dollop of scalloped potatoes, her dad got two pork chops. I then understood why Cathy was a wiry, skinny little thing. At our home, I would eat three or four pork chops by myself (they were, after all, sliced thin, not like a beef steak). I never remember running out of food or being chastised for eating more than my fair share.

Not all my correspondence was with girlfriends.

My first "real" boyfriend was an AFS exchange student from Sweden. Sven (yes, his real name) and I went to Prom when he was a senior and I was a sophomore. We wrote letters weekly for over three years. I often think Sven got me through high school and the first months of college by being my confidant and "safe" boyfriend. He also encouraged me to be more "intellectual" and look beyond the borders of my Montana world. Because of Sven, I became an AFS exchange student myself—spending the summer of 1971 in Finland; he challenged me to read more; he let me dream big. I often think of how expensive it was to write those letters to Sweden, but there were two things my folks never questioned me buying— postage and books.

And as prolific a letter writer I was as a youth, even more exciting was receiving letters in return. The walk to the mailbox was filled with anticipation—finding letters addressed to me, pages filled with ongoing sagas of summer romances, or mundane daily life; counting the days to the next fair or trip to town when our paths might cross; planning for the upcoming school year.

I saved many of the letters from that era. For years, I had every letter from the Swedish boyfriend. But time takes its toll. Moves forced me to jettison non-essentials. Getting married and having kids put a big dent in my letter-writing time. I had less time to reflect, needed more time to get through the day, meeting the demands of work and family. Email, texting, and Facebook have changed the communication process.

Some may think technology ruined good old-fashioned letter writing, but I don't. I love technology; I love how Facebook has connected us in a way letter writing could never do. I can "write" on Facebook and reach hundreds of friends. I can go offline if I want to say anything personal. And photos are so much easier to share now than in the olden days.

I would never go back, but no one can ever take away the thrill I still feel of seeing my name on an envelope, the anticipation of

opening a letter with words crafted for my eyes only, and the satisfaction of knowing for a brief moment, our worlds aligned.

215

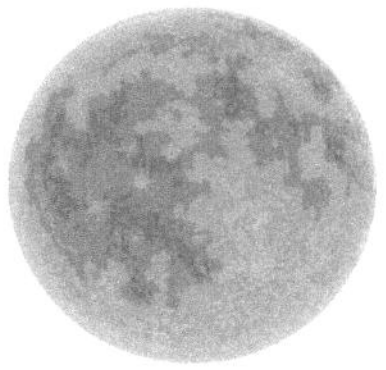

CETI ALPHA DESMOND

ANDRÉ FLEUETTE

The executive stopped, expensive leather heels coming together so quickly they clicked, but the smile remained, the eyes soft and welcoming. "Doctor Rathbun knows why you're here, Detective." She looked both of them in the eye, in turn. "And he's quite aware of the bench warrant you're carrying."

"So, he's ready to answer for the missing workers?" Maisie asked. She noticed only the slightest hesitation in their host.

"Of course." Cassie's smile only got bigger, brighter. "As I said. Desmond is eager to see you. I expect that you will be pleasantly surprised by your conversation." She waved a hand back along the corridor. "This way, please," the assistant said, resuming the clack-clack cadence of impeccable heels on the flawless black floor. The hallway was polished like a movie set, an ostentatious revenant from the old science fiction features pledging a lateral glimpse at an optimistic future, each surface mirrored and bright. Broad white panels lined their walls, reflecting the pair of detectives marching in syncopation along the burnished black floor as they followed the trim, priggish woman

217

in the plum-colored business coat-and-skirt combo, complete with matching and anachronistic pillbox hat. Doctor Rathbun's assistant introduced herself when they met in the glass-and-steel lobby: Ms. Cassandra Kindle, emphasis on the feminine singular. Detective Maisie Fox felt underdressed in the executive's presence, unkempt, despite the navy jacket and tie combo she had chosen special for to-day's visit. Cheap, even. Slovenly, indeed, by comparison.

"Assistant? Or something else?" Maisie whispered to her part-ner, Detective Dan Conklin, earning a shrug and a raised eyebrow that suggested much more of something else. A man of Dr. Rath-bun's lofty stature? A henchman-cum-concubine wouldn't be out of the question. A partner, maybe. Or an accomplice. There was enough crime to share between the two of them.

They had been met outside by a uniformed valet, keen on re-lieving them of their black-and-white, the archaic term remaining despite the vehicle's tricolor abstract-geometric paint scheme in blue, orange, and white. Politely, they declined, citing regulation, vacating the vehicle in the fire lane out front, defying ordinance in the name of expediency. At Conklin's suggestion, they left the lights flashing, leaving a second black-and-white and its accompanying backup to keep watch over it.

Once inside the headquarters of Rathtec, the massive building a fusion of stone baroque and modern glass-and-steel on the center of dozens of acres of plush, unspoiled green, their coffee orders were taken; a small, regular latte for her, a double-sweet white chocolate mocha (extra whip) for Conklin. No charge, of course, and deliv-ered with expansive smiles. The pair sipped while they waited, Ms. Kindle's efficiency evident as the executive arrived precisely at the top of the hour, the exact moment of their agreed visitation.

Ms. Kindle escorted them, cold business-chic, into a glass el-evator compartment at the center of the capacious, sunlit lobby. The car deposited them ten levels down at the bottom of the shaft, four levels below employee parking, into this seemingly endless hallway. Steel conduit snaked out from manifolds, junction boxes were marked off with white-and-yellow striped paint with warnings to steer clear, while protrusions of red, green, and blue—functions unknown—disrupted the otherwise smooth, featureless walls. Even the doors were hidden. Maisie wouldn't have even known they were there if they hadn't opened periodically, discharging technicians in white lab coats, more suits, and the occasional neat-but-unkempt, bearded, and/or dreadlocked look of the information-technology geeks. Periodically, enormous oil paintings depicting fantastical landscapes, stunning waterfalls, and skies the wrong hue of blue broke up the seamless white of the walls.

"I'm sorry, miss…" Conklin started before remembering. "Excuse me, *Ms.*?"

The assistant turned to face them, short, luxurious, auburn hair spilling as if sculpted from under the pillbox. "You can call me Cassie," she smiled, perfect teeth under perfect nose and radiant, powder blue eyes. She clutched a terminal in her hands, glossy nails in a color Maisie couldn't identify but one that faultlessly complemented her outfit. Sonic Tango or Grape-o-licious Berries: certainly, a tortured and ridiculous brand name.

"Sure. *Cassie.* Thanks. How much farther?" Conklin was an impatient man, what you might call prickly, and uncomfortable with female authority. Though she knew, not a woman-hater, he'd confided over cheap whiskey and draft beer one night at his local. Leery, thanks to a controlling, domineering mother and absent father. The calm, erudite, and self-possessed Ms. Kindle was surely causing his internal mechanisms to twitch.

Maisie bridled a little at Conklin's impatience but was, in a way, glad he asked: the papers in her pocket—the list of names of the missing, the warrant for Rathbun's arrest—weighed down her affordable cotton pants as if they were a bulky bag of coins. "It's a long hallway." She smiled at Cassie.

"We're almost there. Just this way a short while longer. I am assured that Dr. Rathbun is awaiting your arrival in the Hub with some eagerness."

"Eagerness?" Conklin snorted, earning a glare from Maisie. "Not to be rude, mind you. I mean…we're, uh, the police. We're not used to…eagerness," he explained.

. . .

The Hub, Cassie explained as they walked, was the nucleus of the Rathtec Center complex. "The Hub accesses the cortex of the research corporation's massive intelligence. This whole facility, everything," her hands widening to encompass everything around them, fingers splayed open, "is one symbiotic organism, all working together. And the Hub is the brain." Maisie marveled at how Ms. Kindle could speak, walking backward in those heels without missing a step, footfalls as regular and precise as a metronome. She reminded the detective of a White House tour guide, repeating the same lines by rote after many thousands of repetitions: "And we're walking…"

The trio stalked down a long ramp—the executive much more confident on the slick surface in heels than Maisie was in Oxfords—toward a massive, curved door, a semi-circle that partially blocked access through the hall. As they grew near, the detectives could see that the door was, in fact, moving, albeit slowly, a steady stream of personnel entering and leaving as they approached.

"Shift change was just a short while ago," Cassie explained, waving at several workers who smiled at her as they passed, eyeing the detectives quizzically. "There usually aren't so many people in this area." They stepped aside as a pair of electric forklifts escaped the Hub, dodging the moving door and gliding up the ramp.

"The door?" Maisie asked, concerned as it closed the gap leading into the complex.

"It will close behind us," Cassie said, waving the pair forward. "It's on a timer once the countdown starts. There's no way to stop it from closing at this point."

"So, what? We're going to be locked in there?" Conklin asked, an edge to his voice.

"Does that bother you, Detective?"

"I'm not sure how that helps us," Maisie said, answering for her partner. They'd only been together a short while, a matter of months, two bundles of raw nerves, poor performance reviews, and square pegs paired together by their shift captain. Maisie, recently cuckolded and divorced, and Conklin, widowed and orphaned in the same car wreck, comfort only found at the bottom of the caliber of alcohol sold in plastic bottles. They were not united long enough to develop the true instincts that one evolved with a partner after years together despite their shared traumas. "We have official business…"

"Of course," Cassie said, waving them forward as the door inched closer to sealing shut. "You will be able to leave after Dr. Rathbun's presentation. I do apologize for any inconvenience this may cause, but we must enter before the door closes, or I'm afraid you'll have to come back another time."

"You do know what a warrant is, right?"

Cassie smiled, though this time, Maisie could see a crack in the assistant's façade, an edge in her eyes that telegraphed annoyance. "Doctor Rathbun is a visionary."

"So was Jim Jones. And Pol Pot," Maisie said. "A thousand others."

"As well as Noah, Marie Curie. And a thousand others," Cassie said, restoring her urbane composure. "Right this way, please." She strode confidently through the closing gap between shiny-black door and wall.

"This is stupid," Conklin said, pausing. "Why would they have to lock us *in* their secure facility?" There were just moments left before the door would seal them out of the Hub and block their passage to Dr. Rathbun. "What do you think?"

"I think," Maisie said, frowning and straightening her jacket. "I think that it's now or never. And I really don't want to be the one to tell Captain Frasier that justice was deferred by a door."

"I think if she saw the size of this door, she'd understand," Conklin said.

"You coming?" Maisie jerked her head into the Hub, then stepped through, Conklin tight on her heels as the enormous portal closed behind them with a soft hiss and clack.

• • •

Maisie stopped just inside the Hub, in a surprisingly small clear area, taking a moment to orient herself. The room was entirely circular, with two elevated platforms on either side, split down the center by the wide, formless black walkway. A double stairway flanked by wire-and-steel railings led up to each platform, which was crowded with workstations, transparent monitors filling the vertical spaces like individual glass windows. At least a dozen white-coated technicians bustled about on each platform, the low buzz of serious conversations filling the air, jostling for auditory space with computer-voiced announcements that seemed to come from everywhere. Metal pallets bulged with cargo-netted gear, boxes, and bundles overflowing and rising high above the floor, filling the wide central corridor.

"Initial rotation complete. Secondary ignition initializing. Window optimization in Z-minus seven," the computer intoned, in a voice Maisie recognized as belonging to Ms. Cassie Kindle. The real Cassie, she realized, had disappeared. Studying the room, she noticed something, tapping Conklin on the shoulder. "Look, Dan." She pointed at the door they'd come through moments before. "The 'door' isn't moving. The whole room rotates."

"Huh," Conklin said, crouching to get a better look at the seams. "I'll be damned."

"Detectives!" A cheerful voice called to them, and the two turned to look. Maisie recognized the man instantly, though she'd never before seen him in person, just the famous image that graced magazines, news feeds, and the kind of snarky t-shirts worn by clove-smoking hipsters. He was a spectacularly homely man, unique in his unfortunate huckery, bent of spine and limb, and blind in one eye, evidenced by the pirate-style eye patch that graced his face. Maisie was unsurprised to find that the patch perfectly matched the plum color of Kindle's ensemble.

"He looks like a naked mole rat," whispered Conklin, earning a snort from Maisie.

"Quiet," she whispered back, though she agreed. Rathbun was profoundly unattractive. And, she reminded herself, despite the lavish exterior and show of hospitality, responsible for the presumed death of nearly two dozen people. "Detective Fox," she said, keeping her voice professional, then nodded to Conklin. "This is my partner, Detective Conklin. Dr. Rathbun, I assume?" He only came to Maisie's shoulder.

"The one and only," he smiled, revealing a set of gleaming ivories. He shook her hand, then Conklin's, and guided them up the platform on the right, apologizing the whole way for the clutter. Technicians smiled at them as they passed, parting to reveal a small table and a set of stuffed leather chairs in the center of the maelstrom. They took their seats. An attendant, dressed in a white kitchen uniform, immediately appeared at their sides with a tray of drinks and profiteroles, choux à la crème, and other treats. She set a coffee cup in front of each, Maisie not at all surprised to find a precise duplication of her earlier order, corporate logo decorating the foam of her latte.

By agreement, while stuck in Houston traffic en route to Rath-tec, Maisie was to take the lead. Be the good cop. Conklin was to watch, remain silent, preserve his opportunity to be bad cop should the need arise. It was a role for which he had spent a career perfecting. "What is it you are working on here, if I may ask?"

"Mission to Mars-type stuff?" Conklin interjected, reaching for a puffy cake. Maisie shook her head, annoyed that Conklin had, in only the first minute, deviated from the plan. "I saw a piece on CNN. Something about that botched launch. That rocket that exploded." The detective shoved the cake in his mouth, then reached for a napkin, finding the cake larger than he'd expected.

Rathbun laughed. "No, not that. I mean, yes, we're involved as an organization with the Mars insertion project. But I have my nephew Todd overseeing that sector from our Florida location."

"How's that going? The news isn't very, uh…reassuring."

"Todd's an idiot," Rathbun said. "The project is failing, as noted by the payload that, as you brought up, recently exploded."

"That's a problem," Conklin said around the cake.

"Not at all. Nobody was killed. A setback. A few, mostly minor, injuries, unfortunately. But they were handsomely compensated."

"So, behind schedule and losing a ton of money?" Maisie asked, reaching for her latte.

Rathbun smiled at her. "Like I said, he's an idiot. But a useful one." He shifted in his chair, folding his legs in front of him.

"How so?" Conklin asked.

"How?" Rathbun shifted. "Todd the Idiot is behind schedule and losing a ton of money because that's precisely what I wish him to be doing. If the Mars mission were terribly important, I'd be handling it myself." He looked up, noticing movement, and rose to his feet. Maisie looked over her shoulder, spying Cassie weaving her way through the workstations to join them, the tablet still in her hand, now with a paper folder as well. The translucent screens displayed lines of data, various planetary orbits, by the look of them, and many fields of data incomprehensible to a police detective.

Cassie had changed from the plum business outfit into gear more suitable for a winter hike in the mountains, complete with sturdy-looking footwear.

"Welcome," Rathbun said, rising to his feet. Cassie nodded, then took the fourth seat, the doctor sitting only after she was settled.

Conklin pointed a finger at her, shifting it between the two of them. "Are you two…"

"Fucking?" Kindle said, raising an eyebrow at the detective. "That's the word you wish to use, isn't it?"

"Uh…" Maisie shook her head, embarrassed by Conklin's forthrightness. "We didn't…"

Rathbun laughed and reached a hand over into the space between them, Cassie reaching down to take his with her own. "Of course we are," she said, settling back in the chair.

"We are…a couple," Rathbun said. "Surprising, I know, to look at us. But…"

"Look, I'm sorry," Maisie said, interrupting. "Not to be rude, but we need to get to business." She set her cup on the table, then reached into her pocket. "As I've heard you are already aware," she shot a look at Cassie, "I have a list here of individuals who have, at various times over the past few years, gone missing while in your employ, Mr. Rathbun."

"Doctor," Cassie said, the look on her face inscrutable. "It's *Doctor* Rathbun, please."

"*Doctor*, my apologies," she said, despite her revulsion of the man. "Twenty-two individuals have gone missing in the past two years from this facility. Despite repeated attempts for information, multiple visits, your office has refused to cooperate with us, and have stalled or, frankly, completely ignored subpoenas for yourself and others in your employ."

"We're quite busy, as you can see," the doctor said, winking at her.

"The families of the missing individuals are quite upset," Maisie said, irritated by the wink. "And rightfully so. They demand answers." She held out the paper to the doctor, only to have it taken from her hand by Cassie. "And so does the HPD."

"That was an error," Rathbun said. "Contracting people with families, I mean."

Cassie unfolded the paper, then scanned the list. "We've corrected that," she said, her eyes running down the list of names. When finished, she set the paper on the table, then nodded at Rathbun.

"Corrected what?" Conklin asked.

"Families," the assistant said. "That was my mistake, if I am to be honest. An oversight. We no longer utilize individuals with families. Anyone who will miss them."

"No longer…" Maisie said, astonished. What kind of monsters were they? How involved was Kindle in this?

Conklin leaned forward, his coat falling open to reveal the sidearm in a shoulder holster. No doubt a calculated move. "So, people without families are okay?"

Rathbun shrugged. "For our purposes, yes."

Maisie stood, reaching in her pocket for the other paper that it held, the judge's bench warrant for the doctor's arrest, should he decline to appear on his own. She held the paper out, pulling it away from Kindle's grasp and pointedly extending it to Rathbun. "This is a bench warrant for your arrest, should you fail to come willingly," she said. "For the murders of Erin Lobdell, Angelika Hidalgo, Ray Schuyler, Urjeet 'Eddie' Ramachandran…" Maisie had memorized all twenty-two names, such was her disgust.

"No one is missing," Rathbun said. He turned to Cassie, who handed him the folder she had been carrying. Rathbun flipped it open, then pulled a sheet out and handed it up to Maisie.

"Lewis Casey, age thirty-seven. Architect," Rathbun said.

Maisie took the paper. In the top left corner, a photo showed a pudgy, balding man with glasses. The right quadrant held Mr. Casey's personal information: employee number, height, weight, blood type, and the like. The lower half was blank except for one sentence:

"I, Lewis Arnold Casey, hereby declare that I am of sound mind and body and am of free will and without duress retained in the employ of Dr. Desmond Rathbun and Rathtec Industries for the foreseeable future."

A bold, scrawling signature accompanied the declaration.

"Hiromi Hando, age twenty-six. painter." The photo showed a young Japanese woman smiling with bright eyes. The page contained the same disclaimer.

"Nasir Malik, age forty-two. Heavy equipment operator." The next sixteen pages were the same: each contained a photograph, the disclaimer, and a signature.

"Note the date," Cassie said, pointing at the top of a page: July 14, 2027. Two weeks ago.

"I'd like to see them in person," Maisie said. "If you don't mind, of course." She handed the sheaf of papers to her partner.

"We came all the way out here," Conklin said, leafing through the pages. "If you don't mind indulging us."

"That would be a major disruption," Rathbun said. "Would a spot-check suffice for your needs? Pick two or three names at random, and I can have them meet us here. We can talk over coffee."

"Well," Maisie thought, her mind racing. If they were here and working, why the secrecy? "What's the hesitation in showing us? And why have you ignored the summons we've sent you? The requests for information? We very much would like to confirm the veracity of…"

"There's three missing," Conklin interrupted, shuffling the papers. He counted through them again, then nodded. "Yeah. There's twenty-two names on our list, nineteen pages here."

"Who's missing, Doctor?"

"There's no one…missing," Rathbun said, looking away from Maisie. Rathbun and Cassie looked at each other, silently communicating through their glance, then Cassie nodded.

"Let's do it," she said. "Like you suggested before."

"Okay," Rathbun said. He looked up at the screens surrounding them. "Just about ten minutes," he said, and waved at the tray of food on the table. "And I think all your questions will be answered. In the meantime; relax. Enjoy the cakes. We bake them here, and they're delicious. Our chef is a genius."

Maisie ignored the food, turning instead to the list, pen in hand. She went through Cassie's papers, checking each name off her list as she found them. At the end, three remained unchecked: Jodie Wetzler-Van Valkenburg, Yan Xiuying, and Raymond Schuyler. Even if, though she doubted, the other nineteen were safe and well, three people were still missing. Three families who needed answers. Three charges—many believed murder—to be levied against the great Desmond Franklin Rathbun. "You led us to believe that there would be a presentation?"

"Yes. In ten minutes," Cassie said in a tone that ended the conversation.

The warrant weighed heavy in Maisie's hand while they waited.

• • •

They had no way to notice, given the featureless nature of the walls and the lack of exterior clues, but the room had, apparently, continued to spin while they talked. Maisie noticed a countdown timer on one of the screens, prominently displayed in black numbers on yellow. With five minutes left, the uniformed attendant returned, bearing a pair of yellow-and-royal blue parkas emblazoned on the left breast with the Rathtec corporate logo, a stylized rocket leaving orbit. Everyone recognized that mark. Maisie was surprised to see her name, "Fox," embroidered on the right; Conklin's on his as well.

"Compliments of Dr. Rathbun," the attendant said when she delivered each neatly tied bundle. "And yours to keep, should you desire." She floated away as silently as she approached, leaving Maisie to wonder if Rathtec also offered advanced courses for obsequious lickspittles.

"You'll want to wear that," Cassie said, encouraging the pair to put on the coats, which they did.

The jackets, unsurprisingly, fit perfectly. In the left pocket, Maisie found a thin fur hat and, in the right, a pair of matching, insulated gloves.

"It's July," Conklin said, stating the obvious. "Why do I need a winter parka? And gloves?"

"One minute to break seal," the computer-voiced Kindle said.

"Patience, Detective," Cassie said in her practiced monotone.

A moment later, the attendant returned once more, handing a small black box to Maisie, Conklin, and Cassie. Opening hers, Maisie pulled a plastic mask, like a hospital oxygen mask, with a cylindrical filter hanging beneath, also bearing the corporate mark of Rathtec. She scanned the room, noticing that the technicians each were securing similar masks to their own faces. Dr. Rathbun, for his part, removed a sleeker model from inside his coat pocket.

"I'll want this as well?" Maisie asked.

"Certainly," Dr. Rathbun said.

"Thirty seconds to break seal," the computer voiced.

"Receiving telemetry," a technician said calmly, studying his console. "Be advised, we have a code blue. Code blue. Code blue," the man said, then entered a series of keystrokes. A bank of lights along the wall switched to a deep, pulsating indigo, and a quiet buzzing alarm sounded. Across the circular room, a door crashed open, and a trio of blue-clad personnel, also wearing the facial filters, hurried into the room and down the stairs, taking a position near the wall opposite from where Maisie and Conklin had entered. The corps of technicians dutifully remained at their stations, working as if there had been no interruption.

"Come on," Cassie said, rising to her feet, fixing a mask in place, and nodding at Maisie, who donned hers. Conklin fumbled with his straps, and Cassie stepped up and assisted, the hands of practice quickly fitting the mask to his face.

"What's going on?" Conklin said, his voice muffled by plastic.

Rathbun stood, reaching up to pat the detective on the shoulder. "Minor medical emergency. Nothing to worry about."

"Minor?"

"It wouldn't be a code blue if it were more serious," he answered. "Whatever it is, we have staffed and prepared for this, as you can no doubt see."

"Five…four…three…two…one…break. Break. Break," the computer said. A seam of bright white light appeared above the black walkway on the third 'break.' Maisie watched as the seam grew wider, the rotating room once again creating an aperture into the outside world. What the point was, she had no idea. Just Rathbun's calm, repeated insistence that the wait would be worth it.

As soon as the gap was wide enough, a gurney rushed through, led by a pair of red-coated individuals, also wearing mask filters. A second later, Maisie felt a chill as the temperature in the room dropped, eddies of swirling snow following the emergency team inside, steam appearing in their exhalations. A single figure rode the gurney, writhing in obvious discomfort, the trio of medics inside the Hub jumping to assist.

"Come," Cassie said, tugging Maisie and Conklin, who stared wide-eyed. "We have to go." The pair followed their escort, passing close enough to the gurney to see clearly the person it contained, visible as a young woman despite the bandages and face mask. Cassie held onto the sleeves of their jackets, pulling the detectives with her, not pausing to witness the spectacle the injured person created in the calmness of the Hub.

"Who was that?" Maisie asked her, turning toward the bright light and Cassie.

"Who was that?" Cassie echoed, back ramrod straight as she strode into the light. "That was Angelika Hidalgo, wastewater technician. One of your missing employees, Detective."

Maisie glanced back to the medical team, losing sight of them as she passed into the bright light of the outside world.

• • •

"Where are we?" Maisie stumbled, supported by grabbing hands that her senses ignored. Her sense of place shattered like a crystal on pavement; everything she knew twisted upon itself. The Hub exited to a stone walkway, buzzing with activity as parka-clad workers, a rainbow of colors bright against gray stone and blue-white sky, swarmed around them, a rumbling roar filling the air.

"Easy," a voice said, a strong grasp on her upper arm, a warm hand on hand that she returned, clutching as an anchor to reality. When her balance returned, the hands withdrew, and Maisie bent over, hyperventilating.

"Jesus tap-dancing…" Conklin muttered next to her, his voice a sibilant whisper.

Cassie's steady voice moored Maisie to the ground that held her full attention: individual gray bricks with the appearance of being hand carved, fitted together to make a nearly seamless roadway. "If it helps, I had the same reaction my first time." A hand, Maisie had to assume was Cassie's, rubbed her back in slow, circular motions, continuing until she could remove her hands from shaking knees and rise to her full height.

They were on the side of a mountain, their backs to a sheer wall, impossibly high in the sky. A range of similar violet-gray peaks, dappled with white snow, surrounded them on three sides, sheltering a deep valley, a mosaic of natural colors blanketing the floor. Cassie hooked her arm in Maisie's, drawing her toward a hip-high wall, out of the bustle of workers. Her breath caught in her chest again as they approached the drop, the mountain disappearing far below roiling gray and white clouds. A vast river, more than a hundred feet across, thundered over an edge, disappearing in foam and mist into the distance. On an outcropping of stone on the far side of the river, a large building in the Classical Greek style occupied the lip of a precipice, connected to where they were by a long steel-and-wire bridge. At the fore of the building, leaning over infinity, a tall statue of a woman, arms spread wide, graced a tall plinth. On the near side and to their right, a long, glass structure hid the river from view, a long, double-rainbow fluttering in the wind-blown mist that rose over the building.

Behind her, Conklin was held up in turn by a dark-skinned man in a red parka, a patient, kind look on his face.

"Where," Maisie repeated, "the actual *fuck* are we?"

"Take a moment," Cassie said. "Deep breaths, concentrate on breathing."

They stood that way for a few minutes, the four of them, as forklifts unloaded the Hub, the steady noise of people at work a welcome bulwark against the madness their eyes showed them. It was, without a clear second choice, the most beautiful view that Maisie had ever experienced in her life.

"Is that…two suns?" Conklin said, looking up, squinting.

"Ariadne Alpha and Beta, yes," Cassie said. "We're orbiting a binary system." With a nod, the man in the red parka released Conklin.

"I'm going to need a minute," Conklin said, spinning in circles, taking it all in. Behind them, the unloading of cargo from the Hub went on as if normal.

"Thanks, Eddie," Cassie said. The man waved and walked away. "That was Eddie Ramachandran, by the way, our chief of emergency response. Another of the missing whom we can check off your list."

"Two suns? Orbiting?" Maisie said, incredulous. "Ms. Kindle, what's going on?"

"Welcome to Ariadne-313 Alpha six." She was beaming, beatific in her countenance as she viewed the world. She'd smiled before, in the Rathtec building, in the Hub, but her smile was radiant as if the joy within was stretching the seams of her.

"Ariadne…are we on…on another goddamned *planet*?" Conklin asked, choking out words in between gasping breaths.

"Yes, that's why the filters," Cassie said. "The locals call it Ceti Alpha Desmond, after Dr. Rathbun." She waved a hand dismissively. "I agree that name is ridiculous, of course. As a group, I think the local team watches too much *Star Trek*."

"Locals?"

"In addition to the twenty-two names on your list, there are an additional three hundred and sixteen human souls on Ariadne…or Desmond, if you'd prefer," she said. "All without families," she said, smiling beneath her mask. "For what I think are becoming obvious reasons."

"But they live here?"

"Full-time, yes," Cassie smiled.

"How? How did we get here?" Conklin asked as a petite woman approached, middle-aged, her black hair streaked in gray and conspicuously not wearing a mask.

"What do you know of quantum entanglements? Particle transference?" The new arrival said, a broad, welcoming smile on her face.

"Nothing," Maisie said.

"It'll be kind of hard to explain then. For now, and for the sake of your noggin, call it long-distance spatial teleportation."

"Detectives, this is Fang Nguyen, our resident sculptor and president of the worker's council."

"A sculptor?"

"Yes," Fang said. "The worker's council is the local leadership here on Desmond. We're an elected body comprised of representatives of the arts, science, and labor. We guide the development of this planet with a focus on long-term sustainability, small footprint, and intelligent, non-destructive growth."

"This doesn't look small," Maisie said, encompassing the settlement.

"It's a big planet. Almost twice the size of Earth," Cassie said.

"We had to put a footprint somewhere," Fang interjected. "To avoid impacting the natural beauty of Ariadne, this site was accepted as the least attractive location that suited our needs."

"*Least* attractive?" Maisie was dumbfounded.

"What about Rathtec," Conklin asked. "And Dr. Rathbun? Don't they run this place?"

Cassie smiled, releasing Maisie and putting her hands in the pockets of her sky-blue parka. "Not at all," she said. "Desmond Rathbun is a visionary, as I said. I am the only member of Rathtec's leadership to hold a seat on the council, but strictly as an advisor. I have no voting authority in development matters. Although I do control Hub access as the point of contact through Rathtec."

"And Dr. Rathbun?" Maisie asked.

Fang answered. "To my knowledge, he's only been here twice. Once when Cassandra…sorry, that's the name of our settlement… was founded, and once for Jodele's funeral."

"Why? Why won't he come?"

"Health reasons, if I must be honest," Cassie said. "High-altitude problems."

"This town. It's called Cassandra?" Conklin asked, eyeing Ms. Kindle.

"Desmond's one and only directive was to name the settlement after me," she said, shaking her head.

"And this mountain," Fang laughed. "Mount Kindle."

"I find it rather embarrassing, if I may be honest. But you did say it was the least attractive option."

At Cassie's urging, Fang led them to the bridge, stopping at the apex of the curved structure, along the railing, and away from the bustle of traffic. "Luckily, water is water," Fang said, indicating the river. "We monitor it constantly to ensure human potability, of course, and it is filtered and purified. But, so far, it's water and drinkable. Food, on the other hand," she pointed toward the long, low glass building on the riverbank. "*Voila*, our greenhouse. The staff jokingly call it *Trader Joe's,* named for our chief botanist, Joseph Nichols, but do keep that here, if you don't mind."

"Are there any local foods that are…uh…compatible? Edible? I mean, for people?" Maisie asked.

Cassie smiled. "Signs are definitely promising. We're taking things slowly, as you might imagine. Hence, the greenhouse. Lab-grown meat. Lots and lots of dietary supplements. But there is one berry we found at 5K Camp…"

"5K? What's that?" Interjected Conklin.

Fang answered: "One of our field camps, below us at five thousand meters of altitude."

Conklin peered over the edge, nodding in admiration.

Cassie continued after a brief pause. "They're calling it the *kakano* berry for now. Don't ask me. Our people are terrible with names. It's similar to calafate, sort of like a blueberry if it was coated in kombucha and stinky cheese. I know, it sounds disgusting. But mixed with soy milk and a little sugar, it's delicious and packs a punch like concentrated espresso. The staff loves it."

"A little too much on the weekends," Fang said, then explained, "They've been experimenting with fermentation, as well."

She led them to the far bank and along a paved walkway that fronted the river, with the Greek-style building, identified as Cassandra's capitol, on their right. The path led them to the rear of the building, site of the statue they'd seen on first arrival. A trio of marble sepulchers fanned in a semi-circle around the statue, which was larger than Maisie had first imagined, nearly thirty feet tall, if you included the plinth; the woman leaning forward, weight on her foreleg, arms spread wide as if embracing the world.

"Is that…" Maisie asked, walking toward the edifices.

"Your three missing people," Cassie said. "Jodele, Ray, and Xiu." She stepped next to Maisie and laid a hand on the center tomb, lowering her head. "Jodele Wetzler-VanValkenburg."

"Who was she?" Conklin asked.

"Our first hero," Fang answered grimly. "The first human to step on Ariadne. Scientist, explorer, and legend."

"Fang's wife," Cassie said. "Someday, she'll be as famous as Neil Armstrong, Robert Falcon Scott, and Amelia Earhart. Someday, when the world is ready for us to tell them about this place."

"I'm sorry," Maisie said to the sculptor.

"Thank you," Fang said, her eyes glistening but not from the cold. "It's been two years now. She is…missed."

Maisie looked at Conklin, who had the same confused look in his eyes as she did. "Will you excuse us?" she said, drawing her partner away from the others toward the railing at the cliff face beneath the towering statue above them. Looking over the edge, she could see a terraced hillside stretching beneath them, holding avenues and buildings in that same Classical Greek style, timeless beauty juxtaposed with the confounding alien landscape.

"Now what?" she asked, laughing beneath her breath. "I went to work this morning expecting to arrest a serial killer at worst or indifferent corporate asshole at best. I didn't expect the brilliant visionary to take us to the other side of the galaxy."

"I really have no idea," Conklin said. "Though right about now, I wish I hadn't quit smoking."

"No shit," Maisie agreed. "I wonder if that fermented Koko-mo-whatever berry is on tap somewhere. I could use a drink."

"Me, too," Conklin said. He sighed, gripped the railing, and looked over the edge. "How are we going to explain this to the Captain?"

Maisie shrugged. "I guess…figure it out?"

"Sure." He laughed then, looking over the vista before them. "Or don't," he whispered after a long, silent pause.

They returned to Fang and Cassie, who was laughing, Maisie realized, for the first time, her face lit up with suffused joy. The pair looked at the detectives as they approached.

"What have you decided?" Cassie asked.

Maisie held her hands up in surrender. "I'll admit it. I have no fucking idea how to approach this one."

"Maybe this will help?" Cassie handed each of them a folded piece of paper retrieved from within her parka, followed a moment later by a pair of pens.

Maisie unfolded the paper, recognizing it instantly. Her own face looked out at her from the upper left corner, personal details in the right. The bottom half held a single sentence:

"I, Maisie Eleanor Fox, hereby declare…"

"You weren't assigned to this case randomly, Detectives," Cassie said, extending the pen to her.

Maisie and Conklin shared a look, then she turned back to the executive. "No families," she said, getting a nod in return.

"Nobody will miss us."

"Exactly. Doctor Rathbun saw to it that you'd be paired together and then assigned here today. A generous donation was made to the Fraternal Order for their consideration, of course."

Fang leaned against the railing. "We had a fight in the tavern a few weeks back. Nothing serious. But it did highlight our need for some security to enforce the local ordinances. It would make some people feel better as well. Eddie's a medic, he's not cut out for such things." Fang looked Maisie in the eyes. "We could use you."

Maisie took the pen, clicking the end cap nervously. "What do you think?" she asked Conklin, whose actions and body language mirrored her own. He shrugged, fidgeting with his own pen.

"Your call," he said.

Maisie looked around at the vast mountain range, the steep drop to the valley below, and the river, spilling over with beautiful, monstrous intent, then turned to Cassie. "That tavern you mentioned…is it open?"

"We can make it so," Cassie said, tapping instructions into a data pad that appeared from a coat pocket.

"What about dogs?" Conklin asked. "I can't live somewhere without dogs."

"Of course," Fang smiled warmly. "Dr. Rathbun and Ms. Kindle feel the same way. And the kennel is conveniently next door to the tavern." There's a totally adorable beagle puppy named Emma that I want you to meet. Right this way, constable," Fang said, leading the detectives down a ramp into the town, with Cassie on their heels.

THE DUMPSTER

P.J. CHRISTMAN

I'm the guy you saw during Christmas week, the one upon observing you felt a mixture of pathos and loathing. I was bending over a dumpster, 'diving' to find what I could to eat that morning. My clothes were stained and tattered, my face badly in need of a shave, my hair a greasy, ragged mop with no luster, and I moved slowly and in a circumspect fashion. You see, I didn't want anyone to see me, especially someone like you, capable of the most critical contemplation after casual scrutiny. I looked vaguely familiar, right? Your hunch was correct. We went to high school together, but I'm glad you weren't able to make the connection.

What good would it do to tell you that over the past five years, I haven't slept soundly? That I often spend the night under noisy highway overpasses, in discarded Japanese appliance boxes, or under damp newspapers on obscure benches. You cannot know the ineffable damp experienced from the perspective of a distraught soul who wakes up intermittently each night from exposure. Such torment is beyond the comprehension of all those never having had it thrust upon them. They cannot fathom how a long-term lack of hygiene insidiously erodes a person's self-esteem. Nor empathize with the denigrating feeling of true rather than popular grunge when excess clothing has caused sweat to occur and dry during almost insufferable interludes of varying temperatures. They cannot know the silent lament one feels when, over time, the teeth begin to loosen in their fittings. Nor how the skin, without proper nutrients and emollients, can turn to a dark, pre-cancerous snake hide that cannot be shed for another.

I know, you don't want to hear it. And you're right, it would appear appallingly easy to extricate oneself from such deplorable behavior and circumstances, at least with a background such as mine. But oddly, it isn't. Such privations become a way of life, sort of surrealistic and seamless, as if the vice of a death one might simply avoid is slowly tightening. Every day becomes another day of desperation. One of fruitless hope that your luck will turn when, of course, luck has nothing to do with it. A day of anguish over one's condition, of interminable waiting for a redemption that never comes. A day of passionate entreaty that you will not again find yourself in the food line at a soup kitchen, nor again find yourself panhandling because your dumpster diving has produced only wrappers with decaying mayonnaise and ketchup, only shards of pizza with teeth marks, or de-fizzed carbonated beverages flatter than your last cheerful thought.

Your pace increased slightly when you observed me, my feet off the ground as I leaned down into the dumpster. I could see that just before losing sight of you through the falling snow. You were appalled, but doubtless, it all seemed part of the fabric of urban existence to you. An unpleasant phantom had appeared but then had been quickly put out of mind. There was nothing you could do. I, and my fellow *al fresco* co-conspirators, remained a part of urban life to be tolerated but largely ignored. We were to be pitied as Victor Hugo's *Les Misérables*, Franz Fanon's *Wretched of the Earth*, or Eldridge Cleaver's *Soul(s) on Ice*.

You may yet shake your head in disgust over such ravings. But mark well such thoughts. For someday, your pleasant, financially sound, and comfortable situation could take a turn as quickly as potato chips left out in your city's less-than-pure air. Indeed, very few of the souls you see sleeping over steam vents, diving in dumpsters, or hovering on street corners in tattered mittens ever intended to slide that far into oblivion. Oh no, my friend, not a one ever imagined the horrors in store for each interminable evening. For *days* most indigents can deal with. There remains a fleeting but recurring sense that a change for the better may occur. Nature provides that almost inexhaustible optimism keeping you just on the precipice. You are aware that you can sink deeper, that things can get worse, but days give you mindless activities to divert such untenable musings. Moving from one location to another becomes a temporary diversion. Seeking scraps of food or a cheap bottle of beer occupies time of no known value. Chatting with a fellow pariah momentarily stops the low-grade mental torment and physical pains that are your constant companions. Yet even daytime becomes a tendentious keeper that wishes to keep you a semi-conscious somnambulist for eternity. Minutes seem like hours; days appear as slow-motion blurs. Weeks, months, and years remain notions of an indeterminate nature you no longer wish to comprehend.

You, on the other hand, still wonder how such predicaments ever take on a destiny of their own. How someone of seemingly educated background and once reasonably sound mental faculties can allow himself to stoop to such dissipation.

Suffice it to say, that it is a gradual process. One of which the downward spiraling individual initially is unaware. With a few bad twists of fate, a few too many drugs of choice, and a work attitude that in several instances is diagnosed as unprofessional, unfocused, or lazy, and you can find yourself ineluctably drawn downward into the whirlpool with no bottom.

My drugs of choice were alcohol and caffeine. Sound familiar? But the extent of the decline a bit farfetched, eh? Well, take care, my friend, that the sirens of stress relief don't envelop you too far into their web. When I began the use of such drugs, they were rites of passage and were considered *de rigueur* adult behavior. While in high school, and with the use of phony IDs, the sneaking of six-packs of beer and half-pints of spirits constituted an indoctrination. Then every college has its dens of iniquity, featuring wooden tables etched with initials, ceilings charred by cigarette lighter-burned graffiti, and the mildewed smells of hundreds of coats of stale beer upon the floors. Many a night was spent in such pleasant haunts, my youthful body quite prepared for such repeated indulgences. Hangovers became a badge of respectability, one signifying that you were '21' or had the expertise to provide yourself with identification rendering you acceptable to the sextons of such emporia for frivolity.

Of course, during these youthful periods, others were shunning the use of coffee, alcohol, marijuana, and other drugs of choice. But they risked social ostracism by our adventuresome majority and were forced to suffer ignominious monikers like 'nerd' or 'wimp'. Their futures were predicted to be lifeless and passionless, and their prudish temperance frowned upon by many a jaundiced or blood-shot eye.

When I began my first job as an international banker in San Francisco, my usage of alcohol increased in response to my denial of self-awareness that the sea of desks around me and their pilots' requisite duties were of little stimulation to me. A conundrum arose regarding this privilege. Everyone kept telling me what a great job I had, that I would be assigned overseas, and what great contacts I would make for future work as a stockbroker, or mutual fund manager, or analyst. My diurnal outfits included Brooks Brothers suits and ties, wing-tipped shoes, and other fashionable symbols signifying ascending financial status. The flipside continued to be my almost complete lack of genuine interest in any of this work and its perquisites.

Coffee got the engine going for the bus commute in the morning. Alcohol in many a downtown bar sent me into reveries that life wasn't so bad after all. Most evenings, I confined myself to the intake of several bottles of foreign beer, but weekends often included the guzzling of margaritas, Manhattans, bottles of wine with meals, in addition to the occasional cigarette thrown in for striking the right pose. In the mornings and evenings, beguiled by such drugs, I briefly felt on top of the world, that the continual bouts of boredom I was experiencing were a component of paying one's dues, an integral part of mastering the making of money.

Of course, the abuse of any habit has its price. With the intake of more and more coffee and alcohol, my attitude began to fluctuate more and more pendulously. I hated my job; no, I was more than fortunate to have been given such an opportunity. I loathed the corruption in the Southeast Asian country's corporations and banks whose lines of credit I administered, yet my chest swelled with pride when I was able to tell peers I was the Assistant Area Administrator for the exotic land of Pubatra. Such vacillations were increasingly reflected in my attitude. When others stayed an hour after the 5:00 closing hour and took armloads of credit files home with them, I departed promptly at closing, walking with an erect posture out the door. This insouciant behavior must have appeared as if I was saying, 'You are not paying me enough for such additional aggravation.'

This did not go undetected by my supervisors. My lack of zealousness was reflected in my annual review, and after more than a year I was one of the few yet to be promoted from Assistant Area Administrator to Area Administrator. In fact, many of my associates had already been shipped overseas to plum tax-free and rent-free jobs.

All of this caused me to drink even more. Sometimes I forgot where I had been the previous evening. From time to time, I awakened in strange women's apartments. I noticed food and drink stains on more and more of my clothing and quit taking them to the cleaners as often as needed. Had I taken some affirmative action at this point, had I found a pursuit more in line with my true interests, I might today be one of those revered and upstanding members of some community. But I didn't make any move. Oh no, my friend. I toughed it out, convinced that my soothing alcoholic hazes would countermand the ennui, stress, and dealings with those of less-than-pleasant dispositions. During such stuporous evenings, I often convinced myself that my friends were right: I had availed myself of a unique financial and sociological opportunity. Yet every night, the commuter buses were full of silent, forlorn faces from the financial district. I was one of them. Others intoxicated by the nature of the international work and power probably were still at their desks, strengthening their positions in the American dream.

As my self-esteem sank lower with each passing month, any concern for my situation drifted further and further into obscurity. I received a drunk driving citation and could no longer drive. My blood-sugar levels began to become more and more erratic so that I was tired almost all the time, at least until I got an increasingly larger number of sugar-laced drinks into my increasingly toxic system. Counteracting such a destructive course were more and more afternoon cups of coffee to supplement those downed in mornings. The seesaw of the drugs became even more extreme. I looked haggard and unkempt, becoming less and less aware of this visible deterioration.

One summer morning, I awoke in my car. I had thrown up and was forced to drive home in humiliation. I couldn't remember where I had been the previous evening. I spent the day thinking how little I cared for the view of the San Francisco Bay I had from my Presidio Heights apartment windows.

THE DUMPSTER

Eventually, I was asked to resign. Like many young optimists, I had always lived like there were no tomorrows, and my savings quickly dwindled. Friends began calling less and less. I started avoiding the use of heat in my apartment to save money. My collars and cuffs slowly acquired the ever-so-tattered edges seen on those in financial transition. The final blow to any remaining shred of self-esteem was the eviction from my apartment. Further pleas to relatives for loans fell on deaf ears, and my father and mother had been dead for years and had left me nothing but best wishes. The end of a patina of respectability was nigh. The demimonde of the destitute was rapidly approaching.

When interviewing for jobs, lack of confidence, poor grooming, and long, unexplained periods of time missing from my résumé were telltale signs. Keenly observant eyes were forewarned that test results need not be consulted. Second interviews never occurred. The money I received from selling my car only lasted for the several months, during which I prevailed upon friends for housing at modest rent. Only one of my credit cards was still free of danger signals, and in desperation, I used it to purchase a bus ticket to hopeful salvation. However, the appearances and demeanors of my fellow travelers let me know we were gaining miles but going nowhere. We shared the common destination of oblivion. The beginning of the end had finally come.

Still, the human body is actually quite resilient, as you know. I now have my good days. During warm weather, I can bathe in streams or under faucets, and over the recent years, at least twice families have invited me for a fine holiday dinner. I do miss my old friends, though. And I do wish I could phone my relatives to give them some compelling news in my favor. But outdoor life is sometimes pleasant. And during inclement weather I often spend time in warm laundromats or with my closest companions: books in the city library. Sometimes the librarians ask me to leave when I fall asleep, but it's a small price to pay for a respite from the winter and summer elements.

It's just unfortunate you caught me in that dumpster. I know I said luck has nothing to do with it, but things could change. Sometimes I get day work, sweeping up and such. It's not much, but I usually earn enough to send my nieces each a card on their birthdays and at Christmas. I never tell them where I am, of course. They, like you, would probably never understand how I ever arrived at my current destination.

LUKEWARM GIRL-ON-GIRL ACTION

STEF WILLEN

Lesbian Really Enjoys Her Massage

Two women sit in their underwear on a futon, facing each other. Their unshaven legs are intertwined. A tube sock is almost all the way off. A bottle of Astroglide is approximately four-and-a-half miles away at the nearest Walmart. A soft moan grows louder.

"Oh my God, that feels so good. What are you doing?"

"Absentmindedly rubbing your foot."

"Well, keep doing it."

"I always do it this way."

"No, you don't."

"You always like how I absentmindedly rub your feet!"

"I do. But you're doing something different. What are you doing different?"

"I think I was just using my knuckles more."

"Oh, please. Use your knuckles more."

"Or, maybe I was digging into your arch more."

"Oh, please. Dig into my arch more."

"Actually, I think I was just processing."

"Oh, please. Keep processing. I'm just about to process."

Dominant Brunette Convinces Blonde to Try Something New

A brunette and a blonde are sitting on a couch watching *Chopped* on the Food Network when the brunette hastily grabs her partner's hand. Her eyes flicker with some kind of plan. Her cargo shorts stop just below the knee.

"Ready?" she teases and interlaces their fingers. Their naked palms are touching. She is not done. She cups their joined flesh with her other hand. "This is going to blow your mind, trust me," she coos.

"Wait a minute," the blonde says. "Didn't we see this episode?" Pre-cooked pigs' snouts are being drawn from the contestants' baskets.

"Yes, probably twice," the brunette says in a low, soft voice. "Now shut your eyes," she demands.

The blonde does as she is told, and as the warmth of her lover's hands enters her own, she begins to imagine how she would prepare a pre-cooked pig's nose. A fine chop and a slight pan fry? Maybe a rough chop and then put it in the fryer, like how bull calf testicles are served? Great, now she's thinking of putting testicles in her mouth. Suddenly, her interlaced hand is being shaken up and down and all around, causing her snap-button Western shirt not to slide off her shoulder at all because it's all buttoned up.

"What are you doing?" Her heart pounds wildly. "This doesn't feel good at all!"

"Look down," the brunette orders, moving her cupped hand just enough to expose only their two naked thumbs. "Tell me," she says, her almost identical snap-button Western shirt not even beginning to slide off her shoulders, either, "which one is *your* thumb?"

"Oh my gosh," the now-willing blonde gushes. "I don't know… I can't even feel which one is my hand! It's like you made me totally numb!"

"Freaky, huh? My mom used to do this with me."

"How is your mom?"

A Couple O' Cats

"Take your shirt off, baby," the mature lesbian softly instructs her young lover. She rubs a leash between her fingers.

"Right here?" Her young lover looks around nervously.

"She won't come near you unless you do because she can smell your dog."

"Oh, wow. Okay." Her young lover slowly removes her shirt. She is not wearing a bra. She is wearing a sports bra. It only partially covers her tattoo of…a dragon? An angry chick with messy hair? Something meaningful exploding out of a feather? "There," she says tentatively. "Pssst, pssst," she tries.

The mature lesbian crawls behind her young lover, wraps her legs around her, and pulls her into her own spread thighs, which are clad in a quick-drying fabric great for hiking or tooling around. She rhythmically pats the floor between her young lover's open legs.

"Pssst, psssst, psst, psst, psssst, psst," the mature lesbian says.

"Pssst, psssst, psst, psst, psssst, psst," the young lover says.

The two lovers explode with a gentle "Awww" at the exact same time in a urine-stained concrete hallway of a Los Angeles animal shelter.

"I really want another cat," the young lover whimpers, her fingers glistening with feral kitty slobber.

The mature lesbian cannot restrain herself. She wraps her sagging arms tight around her young lover and squeals, "We can name him Oreo!"

UNFORGETTABLE SONG

SUE BRYAN

Phoebe is the new girl. I fell in love with her when she said she'd introduce me to a ghost.

"Did you bring your gift?" she asks me. The ghost likes shiny things. I've brought a quartz crystal I don't need anymore. When the house is quiet, we slip out. Our sneakers squeak through the wet grass. We cross the creek into the forest. Witch-finger branches snag our jackets, warning us to turn back. I have never been this far into the woods.

The full moon reveals an abandoned foundation in a clearing. A maze of rock walks. Phoebe lays her white feather and a shard of green glass on a smooth step that leads nowhere and elbows me. I put my crystal next to her feather, and we back away.

A thick, white mist swirls around our offerings, and then I hear…no, feel…the song. I can't tell if the music is coming from outside me or rising from the marrow of my bones. I leave sight and hearing behind. The song embraces me from between my shoulder blades like a warm woolen cape. I lose time until Phoebe pulls on my arm.

DUST UP

Back at her quiet house, we tousle towels through our damp hair and sit back-to-back in the dark. "Wow," I say. I feel her nodding. I try to hum a note from that song. She laughs. Leaning on each other, breathing. Neither of us sleeps.

JUST THE HAFNIUM, PLEASE

GREGORY L. WAGNER

I have become so accustomed to a bile-hued landscape red hurts my eyes. It's not the whole planet that throws the color of stomach acid in your face, just the smallest of the twenty-three continents. But that's the one with the potential hafnium deposits. Yeah, I know, that's not normal. Drastically so. But I've discovered that everyone else's normal isn't mine. It's not normal to lose every family member one at a time to completely separate incidents without a one of them reaching retirement age. It's not normal to trek around uninhabited, lifeless planets by yourself with no backup structure to haul your dying ass back to civilization. And there is nothing normal about Ellyana. Not one damned thing. It is somewhat normal to try to stake claim on the best mining deposits of these dead planets while other prospectors are doing the same. And it's completely normal for said other prospectors to try to kill you so they can log the claim and get the percentage. This is a risk-reward business.

"The scans from sector three eighty-seven by two-eleven are coming in," Ellyana says. She doesn't turn around.

I grunt and give the top of the seismic transducer a hearty twist. "Interesting data?"

"No, not ye … hmm." Ellyana pauses mid-rebuttal.

I go still and embrace the moment. Mother used to call it "Grasping the Savor." We mining prospectors live for the liminal spaces. Our entire existence is built around them. We need those moments of potential where you stand between your current shitty existence and a completely different type of future. For us, liminal spaces contain the purest form of distilled hope. Hope is our addiction.

Ellyana sighs and slams a fist onto the outdated control console. "Not yet." The screen starts to blink on and off. She smacks the side for good measure. The data image settles.

I have no impulse to smash the transducer against the workbench in frustration or rush over and double-check the data. Curious. I set the malfunctioning component down gently on the dented metal surface. "I'll prep the next batch of deploys. When can we pull the ones from the current grid point?"

"Two hours, plus or minus."

I nod. "I'll have the next set prepped in an hour." I turn and head for the pressure bay. We should have been off this dead rock weeks ago. The longer we dwell, the more likely we are to end up in a contest with other prospectors to see who can manage not to die. Then again, both of us shouldn't be here right now—not together, at least. Like I said, nothing about my life runs along the normal.

• • •

There is exactly one long-term advantage to spending most of your outdoor existence confined to an environmental control suit. You keep yourself in shape. Suits that allow you to work effectively in a vacuum and hostile-air planets are custom-built to your precise dimensions. If you wear a suit that is too small in the shoulders or waist, too large in the legs or arms, you will spend unnecessary and wasteful amounts of energy. Worse, ill-fitting suits wear in odd places that lead to failure. Most importantly, ill-fitting suits don't let you move efficiently and accurately at critical moments.

This is why professionals pay the credits to have their suits custom-manufactured and precisely tailored. At the price of more than a year's typical income. So yeah, you make damned sure your suit fits the same way today as it did eight years ago. Nobody but the big prospecting combines is affluent enough to drop down a gravity well with more than one personalized suit.

My father taught me the importance of causal chains. It's a survival lesson every prospector teaches their young. You and your suit don't fit properly; you can't move well. You can't move well; your reaction time in critical situations goes to shit. Your reaction times go to shit; you can't clear the other prospector's weapons fire. You can't clear other's weapons fire; you die. Ergo, keep you and your suit tuned up and in synch or die. He taught me this, of course, before a sniper round made his head explode in his suit helmet like an over-ripe tomato that a particularly aggravated person stomped on.

"I'll drill in the thumpers," Ellyana says as she enters the pressure bay, already suited up. She stops to close and latch the pressure door.

I check the plumbing system's gauges and exchange inside air with outside air. "That sounds good. I'll start the sensor implantations." We wait in silence until the outside pressure equilibrium telltale turns green. Then, with two hands and a totally necessary grunt, I haul the three-inch-thick safety latch on the bay door back.

"You need to get that thing oiled before it seizes," Ellyana says. Her voice is perfectly neutral. She straps two thumpers to her waist belt and throws the drill over her shoulder.

I smack the door opener and watch Ellyana stroll past and out the door. The thumpers hanging against her hips sway vigorously as she walks down the short ramp. I take the moment to study this particular instance of that particular motion. Have I mentioned that top-of-the-line suits fit like a second, molded skin? That top-of-the-line suits require absolutely no imagination to fill out the details of a carnal thought? Ellyana's suit is of the finest construction I've ever seen.

My parents taught all their kids, from our first steps, to never turn our back on someone from a different crew. Never. It got coded into our fast-twitch nerve clusters. I grab four seismic sensors and head out of the bay, turning opposite Ellyana. My shoulders don't have an uncontrollable itch. I don't feel any need to turn and track her position to cover my back. And I've only known Ellyana for a little over five weeks. Curious.

• • •

I take an old rag, dip it in the jar of used surfactant cleaner, and wipe down the dented workbench. The smell of warmed beans mixed with reconstituted rice and vegetables drifts from the tiny kitchen nook.

Ellyana pokes her head around the edge of the nook. "Dinner will be ready in just a moment."

A warm flush surges through me at the simple proclamation. I grab two chipped plastic plates from the cupboard and use the damp rag to move the smears of old meals around the plate's surfaces before setting them on the workbench. The old rag still has the remains of the letter "C" stitched into it. The C stood for Cecil, my oldest sister. The rag is what's left of her environmental suit onesie. The fit and comfort of the onesie are critical for proper suit wear. If the onesie bunches or tears, it leads to bad chafing. Cecil taught me that a chafing suit can really downgrade your entire quality of life. It was a curated lesson she put together for me. This was before one of the big mining combines out of Vorrel Six left a little present for her to find at a sampling site. We didn't even bother to try and bury her. What was left wouldn't have filled a can of beans.

Ellyana brings the small pot of dinner over to the table. We scoop out our own portions and start to eat.

"I have a feeling about the current grid point," Ellyana says. She looks up and smiles at me. Little dimples pop out on her cheeks. Her hair is somehow not oily or hanging down her skull like mine. I don't know how she keeps it so clean. Maybe she was able to scavenge dry-clean ointment from the remains of her busted-up ship.

"This is going to be our lucky setup," Ellyana says. "This is the place; I can feel it!" She holds my eyes for a long moment, drawing me into their deep brown depths. Her eyes have the same gold flecks around the irises that Mother's did. She looks back to her meal.

I nod slowly, accepting her enthusiasm. Who am I to argue? Ellyana is a being of luck. Her partner and entire crew were killed in the accident aboard their ship. The last died only a few moments before I arrived to lend aid. Ellyana escaped without even a bruise.

My second oldest sister, when she inherited charge, would never have gone to another prospector's aid. None of my family would have. The risk was too high, and the reward nonexistent. At best, you got more mouths to drain your finite resources and bodies to crowd your limited space. But I've been doing this for years since the last of them, my brother, just older than me, died. There is no one left to pick at my decisions.

It wasn't a prospector that took out my last brother. He got lazy and didn't maintain his suit properly. I warned him about it repeatedly. He didn't pay my warnings any heed. And he wouldn't let me touch his suit. He wasn't big on talking at that point. Didn't say a single word the last four months I knew him.

• • •

The data alarm wakes me from a dream. It's an old dream that used to leave me in shivers, huddled in a corner. Now, it only bothers me when I'm asleep. Ellyana rolls out of our bed, still naked. I ignore the cool air licking my body to watch her walk to the data console. I try my best to study every detail in the variable illumination. The inside lighting isn't as uniform as when I was a kid. Our family's ship isn't in good repair. I've tried to keep it up, but prospecting solo isn't the best money-making proposition.

Ellyana goes perfectly still as she scans the data screen. After a long moment, she straightens fully and turns to look at me. I stare. She hasn't seemed to mind my stares. Her's is the second most impressive topology I've ever witnessed. The six-hundred-mile gulch on Thesbal Four still holds top place. I finally look up at her face. Her eyes are quiet for a moment, then a beautiful smile parts her lips. The dimples make an appearance. "We've hit it!" she says. She claps her hands and starts jumping up and down.

I roll out of bed, tug on my least-soiled underclothes, and walk over to the data console. I triple-check the seismic high-resolution frequency scans. We didn't just hit it. This is the largest concentrated hafnium deposit I've ever heard of. By a factor of three. One of the big mining consortiums will send an armada to protect this claim. Here lies far more than mere riches.

I turn to look at Ellyana. She throws her naked body at me and wraps herself around my sparse frame. Slowly, I feel her start to cry. I wait for it to pass. A hafnium find this large would set anyone up in a mansion in one of the core cities for life. And all their descendants' descendants. I'm not in any hurry to drop the claim beacon. Nor to lift for the nearest claim station at best speed. I can see no further than where I am right now. Curious.

• • •

Ellyana keeps turning to look at the data screen as if to reassure herself it's still there. Finally, she takes a deep breath and settles.

She looks at me and produces a smile that carries every lascivious thought I've ever had. "This calls for coffee." She looks down coyly. "I have a small serving left. I've been saving it for the right moment." She turns and heads for the kitchen nook.

Soon, the thin aroma of reconstituted coffee reaches me. I sit down at the workbench and wait. Ellyana comes to the table with two steaming mugs. A loose robe, untied and hanging open, rests on her shoulders. It's all she wears. She sets the coffee mugs on the table and looks at me in a way no one ever has.

"What's the depth profile ratio?" I ask.

Ellyana turns and steps over to the data screen.

I look down at the two coffee mugs she has brought to the table. One for me. One for her. I have no impulse to quietly switch our mugs.

"Fourteen to one," she says.

Ellyana returns and sits down. "To our future," she says, raising her mug.

I raise mine in toast. We drink. The poison she put in my coffee starts to take effect almost immediately. Disappointment washes over me but leaves no discernable trace. Curious.

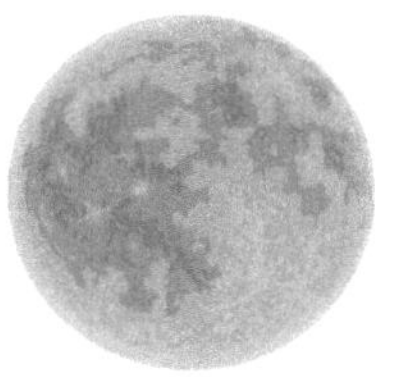

MODERN AUTOMATA

JENNIFER EDELSON

I follow August into the roiling river. Tiny bubbles tickle my ankles, popping as they rumble to the surface, beckoning me to sink down and revel in it all. Near the center of the tributary, I drop, squatting so the murky water touches my chin. Steam rises around my face, obscuring the flowers dappling the shore, growing between sharp blades of tall, tapered grass and smooth boulders.

August squats down beside me, moving his arms over the water's surface, creating steaming waves that ripple out toward the riverbank. "Let's build a house right here. On stilts. Out of glass. With a trap door. And a slide." He grins. "We'll drop on down whenever we need a swim."

"I wish," I say quietly. Around us, snowcapped mountain peaks loom over the valley, staking the now plum-hued sky. "It's so beautiful." My chest thrums with it. "The end shouldn't be so perfect."

August floats closer and gently tugs my arm, pulling me off my heels. He drops his head, resting his forehead against mine as he looks down at the water between us. He looks up at the sky, at the plants crowding the bank, at the diamond-cut mountains.

"August?" I press.

Finally, he looks at me. "But maybe it won't end."

August wipes a damp piece of hair off my cheek, tucking it behind my ear. He's so keenly aware that the universe has decided to stamp us out, yet still so committed to living. "We'll run out of code," I whisper.

He puts my wet hand on his damp chest. "Or maybe we won't, and we really can keep willing materiality into existence."

"I . . ." *Stupid, August.* It's not fair making me remind him again that we are experimental ephemera created from memories. Corrupted files. Ghosts in an empty Matrix. It does not matter what we want—because we stole this autonomy. And the architects don't want us to keep it.

I hug my shoulders, feeling the ever-present void close in. "We should go."

August sighs. He stands up, leaving a brief hollow in the steam over the river—a bleak reminder. "I picked Yellowstone. It's your turn."

"Portugal?" I ask hurriedly.

He tries to smile, clasping my hands as he pulls me closer. "Alright."

We close our eyes. From Yellowstone, we materialize in Lisbon, emerging in one of the oldest plazas in Alfama. We visit Baixa, and Alcantara's Aqueduct, and Belem, climbing the tower at Torre De Belem to glimpse the whole of the district. We walk old cobblestoned streets and peer in windows at empty cafés and deserted bakeries. In my memory, Lisbon's districts crackled as though energized by the millions of souls walking its corridors. But without people, it's as if the city's heartbeat has petered out. And the emptiness reminds us of our reality.

We leave Lisbon. August picks Gettysburg. I pick New Zealand. We visit the Statue of Liberty and Easter Island, then Glacier National Park. Then August picks India. We travel to Bangalore and

Delhi, then finish in Goa. But in Goa, especially, the void laps at our toes like the emerald waves sweeping Palolem Beach.

We escape to Rome, closing our eyes and clicking our heels together as we chant, "There's no place like Rome," just because. In the moment, it seems funny.

August remembers visiting before, but I want to show him my Rome, a city enchanted by real ghosts and storied history. Working from a ballpark recollection, I drop us near the Forum under a stonewashed sky. Rome looks worn, the way an old photo fades over time. And its streets are crooked, as though someone took the city apart and put it back together a hair off-kilter. Still, August stands on the Forum's main road, Sacra Via, quietly staring at the many visible ruins. Despite my bizarro recreation, he looks awed.

"The Romans, they just paved over everything whenever they wanted something new." Mostly I remember that being true. But I'm also kind of winging it. "The Sacra Via is the oldest road in Rome. Imagine all the things that went on here."

"I almost can. It's incredible."

August's enormous grin lights his face. Standing here, for a moment, it doesn't matter that we are the only two people in the city. His eyes dance as he imagines the Forum's streets thousands of years ago, filled with market stalls and people in laurel wreath hats and linen sheaths.

We hold hands while we walk. My memory isn't always reliable, so I have to guess at different ruins. August and I, we give them all made-up names: Temple of the Lost Goat, Pillars and Piles Gateway, Clash of the Titans Temple, I Claudius U. When we get tired, we decide to stop and sleep in the spot where Julius Caesar was cremated, Temple of the Comet Star, or Caesar's Little Pizza Heaven.

"Being here makes it easier to think about disappearing," August says, settling down over a large pile of golden straw he conjures out of the ether.

I sink beside him, slinking into his arms. "How so?"

"So many people died here." He shrugs, displacing the hay around his shoulders. "It makes me feel like part of something bigger. You know, like part of the big boy's vanishing club. All the super cool kids do it."

August has an odd way with words. But he's right. Looking around, it's easier to accept that no matter how we fight, ends are part of the order of things. "You're the only person I want to disappear with," I whisper in his ear.

He turns his head sideways. "I'm the only person you know."

"Good enough," I grin. I contemplate while I tap my lip, attempting to look at my eyebrows. Every second that passes, there's a new chance I may never see him again. And because of it, I want to do all sorts of things with him that probably wouldn't have gone over so well a thousand years ago down the street in the Complex of the Vestal Virgins.

Overhead, through the cracks in the ruin's roof, the sky blots, and purple-gray streaks seep across the firmament like ink in water. As color winds between burgeoning stars, my mind blurs. August is all I know, and tonight especially, *all* I want to do is lay in this pile of golden straw next to him.

He closes his eyes. "Find a truth that's true for you."

"What?" I ask dreamily.

"Kierkegaard. I just pulled it from the Net. If we can think ourselves here, maybe we can think ourselves to someplace where ends don't exist."

I twine my fingers in his. Has he found the answer? Or is this seed pre-determined? Our coding is a mystery. "But how can we if it's not from a real memory?"

"I'm not a memory, and you found me."

I stare at my soul mate—a glitch—and answer eagerly. "Okay. Pick a truth. On the count of three."

August looks up at the fading sky and grips my hand tighter.
"One.
Two.
Three."

ABOUT THE AUTHORS

Andee Baker is a retired sociologist originally from the Midwest. She moved from academic writing on social movements, fan communities, and rock musicians to writing for popular audiences with her memoir *My Men, Mick and Me*. She also acts in theater and film productions from time to time. You can find most of her writings at www.andeebaker.com.

Cristina Browne was born in Colombia, South America, grew up in New Jersey, moved around a bit, and came to Santa Fe in 2021. She was compelled to write as a creative outlet from work and gained inspiration and encouragement from the wonderful Santa Fe Kooks writing group. Thank you all! When not at a desk, she can be found hiking, reading, walking her cats, or enjoying concerts, art, and culture around the Southwest.

Sue Bryan is a Santa Fe author, Self-Actualization coach, and quantum activist. Her happy place is on the line between ordinary reality and the world of magic and miracles. Her work has appeared in *Godtalk* and *Portals, Sacred Sentience* anthologies, and *Cemetery Stories,* an anthology about death and dying by the New Mexico Council for the Humanities. Find out more at www.inwardjourney2020.substack.com

Jennifer G. Edelson is a trained artist, former attorney, and the author of three award-winning YA novels, *Between Wild and Ruin, Wild Open Faces,* and *True North,* as well as numerous published award-winning short stories. She resides in Santa Fe, New Mexico, with her brilliant husband and perpetually FOMO dog, Hubble. Other than writing, Jennifer loves hiking, tacos, Bollywood, Albert Camus, dark chocolate, exploring mysterious places, and meeting new people—if you're human (or otherwise), odds are she'll probably love you. You can find her work and more at www.jennifergedelsonauthor.com

P. J. (aka Paul) Christman is the author of *The Purple Runner*, seven other published novels, and two plays. For twenty-three years, he was the Editor/Publisher of the late *Running Stats*, while his articles have appeared in publications including *Athletics* (CAN), *Athletics Weekly* (GBR), *Prick of the Spindle*, *Running Times*, and the *Santa Fe Reporter*. Christman is the recipient of the RRCA Jerry Little Memorial Journalism Excellence Award and is a member of the Colorado Running and Illinois Striders Halls of Fame. Residences have included Park Ridge, Lake Forest, Champaign, Madison, San Francisco, Westwood, Highgate, Remuera, Boulder, and Santa Fe.

Melinda Cross is a former advertising creative director and communications consultant who broke free from the corporate world to return to her first love of books. She works as a nonfiction developmental editor and has been a ghostwriter on more than a dozen published books. Melinda is a graduate of Northwestern University's Medill School of Journalism and is currently enrolled in Stanford's Certificate in Novel Writing Program, where she is completing her first novel, *The Bargains*, set in Chicago, where she lived for thirty years. She splits her time between Chicago and Santa Fe, where she finds endless inspiration, immersing herself in the nature, culture, and people of The City Different.

André Fleuette began writing earnestly to keep himself objectively sane during lonely nights in a dispatch center over a long, cold winter in Antarctica. He has been a filmmaker, graphic artist, hazardous cargo technician, and firefighter. He is an avid traveler and has lived at the South Pole, gone diving with sharks in Australia, and gotten lost somewhere between the Full Moon Party and New York City. He currently makes his home in Santa Fe and dreams about living in a hut somewhere near an ocean. With a dog. On Mars.

Victoria Gregg is a writer of dark fiction. She currently lives with her husband and son in Santa Fe, New Mexico, where she works as a research analyst. When not chained to a screen, she can be found hiking with her family and a perpetually disgruntled husky.

Daniel Huantes Jr. grew up in San Antonio, Texas, with his parents and two siblings. He spent summers in south Texas with his extended family. He graduated from Fort Hays State University in Hays, Kansas. He currently lives in Santa Fe, and he loves drinking coffee.

Elaine Koyama grew up on a sheep, wheat, and sugar beet farm in eastern Montana, the youngest of eight sansei (third-generation) Japanese American siblings. She was a cheerleader, shot putter, and Stanford University graduate. She spent twenty years at Cargill and twenty years running a technology consulting firm and plans to spend the next twenty years writing. Koyama now lives in Santa Fe, New Mexico, to pursue her writing career. The mother of three and the grandmother of five, Koyama continues to play tennis and pickleball, downhill ski, and meet with friends at The Shed for Friday Happy Hour. Find out more at: www.elainekoyama.com

Patrick X.L. Lee is a former award-winning newspaper, digital, and public radio journalist and editor who now does copy editing and writing for various clients. He lives in Santa Fe with his wife, Maria, and French bulldog, Ruby.

John Self is a humorist and author of *The New Restaurant Manager, The New Restaurant Manager, Part 2, The Restaurant Compendium for the Curious*, and the forthcoming *The Santa Fe Compendium for the Curious*. He lives in Santa Fe with his wife, Debra, and Chili, the cat, and has an insatiable appetite for trivia, history, travel, and Santa Fe. He has over sixteen years of restaurant management and ownership experience, plus a comedy club. Later, he returned to school to become a university professor and is now a professor emeritus from Cal Poly Pomona.

Amber Train has made her home in Santa Fe, New Mexico, since 2005. She has been a hotel maid, a door-to-door proselytizer, a nursing home assistant, a waitress, a cigarette vendor, a chocolate strawberry dipper, a paid plasma donor, a knife dealer, a Marine Corps Sergeant, and, most recently, an attorney. In the summer, she sometimes sleeps outside so she can be subsumed by the stars. She likes to commune with cottonwood trees. In 2023, she was honored to win the Grand Prize in the Santa Fe Pasatiempo Writing contest.

Gregory L Wagner is a farmer by birthright and a physicist by education. His stories often consider the problems and issues that arise when the complex and simple collide. He lives in Santa Fe, New Mexico, with his wife and, yes, a dog named Hubble. You can contact him at *Greg.L.Wagner@gmail.com*.

Stef Willen is an award-winning writer for *McSweeney's*. Her writing has appeared there, in the "Best of 2012 Humor" for *Reader's Digest*, and in New California Writing 2012. She has written for Amazon's "One Mississippi" and co-starred in the film, "Em," which won the Grand Jury Prize at Seattle International Film Festival. Currently, she is working on a documentary and other writing projects.